8140819

Benchley, Nathaniel
All over again                     11.95

| DATE DUE | | | |
|---|---|---|---|
| | | | |
| | | | |
| | | | |
| | | | |
| | | | |
| | | | |
| | | | |
| | | | |
| | | | |

## MID-CONTINENT PUBLIC LIBRARY

**Lee's Summit**
**901 O'Brien**
**Lee's Summit, MO 64063**

**LS**

Books circulate for four weeks (28 days) unless stamped otherwise.

No renewals are allowed.

Books will be issued only on presentation of library card.

A fine will be charged for each overdue book.

*Also by Nathaniel Benchley:*

### NOVELS

SIDE STREET
ONE TO GROW ON
SAIL A CROOKED SHIP
THE OFF-ISLANDERS
CATCH A FALLING SPY
A WINTER'S TALE
THE VISITORS
A FIRM WORD OR TWO
THE MONUMENT
WELCOME TO XANADU
THE WAKE OF THE ICARUS
LASSITER'S FOLLY
THE HUNTER'S MOON
PORTRAIT OF A SCOUNDREL
SWEET ANARCHY

### BIOGRAPHIES

ROBERT BENCHLEY
HUMPHREY BOGART

### PLAY

THE FROGS OF SPRING

### EDITOR

THE BENCHLEY ROUNDUP

### JUNIOR BOOKS

GONE AND BACK
ONLY EARTH AND SKY LAST FOREVER
FELDMAN FIELDMOUSE
BRIGHT CANDLES
BEYOND THE MISTS
A NECESSARY END
KILROY AND THE GULL

### MOTION PICTURE

THE GREAT AMERICAN PASTIME

# ALL OVER AGAIN

# ALL OVER AGAIN

by

Nathaniel Benchley

1981
DOUBLEDAY & COMPANY, INC.
GARDEN CITY, NEW YORK

*Library of Congress Cataloging in Publication Data*
Benchley, Nathaniel, 1915-
    All over again
1. San Francisco—Earthquake and fire, 1906-
        —Fiction. I. Title.
    PS3503.E487S4    813'.54
        ISBN: 0-385-15859-9
Library of Congress Catalog Card Number 80-1800

COPYRIGHT © 1981 BY NATHANIEL BENCHLEY
ALL RIGHTS RESERVED
PRINTED IN THE UNITED STATES OF AMERICA
FIRST EDITION

PREFATORY NOTE

The publishing sensation of the fall of 1907 was a book by a San Francisco madam, describing among other things the earthquake and fire of the previous year. Titled *Dolly Remembers*, the book mentioned no names, but described several of Dolly's more prominent customers in terms that left no doubt as to their identities, and sales were sent skyrocketing not only by the prurient public, but also by those real-life characters who, unaware of the laws of publishing, tried to suppress the book by buying up every available copy. It was estimated that, directly or indirectly, Dolly's memoirs were responsible for five divorces, three estrangements, one suicide, and countless broken engagements, and was in its own small way as effective as the quake in rearranging people's lives. The quake (or "shake," as it was called) had in fact a benign effect on some, in that it gave them a chance to wipe the slate clean and start again; Dolly's book had a tendency to wipe out the future rather than the past. In the larger picture, however, she and her book were simply small cogs in the machine that was set in motion along the San Andreas fault on April 18, 1906.

ACKNOWLEDGMENTS

This is a work of fiction, based on historical fact. For the basic details, two books were indispensable: *The San Francisco Earthquake*, by Gordon Thomas and Max Morgan-Witts, and *The Earth Shook, the Sky Burned*, a photographic account of the disaster by William Bronson. Certain sidelights were provided by *The Little War of Private Post*, a first-hand account of the Spanish–American War by Charles Johnson Post; *The American West*, by Lucius Beebe and Charles Clegg; and *Story of San Francisco*, by W. B. Medlicott, the report of an insurance adjustor for the Atlas Assurance Co., Ltd., which was kindly volunteered by Peter Wilson, grandson of the author. Finally, and with thanks for which only a prayer rug and incense would suffice, I am indebted to Mrs. Wallace H. Fulton, presently of Washington, D.C., who was seven and a half years old and a resident of Berkeley at the time of the quake, and who wrote for me an eleven-page account of her memories, including details that no novelist could ever imagine.

The characters are, with the obvious historical exceptions, all fictitious, and any similarity to persons living or dead and so on. However, Beebe tells of a Denver madam named Ada LaMonte, who once slapped a waiter on the behind with a defective mountain trout, and her story seemed too good to be lost. Her name has been changed, out of deference to the trout.

There is a tide in the affairs of men,
Which, taken at the flood, leads on to fortune;
Omitted, all the voyage of their life
Is bound in shallows and in miseries.
      *William Shakespeare*


If at first you don't succeed,
Try, try again.
    *Anon.*


If I had to do it all over again,
I'd do it all over you.
    *Dorothy Parker*

# ALL OVER AGAIN

# CHAPTER 1

The train clacked slowly through the Southern Pacific switching yards, and finally came to a stop at Oakland Pier. The locomotive gasped like a long-distance runner, then subsided, steam hissing from its various valves and vents. In the cars the passengers, gritty with five days' accumulation of soot, crowded the aisles while they waited for their baggage to be unloaded. Most of them would proceed to the ferry for San Francisco; others would stay in Oakland or go on to Berkeley, San Jose, or other points to the south and east. All of them, in spite of the fabled luxuries of the transcontinental train, would be glad to breathe the clean Pacific air and relax in the April sunshine. Luxurious or not, the train ride was not a rest cure.

For Henry Walden, however, the arrival was inexplicably an anticlimax, mixed with a curious sense of dread that he could neither define nor understand. He had started the trip in a state of high anticipation—looking forward to a change of scenery if nothing else—but as day followed endless day the scenery changed as they went from the wooded, hilly country of the East to the flat farmland of the Middle West to the ocean-like expanse of the Great Plains, then up into the Rocky Mountains and down to the barren deserts of Nevada and the fertile valleys around Sacramento and finally to the Bay area and Oakland, and he realized that a change of scenery was not, *per se*, much of an answer.

As a matter of fact the nights, when no scenery was visible, had been more of a diversion than the days. There was a combination buffet, smoking, and library car, patronized exclusively by male passengers who kept their caps on, but this had less attraction for Walden than the dining car, with its imported wines and champagnes, and the drawing-room car, where passengers gathered after dinner to sing hymns with an organ accompaniment and, when the ladies had retired, to move on to more secular music. It was Walden's dream that some night he might meet a young lady whose escort (brother? uncle? father?) had been taken ill, and with whom he could strike up an acquaintance and then . . . The dream never got much farther than that because of the impossibility of the situation, but every night he cast his eye around for a likely prospect, and while he spotted two or three he'd have been happy to meet, their escorts were all in robust health and were, very clearly, their husbands. At the age of thirty-two Walden felt he should be married, but his luck with the ladies had been so spectacularly bad that he sometimes wondered if God hadn't intended him to remain a bachelor, and was hurling thunderbolts whenever a possible mate appeared.

Now, as he stood on the pier at Oakland, Walden looked at the city across the Bay and wondered if his whole trip had been a mistake. He had first thought of it as being the final attainment of a goal, but looking at it another way it could be just one more in a long string of false starts, and something in the back of his mind told him it was probably the latter. If that was correct, then his best move would be to get right back on the train when it returned to the East, but the thought of another five or six days of travel was more than he could bear, and what was more important it would use up practically all of his money. Better to stay where he was, and give the San Francisco matter a little thought before taking the final plunge. He didn't know what made him hold back, but something about the sight of the city, superficially splendid though it was, seemed ominous and hostile, as though a dark cloud were hanging over it. He turned to a porter, who was trundling a baggage cart toward the ferry.

"Is there someplace here I could get a room for the night?" Walden asked.

"Yes, sir," the porter replied. "There's plenty of hotels."

"Which would you recommend?"

"Depends on how much you want to spend. Some of 'em are kind of pricey."

"Oh." Walden thought a moment, then said, "What about rooming houses?"

"There's some nice rooms above the Empire Theatre, on Twelfth Street. Centrally located, and they won't cost you an arm and a leg."

"That sounds better. How do I get there?"

The porter told him, and Walden tipped him a nickel and headed off for Twelfth Street. Within an hour he had rented a room, had his first real bath in a week, and changed into clean though suitcase-wrinkled clothes. He went downstairs and around past the theater entrance, looking for a poster that might tell what was playing, but aside from the fact that the admission fee was ten cents he could learn nothing, and the gate to the surrounding iron fence was locked. It was by now late afternoon, and Walden headed off for a place where he could have a few drinks while he tried to straighten out his problems and make some kind of sense out of what he was doing. It came to him that his hesitation about working in San Francisco might be based on something real—something his instinct was warning him against—or it might be that his old footloose habits, about which his father had raged at him until he no longer heard the words, were simply reacting against the idea of a commitment for life to one particular job. Whichever it was, now was the time to make the decision, and not after he had started work.

He found a likely-looking saloon, and went inside and ordered a beer. He had a theory that a beer or two before starting on anything else would douse his thirst and slow his pace, and he wanted to remain as clearheaded as possible while sorting through his options. Moving to the free-lunch counter he filled a plate with cheese, crackers, two hard-boiled eggs, a dill pickle, some radishes, and a chicken wing, then went back to where the bartender had set a dripping stein on the mahogany. Walden buried his nose in the foam and drank deeply, and almost immediately began to feel better.

Looking at himself in the back-bar mirror, he saw a faint resemblance to the picture in his college yearbook, taken twelve years before. At twenty, he had graduated near the top of the Class of '94, Phi Beta Kappa, *summa cum laude*, and all the rest of it, and he had sailed out into the world like a full-rigged man-of-war. Time meant nothing, because he had his whole life ahead of him, and a man should do as many things as possible in a lifetime. Four years after graduation, he left a promising job on Wall Street to go to Cuba as a member of the 1st U. S. Volunteer Cavalry, otherwise known as the Rough Riders, and when, on September 15, the Rough Riders were disbanded, he decided not to return to Wall Street but to invest in a putative silver mine in Connecticut instead.

That had been the pattern, and he had no regrets. But when he passed his thirtieth birthday he decided the time had come to settle down, and while he felt this was a sound decision he found he had trouble making himself believe it. There were too many things he could do, and do well, to limit himself to one line of work, and new ideas were always more tempting than an established routine.

He ordered another beer, and peeled one of the hard-boiled eggs. The bartender slid the beer in front of him, picked change from the bar, and rang it into the cash register. "You new around these parts?" he asked, wiping a small puddle from the bar surface.

"Yes," Walden replied. "Is there anything I ought to know?"

"You here on business or pleasure?"

"Ah—I'm not quite sure. Maybe a little of each."

"What's your business?"

"That's what I'm not quite sure about. I've had an offer from the Southern Pacific."

"You can't go wrong on that. Southern Pacific owns the whole damn city of San Francisco and environs."

"I know. I'm not sure that's a good idea."

The bartender looked at him queerly. "Are you one of these reformers—what do they call them—muckrakers?"

"God, no. But some things make me uneasy."

"Like what?"

"I don't know until I feel it."

"Then you're a psychic—is that what you're trying to say?"

"No, I'm not a psychic. I guess I don't know what I am. That's one of the things I've got to figure out."

The bartender polished the already shiny surface of the bar. "You've got a problem there, son," he said. "I've heard a lot of guys' problems, but I never heard one like yours. Most of the guys who bend my ear, they know exactly what they are and what it is that's bugging them, but . . ." He left the sentence hanging, and moved down the bar to pour a drink for a customer.

Walden finished his beer and sampled the chicken wing, and when the bartender came back he said, "Let's try a shot of the house whisky, should we? I need something with a little more authority than beer."

"You need something, all right," the bartender replied, reaching onto the back-bar. "But I'm here to tell you there's not a college education in this bottle. You don't get smarter with every drink you take."

"I've already had the college education," Walden said. "Maybe *that's* my trouble."

The bartender set a bottle of rye and a shot glass in front of him. "Where'd you go?"

"A little college in the East you've probably never heard of. It's called Yale."

"I thought you talked like a Yalie."

"Oh? How is that?"

"You can't tell until you hear it. But you know it."

Walden smiled. "O.K.," he said. "We're even."

"If you ask me, what you need is a little recreation," the bartender said.

"Do you have any you can suggest?"

"Well, since you're a college man, you might try Mills college for women. It's right across town, near the foothills."

"I'm not very good at scaling walls. Think of something easier."

"Of course, if it's real entertainment you're after, you should go across the Bay. There's a variety of talent there that'll knock your hat off."

"No, thanks. I feel as though I've been traveling for a week. Anything I get is going to have to be within arm's reach."

"I'll say one thing for you—you may not know what you want, but you sure as hell know what you *don't* want."

Walden poured himself another rye. "Yes and no," he said.

Three ryes later, he felt he had the answer. It was simplicity itself: all he had to do was take each job as it was offered him, do it to perfection, and then move on to the next. Be a sort of Renaissance man—a modern-day Cellini—and that way milk the best out of each position without ever getting in a rut. He had one more rye, said a warm good night to the bartender, and went out into the soft evening air. The street floated gently ahead of him, and he hummed the strains of "There'll Be a Hot Time in the Old Town Tonight" as he made his way back to the Empire Theatre and up to bed.

# CHAPTER 2

It was the sound of the horses in the stable that awakened Lucille Bender. She had been dreaming of thunder, but as her mind surfaced from the murky depths she opened her eyes, and realized that both horses were stomping heavily in their stalls. Then a dog howled, and Lucille flung herself out of bed and went to the window. The sun had not yet risen, the sky had a greenish tinge, and a thin crescent moon was hanging over San Francisco, across the Bay to the west. Looking down at the stable Lucille could see nothing amiss, but the horses continued their restless thumping, and the dog howled again in a long wail that trailed off into a whine. Lucille looked back at the bed, where her husband was sleeping under a lumpy swirl of blankets, sheets, and pillows.

"George!" she said, loudly. "George! Wake up!"

There was a grunt from beneath the covers, then silence.

"George, there's something bothering the horses!" Lucille said. "Something's in the stable!"

"Chickens," George replied, thickly. "Chickens always bother horses at night. Come back to bed."

"It's not night, and it's not chickens!" said Lucille. "And a dog is howling!"

There was a pause, then George said, "I don't hear anything."

"If you'd get out from under the covers you would." Lucille paused, then said, "Furthermore, I smell smoke."

George whirled into a sitting position, his hair standing out as though he'd had an electric shock, and his long, pointed nose seeming to search the air. "Where?" he said. "What kind of smoke?"

"Smoke smoke," she replied. "Come here and smell for yourself."

George bounded out of bed, looking faintly Dickensian in his nightshirt, and went to the window. He inhaled deeply two or three times. "I don't smell anything," he said.

"I know," said Lucille. "But listen a minute." The horses began to stamp again, and he directed his attention to the stable. "You see?" she said.

Without answering, George Bender ran his fingers through his hair, then turned and stabbed his feet into his bedroom slippers and left the room. Lucille heard him go downstairs and unlock the back door, and from the window she could see his nightshirt, a pale patch in the shadows, moving toward the stable. The houses in Oakland were mostly low, and only every now and then did a taller building stand out against the morning sky. For the rest it looked, in the dim light, like a nondescript collection of houses, a poor relation of its glamorous sister across the Bay.

In a few minutes Bender returned, and sat on the edge of the bed. He scratched himself thoughtfully, and said, "I'm damned if I know what's got into them. Just restless, I guess. They probably need more exercise." He started to lie back, then picked up his watch from the bed table and tilted its face toward the window to read it better. "Ten minutes past five," he said, putting the watch down. "That still leaves me an hour." He kicked off his slippers, lifted his feet, and stretched out.

Lucille hadn't left the window. "How can you think of sleep?" she said.

"Why not?" He put one arm over his eyes. "What good would staying awake do?"

"I don't know. I just have a funny feeling. I couldn't sleep if you hit me with a sledgehammer."

"Speaking of that," Bender said, without removing his arm, "I would appreciate it if you didn't say you smell smoke when you don't. That kind of ruse could lead to trouble."

"What harm did it do?" Lucille said. "It was the only way I could get you up. And you must admit it was worth getting you up, if you took the trouble to go down to the stable."

"That's not what I'm talking about. I am simply reminding you of the boy who cried wolf."

"But supposing there had *been* a wolf there."

"There wasn't! That's the point!"

"But supposing there had been—then the boy would have been a hero."

Bender took a deep breath. "I am not talking about the boy and the wolf," he said, enunciating as clearly as he could. "I am talking about you saying you smelled smoke when in fact you did not."

"If you're not talking about the boy and the wolf, then why did you bring him up? Your very words were, 'I am simply reminding you of the boy who cried wolf,' and you know that as well as I do. Now you tell me you're *not* talking about the boy who cried wolf but instead are talking about me smelling smoke—"

"But you *didn't* smell smoke! How many times—?"

"Then why did you bring it up?"

"Oh, Jesus." Abandoning any attempt at sleep, Bender got up, stepped into his underwear, and went to the dresser where his trousers were hanging with their cuffs closed in a top drawer. He took them down, and had one foot halfway into a trouser leg when there was a roar like an express train pounding through the room; the house shook and the floor heaved and shuddered, and Bender found himself flying through the air. From somewhere he heard Lucille scream, and then he hit the wall with a crash and felt bits of plaster raining down on his head and neck. Lucille continued to scream, and he brought himself to his hands and knees and crawled to where he could see her, lying beneath the curtains that had once framed the window.

"Are you all right?" he called. "Lucille, are you hurt?"

She was quiet for a moment, and then she began to claw herself free of the curtains. "No," she said. "It must have been the shock. How about you?"

"I don't know yet. I hit the wall one hell of a crack." He rose slowly, flexing his limbs and testing for broken bones, but he felt no sharp pain; all he felt was jolted and numb and bruised. "I'm O.K.," he said, and helped her to her feet. "I guess we're lucky."

Lucille looked around the bedroom, and laughed. "I was going to say it looks as though an earthquake had struck it," she said. "I'll have to think of another expression."

"You couldn't find a more accurate one." Bender retrieved his trousers, which had followed him partway across the room, and shook the plaster dust off them and held them up. "Damn," he said. "I hate to have to send them to the cleaner's, but I don't—do you think you could manage to sponge them off, so—?"

"Listen," Lucille interrupted. "What's that?" She went to the east window and looked out, and then gasped. "Oh, no!" she said.

Bender joined her at the window, and saw the sun rising through a cloud of dust. At first he could see no damage, but then he realized that one wall of a building two blocks away had fallen onto the second floor of the Empire Theatre, crushing the roof and spilling debris into the street. From a shattered bow window a figure was hanging out a sheet, apparently as a means of escape. Bender knew that the theater's second floor had rooms for lodgers, and he wondered how many had survived. Another tremor shook the building, and he and Lucille tensed, then relaxed as it subsided.

"I'd better get down there," he said, and stepped into his rumpled trousers. "They may need help." He owned a pharmacy, and in the two years since he and Lucille had moved to Oakland he had turned a seedy chemist's shop into a thriving business, primarily by his own energy and initiative and his willingness to serve the public at all hours. He considered himself an adjunct to the medical profession, and bound by the same code of ethics.

"Aren't you going to want some breakfast?" Lucille asked. "At least let me make you some coffee."

"No time for that." He put on a shirt, and slipped his suspenders over his shoulders. "I'll get something to eat later." He took a jacket from the closet, and was about to leave the room when he saw that Lucille was swaying slightly, like a tree in a high wind. "Hey," he said. "What's the matter?"

"Nothing." She sat on the edge of the bed, and breathed deeply. "Just a spell, I guess."

He looked at her closely. "Take some elixir. That'll fix you up."

"I don't think there's much left. You'd better bring home another bottle when you come."

"All right. Later." He hurried out of the room, and when Lucille heard the front door close she got up and made her way slowly into the bathroom. When she opened the medicine cabinet she was greeted by a cascade of bottles and jars, which had been knocked awry by the quake and now spilled out onto the floor, showering the bathroom with broken glass. Lucille said, "Damn, damn, *damn!*" and then squatted down, trembling, and looked for the elixir bottle. She found it, miraculously unbroken, and she stood up and with unsteady hands worked the stopper loose. There was only about a mouthful of the brown syrupy liquid left, and she put the neck of the bottle to her lips and tilted her head back, letting the last few drops drain slowly onto her tongue. She felt a small glow, like a match that flares suddenly and then dies out, and she hoped it wouldn't be too long before George came home with a fresh bottle.

When Bender reached the street he breathed deeply, to make sure there was no smoke nearby, and all he could detect was the cold and gritty smell of plaster dust. As he headed toward the Empire Theatre he saw that a crowd had begun to gather, and someone had put a ladder against the side of the building and was climbing up. Beneath the sign EMPIRE THEATRE 10¢ an iron fence with a locked gate barred access to the main door, and the only way into the second floor was by climbing. The collapse of the adjacent wall had sealed off the back stairs. For reasons he couldn't define, Bender knew that men had died in the debris; he heard nothing, and he could see no bodies, but he suddenly had the feeling he'd had eight years before in Cuba, when as a private in the 71st Infantry he'd come to the belated aid of troops who had blundered into an ambush. There was the same certainty of disaster that pervaded the air, and the same lack of specific details: in Cuba, he hadn't even seen a Spaniard until the day after the engagement, and here he could see nothing but dust slowly rising from the wreckage, but the knowledge of calamity hung over both scenes like a big, dark bird. Bender hurried the last block to the theater, and arrived just as the first body was being lowered down the ladder.

In all there were five, and as Bender looked at the dusty, ashen bodies, some naked and some in torn pajamas, he reflected that civilian deaths such as these, unexpected and pointless, were somehow more tragic than those in the military, where death was an accepted risk and where, when it came, it was often in such numbers as to stun the mind. He remembered only one death in Cuba that had stood out as an isolated incident: in a clearing in the jungle, when his company was making their way to the San Juan River, they'd come upon the body of a young West Point lieutenant, shot through the heart by a sniper. He was not the first or the only casualty—boots protruding from the brush along the path testified to many others—but a Regular Army major was standing beside him, wringing his hands and crying, "Cover him up, God damn it—somebody cover him up—he's an officer!" Demented with grief, the major tried to get one of the passing soldiers to cover the lieutenant, but the only reply came from one who said, "Cover him up yourself, you son of a bitch." Bender never found out who had finally covered the body, but he could still remember the lieutenant's face: he'd been about twenty-one, had brown hair parted in the middle, and was firm-featured and handsome in an unspectacular sort of way. His eyes were staring at the foliage overhead, and he might have been alive except for the red stain on the front of his yellow undershirt, and the ants that were crawling across his eyeballs. That face hung in Bender's mind, and used to come back to him most vividly at night, but with time it faded, and he hadn't thought about it for a long while until he looked at the five still figures lying uncovered in the street.

There were three survivors in the Empire Theatre, and by the time they were brought out a horse-drawn ambulance had arrived to take them to the hospital. Only then did the rescuers have a moment to relax, and it occurred to Bender to wonder what the quake had done to his pharmacy. With all the jars and bottles he had, the results might well be disastrous, and as he turned toward his shop he glanced out over the Bay to the west. The farther shore had been obscured by a low-lying haze, but now the haze lifted like a curtain, and Bender could see black columns of smoke rising from a half dozen spots in San Francisco.

"I'm glad we're not over there," said a man standing next to him. "It looks like they're in for a busy day."

# CHAPTER 3

Tuesday was usually a slow night at Dolly LaGrange's. One of San Francisco's more elegant madams, Dolly had risen from fairly rowdy beginnings in Denver to a position where she could cater to the clientele of her choice, and avoid the riffraff of the Barbary Coast. Her house, on O'Farrell Street in the Upper Tenderloin, was decorated in a manner suggesting a cross between late Victorian and Louis XIV, and it was one of her many boasts that no enlisted man had ever set foot on the premises. Another boast was that she was able to drink twenty-two bottles of champagne without once rising from the table, but this alleged feat had occurred in Central City, Colorado, and nobody in San Francisco could either confirm or deny the story. It was an undisputed fact, however, that she had once attracted the attention of a waiter in the Navarre restaurant in Denver by hitting him on the behind with an imperfectly cooked mountain trout; that feat was recorded in *The Rocky Mountain News*, clippings of which followed her when she moved to the Athens of the Pacific.

By limiting her customers to the *haut monde* of San Francisco she cut down on her volume, but she more than made up for that by the prices she charged for her services and her wine cellar, and her girls were able to work at a more leisurely pace than those in the waterfront area. The beginning of each week was quiet, with only an occasional well-heeled tourist or politician to be entertained, and the girls were able to catch up on their sleep. Monday, in fact, was so quiet that one of the girls once suggested they have a taffy pull to liven up the parlor, and they were in the middle of the operation when they were interrupted by a legislative commission from Sacramento, investigating sin in the Bay City. The bemused legislators left in short order, and thereafter Monday night was always referred to as Taffy Pull Night.

Tuesday, April 17, started out more slowly than usual. Dolly checked the parlor shortly before ten o'clock, and saw that two of the girls were going through the stereopticon views of Niagara Falls, one was knitting what looked like an impossibly small bootee, one was whistling through her teeth while she repaired a torn fingernail, and two were playing cribbage by the potted palm in the corner.

"Dolores! Maribelle!" Dolly said to the last two. "You know there's no card playing except with the customers! Where do you think you are?" The two girls put their cards away in sullen silence, and Dolly turned to the one who was working on the fingernail. "Clarita, ladies do not perform their manicure in public," she said. "And at no time do they whistle through their teeth."

"Where's the public?" Clarita replied, continuing to file her nail. "Show me a member of the public, and I'll listen."

"One should at all times behave as though one were in public," Dolly replied.

"You have got to be kidding," said Clarita, and dropped her nail file down the front of her dress.

Dolly eyed the girl who was knitting the bootee. "Lillybelle, for whom are you making that?" she asked.

"My sister," Lillybelle replied without looking up. "She's in the family way."

"How old is she?"

"Fourteen."

Dolly glanced once more around the room. "Where's Stella?"

"Upstairs," said Clarita.

"I didn't hear anyone come in."

"Nobody did. She's not working—she writing her mother."

"It seems to me she's always writing her mother. She ought to be down here."

Clarita shrugged. "She writes her mother three times a week. She has to take her time where she can find it."

"We'll see about that." Dolly ascended the carpeted stairs, pausing only to straighten an oil painting of the Battle of Trafalgar, and went to the first room on the right on the second floor. She knocked once and entered, and found Stella sitting on an ottoman, writing a letter on a hatbox that rested atop the bidet. The tip of her tongue protruded from a corner of her mouth, and she clutched the pen as though it were alive. "What do you think you're doing?" Dolly demanded. "You know the rules."

"I'm writin' me mum," Stella replied. "She frets if she don't 'ear from me regular."

"And drop that godawful Cockney accent. Did I send you for French lessons just to have you revert to gutter language?"

"*Je m'excuse*, madame. When I write my mozzaire I seenk in Cockney."

"Well, write your mozzaire on your own time. You're supposed to be in the parlor with the others." Stella sighed, put down the pen, and stood up, and Dolly went on, "I've told you time and again this is a group operation, and we have no room for prima donnas. During working hours every girl should be either in the parlor or in her room, and when's she's in her room she should *not* be writing to her mother. Her mother should be the farthest thing from her thoughts."

"I cannot control my thoughts, madame. If I did not allow my thoughts to wander, I should go how you say in Englees gaga." Stella glanced at herself in the bedside mirror, gave a slight tug to her bodice to widen the neckline, and headed for the stairs. When she had gone Dolly looked around the room, and on the dresser spotted a small, gilt-framed oval picture of a couple wearing the pearl-buttoned London costermongers' uniforms. The picture was slightly blurred, and the faces had been tinted an unnatural pink which made them unrecognizable, but Dolly assumed they must be Stella's parents. Also on the dresser was a sailor's hat-ribbon with the legend "Remember the Maine," and for an instant Dolly thought that Stella might have broken the house rule against associating with sailors, but then she remembered that the ribbons were sold in souvenir stores everywhere, and she relaxed. She was about to leave the room when her eye caught the letter Stella had been writing, and after a quick glance at the door she picked it up and read:

> Dearest Mum, Well another day another dollar as they say here in the States. It's a good thing the School lets us sell our baskets and tapestries and the other things we weave, otherwise I might be a bit hard pressed for money. But people seem to like to buy our goods, so I am for the moment on Easy St. (Another Yankee expression.) Our teacher, Miss LaGrange, is very pleased at the progress I have made in my French lessons, and she says if my dancing improves as much as my French she may suggest to the S.F. Ballet director (a personal friend) that he try me out. I told her I come by my talent naturally (ha! ha!) and she says keep up the good work. The only other news is that Enrico Caruso, an Eytie singer, has come to town to vocalize at the Opera, and all the girls are hoping he might visit our School, on an inspection tour in a manner of speaking. My own feeling is not bloody likely, but then you never can tell. It would be a feather in our caps, I must say. The talk is he's getting $1350 a perf, which works out to be 270 quid, so he could bloody well afford to buy a basket or a tapestry or whatnot if only as a souvenir of

Dolly put the letter down and left the room. On the landing she listened for any sounds below, but all she could hear was the muted murmur of the girls' talk, so she went to her room in the rear of the house, lighted the red-shaded student lamp on her desk, and closed the door and locked it. Next she went to a brass speaking tube and blew into it, and when she heard the faraway, tinny sound of the maid's "Yas'm?" she said, "Petunia, I'm in my room. You take the door, and let me know if anyone calls."

"Yas'm," came Petunia's reply.

From a drawer in her desk Dolly removed a large, leather-bound portfolio, opened it, and began to sort through the papers. She found the last sheet, which was numbered 43, then backtracked until she came to the beginning of the chapter. She frowned as she read, crossing out some words and substituting others, and the farther she read the more irritated she became. Finally, in exasperation, she tore up the entire chapter and jammed it in the wastebasket, then took a clean sheet of paper. Her book, which a client had once told her would be worth a million dollars, was proving to be something of a headache; there was no thread to hold the reminiscences together, and she was aware of a certain sameness in the anecdotes. What she needed was a kicker to start things off, but so far nothing had occurred to her.

The speaking tube whistled, and Dolly snatched it up and said, "What?"

"There's two gentlemen just arrived," came Petunia's voice. "They look like they's out to see the elephant."

"I'll be right there." Dolly gathered the papers together, closed the portfolio and locked it in the desk drawer, then stood up and glanced at herself in the mirror. There's more to this writing game than I'd imagined, she thought as she patted her back hair. But then, I guess there are tricks to every trade; it's all in knowing how to go about it.

When she reached the parlor she saw two men in evening dress, both of whom were talking to Stella, and Stella was blinking her eyes and replying with her best French accent. Dolly knew that an acquired accent such as this was risky, because it could easily be confounded by any real Frenchman, but the French had such a reputation for amatory finesse that it was worth the gamble. All along Jackson Street there were so-called "French restaurants," which did indeed serve food but also had private rooms on the second floor, and they did a handsome business simply by dint of their name. Dolly's own name was nothing like LaGrange—as nearly as her mother could recall, her father's surname was Skoda, which he had subsequently changed to Simpson—but she adopted LaGrange for business purposes, and never had cause to regret it. Strictly translated it meant "the barn," which for a Denver girl was not inappropriate.

"*Bon soir, messieurs,*" she said to the new arrivals. "Welcome to my salon." She nodded at Clarita, whose fingernail was by now repaired, and as Clarita joined the group Dolly went on, "You cannot both have *ma petite* Stella, so here is Clarita, who will please you equally well." Then she clapped her hands and called, "Petunia, *du champagne!*" Petunia, who had been waiting just out of sight, appeared with a bucket of iced champagne and four glasses on a tray, and as the drinks were being poured the doorbell rang. "*La!*" Dolly exclaimed, throwing up her hands. "More company! It will be an evening of *grande fête!*" She went to the door, and Petunia hurried away to prepare the next round of champagne.

"Is this your first time in San Francisco?" Stella said to her companion, who was tall and had blond sideburns and looked faintly ill at ease.

"No—I mean yes," he replied, and took a swallow of his champagne.

The other man laughed. He was shorter, and dark-haired, and somehow gave the impression he had spent most of his adult life at Dolly's or similar houses. "What he means," he said to Stella, "is it's not his first time in Frisco, but it is his first time in a whorehouse."

"Madame does not allow that word to be used here," Stella said sternly, and the man laughed again.

"What'll she do—hit me on the tail with a trout?" He turned to his companion. "Did I tell you that one, Frank? Back in Denver once, she—" He stopped as Dolly entered the room with a florid-faced gentleman in an opera hat and silk-lined cape.

"My God, get me a drink!" the man said in a voice that sounded like a snoring bear. Dolly took his hat and cape and showed him to a banquette, signaling for Maribelle, one of the cribbage players, to join him, and in the same instant Petunia brought the champagne with two glasses, and the man reached out with trembling hands. "I thought if that wop sang one more song I was going to throw my chair at him." He poured himself a glass, and drained it in three swallows. Then he took a deep breath, belched, and sat back. "That's better," he said. For the first time, he looked at Maribelle, and patted her knee. "Hello, there. Have a drink."

Frank, the young man with Stella, looked at the newcomer and said, "Excuse me, sir; did you hear Caruso tonight?"

"Did I ever," the man replied, pouring himself another drink and as an afterthought one for Maribelle. "All I need is a rose in my teeth, and I'll feel like Carmen."

"I heard he might not sing, because of Vesuvius."

"I wish he hadn't."

"What is this Vesuvius?" Stella asked. "Why would he not sing?"

"Vesuvius is erupting," Frank replied. "His home town is Naples."

"Do you know him?" Stella asked, a note of hope creeping into her voice.

"No. I just read the papers."

"Oh." Stella took a drink, and mentally shrugged her shoulders.

"Well, if he was upset he didn't show it," the older gentleman said. "I thought he was going to shout the hall down."

"Do you like to play games?" Clarita asked the dark-haired young man who was Frank's companion.

He looked at her with a faint smile. "You name it, kiddo, and I'll play it," he said. "What did you have in mind?"

"Whatever will please you gentlemen."

"Did you have in mind games for two, or four?"

"As I said, the choice is yours."

He looked at Frank, who was perspiring slightly as Stella's hand massaged his knee. "What do you say, Franko?" he said. "This was your idea."

Frank cleared his throat. "To be honest with you, Art, I don't feel so good," he said. "It's awfully hot in here, and—I don't know—"

"Oh, *le pauvre petit*," Stella said, leaning against him. "Here

—a sip of champagne will make you feel better." She held her glass to his lips and he drank from it, clumsily.

"What you need is a brandy," Art said. "That'll settle your stomach and get you off to the races, all at the same time."

The doorbell rang, and this time two men came in. Both wore derby hats and both were smoking cigars, and they looked like Thomas Nast caricatures of politicians. Dolly greeted them, and the larger of the two, who bore a superficial resemblance to Diamond Jim Brady, said, "Abe Ruef sent us."

Dolly's expression didn't change as she said, "I am honored, *messieurs*. Please make yourselves comfortable. The pleasures of the house are yours."

"I want that one," the large man said, pointing to Stella.

Dolly paused a fraction of a second, then said, "I'm sorry. As you can see, she's engaged. You are welcome to your choice of any who are free."

"I said I want that one." He started toward Stella, but Dolly moved in front of him and barred the way.

"I told you she's busy," she said, without a trace of French accent. "Abe Ruef may have sent you here, but he doesn't tell me how to run my house. If you're such a good buddy of his, why don't you go to one of his houses, anyway?"

The man stared at her, his face turning red, and his companion plucked at his sleeve and said, "What the hell, Sam, what difference which one you get? Let's have a drink, and maybe they'll all look better."

The man continued to stare at Dolly, then said, "I'm not going to forget this," and turned away to sit down.

"See that you don't," Dolly replied. "And if you give me any more trouble you'll be out of here on your fat arse." The man paused, halfway into his chair, and she said, "If you think I'm kidding, just try me." She looked beyond him at Petunia, who was waiting for the signal to call Ralph, the bouncer, but the man subsided, muttering, and Dolly gestured for Petunia to bring champagne.

"Who is this Abe Ruef?" Frank said in a low voice, to Stella. "It sounds as though he carries a big stick around here."

"He's the power behind Mayor Schmitz," she replied. "He gets money from all the French restaurants, and owns a big three-story *maison* on Jackson Street." She wrinkled her nose in disgust. "Like a big love factory. Not like here." She took her hand from Frank's knee, and began to massage the back of his neck.

"I'm fascinated by the idea of Vesuvius," Frank said, trying desperately to keep the conversation from getting out of hand. "I mean, a convulsion of nature like that is more than the imagination can handle."

"Oh, I don't know," Art replied. "I had a cousin once who was a convulsion of nature. Once we got him tied down he was no trouble."

Stella collapsed with laughter, and Clarita said, "Speaking of convulsions, I know a good game we can play. It's called Fun in the Home."

"How does it go?" Art asked.

"You get four people and lie on the floor, each with his head on another person's stomach. Then one person starts to laugh, and pretty soon everyone is shrieking with laughter."

"Then what?"

She spread her hands. "Then it's devil take the hindmost."

"Do you think Dolly would let us do it here?"

"Not in the parlor. But I'm sure she wouldn't mind if we did it upstairs."

Art looked at Frank. "How about it, kiddo? Think you're up to it?"

Frank ran a finger under his collar. "Isn't it getting a little late?" he said. "I mean, that sounds as though it would take a long—"

"Oh, for chrissakes stop stalling. You said you wanted to get laid, and I'm trying to accommodate you."

"That's not exactly what I said. What I said was—"

"You said you wanted to do the town. It comes to the same thing."

"Well . . . let's have another drink first, and then we'll see."

By eleven-thirty the gentleman who'd been to *Carmen* had ordered a third bottle of champagne and had taken it and Maribelle up the stairs; the two politicians had finished a bottle of champagne and one of brandy, and had retired with the two girls who earlier had been looking at the stereopticon views of Niagara Falls; two more fugitives from the opera had come in and were in a chug-a-lug contest, drinking champagne with Dolores and Lillybelle; and Stella and Clarita were alternately suggesting games to Frank and plying him with drinks, while Art sat glowering over a brandy snifter.

By one o'clock Maribelle was back downstairs, having had the *Carmen* gentleman pass out beyond any hope of immediate revival; the two politicians had made their noisy departure, and the girls were listlessly looking at pictures of Old Faithful; the gentlemen with Dolores and Lillybelle had been overcome with hiccups to the point where they were good for little else; and Frank had finally agreed to go upstairs for one—but only one— round of Fun in the Home.

By three o'clock the parlor was deserted, and the only sounds in the house were those of distant snoring. Leaving Petunia to clean up the parlor Dolly went upstairs to her room, where she made out a list of each girl and the work she'd done during the evening, and also which customers were to be charged overnight rates. It was much simpler to bill a man for the use of a room than to try to remove him from it, and his vulnerability the next morning was such that he seldom protested even the most exorbitant rate.

Not feeling sleepy, Dolly unlocked the drawer and took out the portfolio with her manuscript, and reread her latest start on Chapter Two. It seemed more promising than any of the others, so she went on with her story, telling how her first love had been an Arapahoe named Sick Wolf, who had helped her father rustle horses. Her defloration by Sick Wolf had been the one bright spot in the generally gloomy atmosphere following her father's execution by the vigilantes, and even after Sick Wolf met a similar end she treasured his memory for having been the first to show her that life had its ups as well as its downs.

She was so carried away by her narrative that she failed to notice the faint hint of daylight behind the drawn curtains, and she had just dipped her pen in the inkwell when the house jumped and shuddered, and a roaring filled the air, mixed with the noises of screams and crashes. The house was lurching like a ship in a storm; plaster fell and glasses shattered, and then everything was still, with the only sound the insane jangling of church bells in the distance. Dolly tottered to the door and flung it open, and was greeted by the sight of the opera-goer in his long underwear, staring bug-eyed as scantily clad girls rushed about like demented chickens.

"Good God, woman, get me out of here!" he bellowed. "I can't be found here like this!"

"Find your own way out!" Dolly replied. "But put on your trousers before you leave—I won't have you giving the place a bad name! Maribelle, help the gentleman into his clothes, and then get dressed yourself." Then she turned and shouted, "Be calm, girls, be calm! The worst is over!" just as Frank came rocketing out of another room stark naked and collided with Lillybelle, sending her sprawling. "Young man, get back in your room!" Dolly commanded. "And don't set foot outside until you're decently dressed!" Frank turned back and collided with Stella, who was trying to get a kimono around herself, and Dolly pushed them both into the room and slammed the door. Then she clapped her hands and shouted, "Girls! I want all girls to listen to me! When you are properly dressed, and not before, you will gather in the parlor and await further instructions! I don't want anyone going out in the streets on her own! Is that clear?" There were muffled sounds of assent. Dolly looked in the mirror and rearranged her hair, then with icy dignity descended the staircase into the parlor, which was strewn with fallen plaster, broken crockery, and shattered glass. She stared at the scene in silence, then went back upstairs and got the ledger in which she kept her accounts, and with that and her manuscript portfolio clutched to her breast she returned to the parlor, prepared to face whatever the day might bring.

# CHAPTER 4

Oakland lies about fifteen miles east of the San Andreas fault, so the damage was considerably less than in San Francisco. Walls and chimneys fell, some steeples toppled or were loosened, and the flagpole atop the City Hall was bent, but there was only one minor fire and, aside from the five at the Empire Theatre, no deaths.

George Bender's pharmacy, however, was a total shambles. He could tell as he approached the building that his fears had been well founded, and when he opened the door he found himself standing in an expanse of broken glass and porcelain, mixed with puddles of syrup, alcohol, arsenic, salts, vegetable oils, and virtually the entire pharmacopoeia. The apothecary jars in which he stored various items had tumbled from their shelves and shattered, in one case leaving a mass of leeches slithering in the debris. Rolls of bandage had been catapulted across the room in the same way that Bender himself had flown through the air, and in some instances they had come undone and now hung like limp streamers after a maniacal orgy. Puddles of gentian violet mixed with the red of the cherry-flavored cough syrup, which in turn blended into the unattractive brown of sulphur and molasses, and in one corner a broken crock of cocaine was turning a variety of colors as the white powder soaked up the nearby liquids. The only items that had not broken were those that were stored in locked cabinets, and these Bender opened carefully so as not to let anything fall. He told himself it really didn't matter if one more bottle broke; his entire stock was going to have to be replaced, and at the moment he had no idea where the money would come from.

In one of the cabinets—and why he had put it there he could not imagine—was a bottle of the elixir of which Lucille was so fond, and that reminded him that she had asked him to bring home a new supply. As he took the bottle down and put it aside, he reflected on the curious popularity of those tonics, elixirs, and medications that contained alcohol. One of his best-selling items was a vegetable compound for female complaints that contained a good slug of alcohol; another was a laxative called Peruna, the name of which implied prune juice but which also contained a substantial jolt in each dose, and the more he thought about it the more he realized that he could equate the popularity of each item with its alcoholic content. He looked at the bottle of Lucille's elixir but the label was vague about the proportions, and when he smelled it he could identify certain herbs and spices and, like a mist rising from a marsh, the sharper smell of alcohol.

He recorked the bottle and thought back to Lucille that morning, weak-kneed and trembling and looking as though she were about to faint. He'd ascribed it to the shock of the quake —the nervous reaction often takes a while to appear after a traumatic event—but now he began to wonder. No, he told himself. It's impossible. She'd have to drink gallons of the stuff to become addicted to it, and besides, nobody ever becomes addicted to medicine. Stew bums in saloons have to have their daily shot of red-eye, but they are a far cry from a lady taking an occasional dose of nerve tonic. It's an insult to Lucille even to think in those terms.

He got out a broom and began the hopeless task of sweeping up the floor. He tried to concentrate on what he was doing, and to find some way to finance the restocking of his business, but he couldn't keep his mind from slipping back to Lucille. He tried to remember the first time she'd had the elixir, and found it was lost in the jungle of trivia of the past. She'd had a cough syrup, he remembered, which she'd taken over a period of time for a nagging throat condition, but he couldn't be precise about when she'd switched to the elixir. He remembered her once saying that the elixir was better for her nerves, and when he asked her why her nerves needed soothing she gave him a sideways look and said nothing. That was the only hint, and he could not deduce a single thing from it.

They had met and married shortly after his graduation from pharmaceutical college. He'd wanted to be a doctor after his discharge from the Army, but a lack of funds and of pre-med training made it necessary for him to take a shorter course, and one that would allow him to start earning money a little sooner. Lucille seemed to respond to his enthusiasm for healing, and for a while everything went smoothly: their new business began to prosper, Lucille learned to be a better than average cook, and she was loving to a point where it sometimes became an embarrassment. More than once, when she snuggled close to him in bed, he'd had to tell her that they could not yet afford to have children, and then she would turn away, and in a short while would be asleep. She'd been perfectly understanding about it, he thought, until one night, when he assumed she was alseep, she spoke to him in a voice as clear as though she were speaking from a lecture platform.

"May I ask you something?" she said.

He opened his eyes, and saw that she was staring at the darkened ceiling. "Of course," he replied. "What would you like to know?"

"Is there anything the matter with me?"

"Anything the *matter?* Of course not—do you feel all right?"

"It's not how *I* feel; it's how *you* feel. Do you find me attractive?"

"I find you adorable! I wouldn't be married to anyone else! What is this all about?"

"Then why don't you prove it?"

"Prove it how? I married you, didn't I? And I haven't looked at a single wom—is that what you mean? Do you think I'm seeing someone else?"

"I don't know what you're doing—no, I don't think you're seeing someone else. I just want to know what's lacking in me."

"*Nothing!* I told you—you're adorable!"

"You take a funny way of showing it."

"How do you want me to prove it? How can I show you?"

There was a short silence, and then she said, "Nature's worked out a way."

"Oh. Well, yes, but that's impossible now."

"Why?"

"I've told you, we can't afford to have any children."

"We don't *have* to have children."

"I know of no other way of getting them."

"I mean—I mean—isn't there some way they can be prevented?"

"There is no way that is one hundred per cent sure. Believe me, I know."

"How do you know?"

"It's my business to know. The only sure preventive is abstinence."

Suddenly she laughed. "I just thought of a saying. Abstinence makes the heart grow fonder."

He reached across, and patted her arm. "There, now," he said. "That's the proper way to look at it."

Next day she acted as though nothing had happened, and it was not referred to again. As a matter of fact, the only big argument they ever had was on a totally different subject, and one he was still unable to figure out. One night at supper, Lucille put a plate of beans in front of him and said, "I wanted trout, but this was all I could find."

Bender looked at the beans, then at her. "Did you ask for trout?"

"Of course I asked for trout but they didn't have any, so this is what I got."

"You mean the fish market had no fish at all?"

"Naturally it had fish, but it didn't have trout. So I settled on beans."

"I should think that if you were in a mood for fish, then anything would be preferable to beans."

"Oh. You don't like my beans."

"I didn't say that. I said if you wanted fish, then why did you buy beans?"

"I didn't want fish, I wanted trout. And if you want to do the marketing for this household, all I can say is you're welcome to it."

"I'm not criticizing your marketing; I'm trying to get something straight. Is trout a fish, or isn't it?"

"Of course it's a fish. Did you think it was a bird dog?"

"I know what a trout is, but—"

"But I don't? Is that what you're trying to say?"

"Look—let's start at the beginning. If you can't have trout, what's the next closest thing to it?"

"Beans."

"But *why?*"

"You needn't treat me as though I'm an idiot, you know. Give me that dish."

"Why?"

"I said give me that dish." She took the plate of beans from in front of him, went to the window, and scraped it out. The beans made no noise, but from the sidewalk a man shouted something.

"Why did you do that?" Bender asked.

"You don't like the beans, you don't have to have them."

"So what will we have for supper?"

"That's your worry. I'm going to bed." She put the plate in the sink, scraped her own beans into the garbage, then ran water on the two plates, dried her hands, and went upstairs. Bender heard her walk quickly across the bedroom, and there followed the squeak of the medicine cabinet being opened, and the thud as its door was slammed shut. He sat at the table for a few minutes, then got up and went out to a restaurant on Twelfth Street.

Now, listlessly pushing the debris around with a broom, he wondered how much of her behavior could be blamed on the elixir. He still found it impossible to believe she was an addict, and if she felt it soothed her nerves it was probably better to give it to her than risk a real crisis by withholding it, so he gave up the futile sweeping and decided to go home for a shovel, at the same time taking the one remaining bottle. With everything that had happened today, and with all the uncertainties about the future, it was no time to deprive Lucille of any solace, no matter what else it might entail.

He left the shop, and out of habit locked it, although he knew there was nothing left that was worth stealing. As he turned toward home he looked at the sky over San Francisco, and saw that the smoke from some fifty fires had joined into one great, towering cloud, which seemed at this distance to be almost stationary but which was actually moving slowly to the south, driven by wind funneling through the Golden Gate from the sea. Most people in Oakland were busy with their own problems, but every now and then they would glance across the Bay, and what they saw made them realize how lucky they really were. A few with foresight realized they would soon have to make ready for an influx of refugees, but for the most part the Oaklanders stared in mute awe, and then went on about their business. Word came that a commuter train had been toppled off the tracks at Point Reyes, and nobody knew how many had been injured.

Bender continued toward home, and as he passed the Empire Theatre he saw a group of men digging in the wreckage. He stopped, wondering what they could be looking for, and it occurred to him that these were no idle scavengers; by the way they dug and clawed into the debris it was clear they were after something important. One of them looked around and saw him, and said, "Give us a hand here, will you?"

"What's up?" Bender asked, going toward them.

"There's a guy buried here." The man lifted a chunk of masonry, and rolled it to one side.

"There can't be," Bender replied. "I was here before, and they got out all the survivors."

"They may have thought they did, but they missed one. We heard him a couple of minutes ago."

Bender took off his jacket, hung it on the iron fence, and joined the men. "Where is he?" he asked.

"It's hard to tell, because you can barely hear him. He may have croaked by now."

At this moment there came a faint, smothered cry, like a distant person calling into the wind. "I think he's over this way," another man said. "It sounded closer to here."

"I've got a shovel at home," said Bender. "It's only a couple of blocks away—I'll run and get it." He turned, and started off.

"If you've got a crowbar it would help," the man called to him, but Bender was already racing down the street, leaving his jacket hanging on the fence with Lucille's bottle of elixir in the pocket.

# CHAPTER 5

Tuesday was the night Gresham Stoddard dreaded more than any in the week, because that was the night his wife Muriel had set aside for the opera. Nothing short of fire or flood could have kept Muriel from her box on Tuesday nights; the news of the sinking of the *Maine*, on a Tuesday night eight years before, had left her completely unruffled, and when two months later Congress declared war on Spain, the Stoddard carriage had taken Muriel and Gresham to the performance of *Der Rosenkavalier* through streets that were thronged with noisy, flag-waving crowds. He'd had a flash of feeling like Louis XVI on his way to the guillotine, but Muriel took the cool, no-nonsense approach, which was that the rest of the world could do as it pleased; what happened in San Francisco was all that mattered.

As he read his copy of the *Call* this Tuesday morning, Stoddard was grateful that Muriel hadn't made Monday their opera night: the previous evening Edith Walker had sung *The Queen of Sheba*, and the review was murderous. At least, Stoddard reflected, they would hear Caruso this evening, and while he held no brief for tenors it would have to be a more bearable evening than Monday had apparently been. Sometimes, when an opera became too long or too shrill, he would feel the icy fingers of claustrophobia plucking at his nerve ends; his heart would race and his feet begin to twitch, and he would have to go out into the fresh air and walk around. Once or twice the claustrophobia developed into a full-blown attack of asthma, but usually the fresh air was enough to return his pulse and breathing to normal.

He had a feeling that this evening might be difficult, because Muriel had invited the Leffert Neppletons to join them, and the Leffert Neppletons were bores beyond the usual meaning of the word. Phyllis Neppleton's father, Crocker Pratt, had come to San Francisco in 1850, rounding the Horn in the S.S. *California* and thereby becoming one of the Argonauts, who organized a reunion almost immediately upon landing and who thereafter looked with what they believed was well-bred contempt on all the subsequent settlers. An evening with Phyllis Neppleton was like a six-month course at the California Historical Society, all told in the regal "we." Stoddard could only hope that Caruso might drown her out, or that between her and Caruso his mind might be diverted from his personal and business problems, which were growing with the speed of a line squall.

It was a forlorn hope, and he knew as they took their places in the box that he wasn't going to be able to last the entire performance. Before the house lights went down he was experiencing a lack of oxygen, and although he took long, even breaths his heart began to race, and his chest to shrink. He tried giving a burst of laughter as a way to relieve the tension, but it was poorly timed, and Phyllis Neppleton thought he was laughing at the Argonauts.

"And when, pray, did *your* parents come here?" she asked. "Or are you a recent arrival? I don't seem to recall your saying."

It was the first time she'd ever asked him anything about himself, and he decided to make the most of it. "My parents were Spanish," he said. "Spanish Indians. Our real name is Seguro."

What the hell, he thought as Phyllis turned away. In another week or so it won't make any difference. Nothing will make any difference, when it comes to that.

He lasted through Act I, which featured "Parlez-moi de ma mère," the duet between Caruso and Mme. Olive Fremstad, and he made it halfway through "La fleur que tu m'avais jeté," Caruso's flower-song aria in Act II, and then the asthma began in earnest. He found himself gasping for air, and decided to leave before he had to be carried out. He could see Muriel watching him out of the corner of her eye, so he stood up, wheezed, "See you at home," in her ear, then took his hat and cape from their hook and all but ran down the carpeted stairs and out into the cool night air.

The Grand Opera House was on Mission Street, south of Market, and to reach his home on Nob Hill Stoddard had to cross Market Street and skirt the edge of the Upper Tenderloin, which began at Mason. When once again he could breathe, he realized it would be some little while before Muriel and the Neppletons got home for the light supper she always served, and he had time for some relaxation of his own. And God knows he could use it; unless he could come up with some spectacularly brilliant idea, he was as good as in jail right now. It was this thought, rather than Caruso or Phyllis Neppleton, that had been responsible for the severity of his asthma.

It had started several years before, when a friend had asked for backing in the mining of a gold strike. It was a sure thing, the friend said; the gold was there, and all that was needed was to get it out of the ground. At first Stoddard had invested his own money, but the mining took longer than anticipated and it became inconvenient to be continually shelling out cash, so Stoddard took some of his railroad stock, used it as collateral to obtain a loan at the bank where he was a director, and then managed, by an extremely delicate bit of bookkeeping, to get the collateral stock back into his own hands. It worked so well that he used the same device the next time the friend asked for money, and although the mine had not paid off, the friend had the word of a prominent geologist that in the long run it couldn't fail, so Stoddard kept pumping money into it on the assumption that it would all be repaid when the mine finally began to produce. The only trouble was that the mine proved to be a washout, and Stoddard was left owing his bank several hundred thousand dollars he was in no position to repay. By dint of his position he was able to cover it up for a while, but now questions were being asked, and it was only a matter of time before the whole thing came out in the open. As he saw it, he had three choices: he could admit to the theft right now, and hope for some kind of leniency; he could wait until it was discovered, and a case made against him in court, and see how the jury voted; or he could take every nickel he could lay his hands on, tomorrow morning, and head for either Mexico or Canada. The last option appealed the most strongly, especially during long stretches of Wagnerian opera or in the company of thundering bores, and the more he thought about it the more he became convinced that the only real choice he had to make was where to go. Mexico was closer, but not by much, and while as a Californian he'd had more contact with the Latin way of life, there was a certain allure in the idea of the Canadian Northwest, the Yukon, and all the rest of it. Stoddard felt that if he hadn't been born and raised in banking, he might have made a good living as a fur trapper. And he'd have been able to choose his own friends.

It was in this frame of mind that he made a sudden decision: he turned left when he reached Market Street, walked west to Mason, and then north to the intersection of Mason and O'Farrell. He knew the way well, having visited Dolly's establishment on and off during the past few years, and she greeted him with warm recognition when she opened the door.

"Ah, *monsieur!*" she exclaimed. "I thought you had forgotten us!"

"Not likely," Stoddard replied, removing his opera hat as he went inside.

"I regret that Stella is engaged right now, but Maribelle is at liberty, and I am sure—"

"I don't care about the girl—it's my throat that needs attention," Stoddard said, heading for the parlor.

"I understand, *monsieur*. I simply wanted you to know that I remember your preference, and to assure you that Maribelle will be every bit as—"

"My God, get me a drink!" Stoddard cut in, and Dolly took his hat and cape as Petunia brought a bottle of champagne to the banquette. The champagne was cold, and refreshing, and for a few minutes he thought of nothing but the slow unwinding that was taking place throughout his body. A young man across the room, who appeared to be Stella's companion, started asking him about Caruso, but Stoddard, who wanted to forget about the opera and all that part of his life, concentrated more on the champagne than he did on his replies. He noticed Maribelle sitting beside him, and for the first time felt a faint spark of desire. He'd reached the age where this always came as a pleasant surprise, and he decided to nurture it as long as he could. When the first bottle was empty he ordered a second, and in the back of his mind toyed with the idea of asking Maribelle to come to the Yukon with him.

By the time the second bottle was gone, his plans were definite: he would spend the night here with Maribelle, who was beginning more and more to resemble Lily Langtry, and in the morning he would withdraw everything from the bank and take her with him to the Northwest Territory. He ordered a final bottle, and when Petunia brought it he took it by the neck, offered his arm to Maribelle, and made his stately though unsteady way toward the stairs. "Come, my Jersey Lily," he said as they started the ascent. "Tonight we revel, tomorrow we flee."

"There's nobody here named Lily," Maribelle replied, following behind him in case he should start to topple. "You must be thinking of some other house."

"Ah, well," said Stoddard. "A man is allowed to dream, I suppose."

"Not on my time you're not. Or if you do, you pay for overtime."

"Money is no object, my Lily. There's always more where the first came from, and that is the secret of success."

"You're cute," said Maribelle. "I think we're going to have a good time."

When they reached her room, Stoddard sat heavily on the edge of the bed and took a long swallow from the bottle. The foam almost choked him, and he coughed and gasped and handed the bottle to Maribelle, then tried to remove his jacket, but he got one arm caught behind him, and she had to come to his assistance. She then undid his tie, and began to work on his collar stud; his boiled shirt buckled, and to make things more difficult he was trying to undo his cuff links while she worked on the collar. "Do you know *The Call of the Wild?*" he asked when finally his collar sprang clear.

"No," said Maribelle, kneeling down to untie his shoes. "How does it go?"

"It's a book, by Jack London. One of the greatest books ever written."

"Is it about love?"

"No. Well, in a way. The love of a dog for his master."

"That sounds filthy." She reached for his trouser buttons.

"No, it's beautiful. This dog is named Buck, and when his master dies, Buck goes off and leads a pack of wolves."

"That's all there is to it? Lift up, so I can get your trousers off."

"That's all, but it doesn't tell the story. The story is about the hidden animal in all of us, and the desire to go back to the wild, and—and—where'd you put the champagne?"

"On the dresser."

"Let's have it."

"Don't you want a glass?"

"Buck wouldn't have used a glass. What's good enough for Buck is good enough for me."

She handed him the bottle. "Are you trying to tell me you want to do it dog style?"

"Do what?"

"What are you here for?"

"I'm here to take you to the great Northwest, where a man can be free and unfettered, and can do whatever comes into his mind."

Maribelle had removed her dress, and was loosening her corset. She stopped, and said, "Anything I do, I do right in this room. You can pretend you're in the Northwest if you want—pretend you're a moose, for all I care—but don't think I'm going to go chasing around any wilderness."

"Don't you want to run through the tundra—bark at the moon—go where the spirit leads you—?"

"Not in a million years. I have a queasy feeling when I go out for the milk."

Stoddard drank some of the champagne, coughed, then stared gloomily across the room. "Drat," he said. "Another dream shattered."

"Oh, no," Maribelle said, sinking down and putting her arms around his knees. "We don't shatter dreams here—this is where we make dreams come true. Think of something—anything to do with love—and you will see if I don't make it come true."

"That's a pretty tall order," Stoddard said.

"Try me out, and see."

He took another drink, then said, "All right. Let's pretend we're eels. Two eels that are passionately in love, and haven't seen each other in years."

She stared at him. "Do we have to get all slippery?"

"I leave that up to you."

She dropped the rest of her clothes. "Boy," she said. "You believe in making a girl work for her living, don't you?"

When, at five-thirteen the next morning, he was hurled out of bed and onto the floor, he had no idea where he was. He heard screams and crashes and the distant jangling of church bells, and it wasn't until he rushed into the corridor and was confronted by Dolly that his memory began to return. With Maribelle's frantic help he got dressed, then dashed down the tilting stairs and into the street, where he stopped, adjusted his tie, and tried to appear casual as he started toward Nob Hill.

If he thought people would notice his evening clothes and wonder where he'd been, he was mistaken. The streets were full of people but most of them simply stared, their faces blank with shock, at the ruins of the city around them. Piles of rubble and masonry littered the streets; sometimes whole houses had fallen and sometimes just their facades, and under the debris could be seen an occasional horse, or a shattered wagon. Some people were in nightclothes and some wore incongruous-looking finery; they had come to the street in the first things they could find, and the one thing they had in common was the gray, stunned look on their faces. The silence was almost absolute: once or twice a brief cry or a moan could be heard, but the most ominous sound that pervaded the silence was the hiss of escaping gas.

Many fires had already started, but none could be reported to the central fire station; the batteries that powered the alarm system had been knocked out, so all reports were either visual or by word of mouth. They did little good anyway, because the city's water mains had been ruptured, and the only way to get water was to pump it from the Bay. The fires grew and multiplied, and in only a very few instances were they able to be controlled.

As Stoddard made his way toward Nob Hill the size of the disaster slowly became apparent, and for the first time he wondered what had happened to his house and, more specifically, to Muriel. She had always seemed indestructible, a figure that would last as long as the city lasted, but now, with the city lying in ruins and God only knew how many people dead, he faced the possibility that Muriel might be among them. It *seemed* impossible but there it was, and there was no special divinity that shielded her. For the last several years his relationship with Muriel had been that of, say, an equerry to the Queen, and in his obedience to her whims he had come to regard her as permanent. He felt curiously detached about the whole subject, and wished he could be a little more worried. I guess that's the problem, he thought: I never have worried about her, so it's hard to start now, especially given this feeling of total unreality. The sight of a woman in her nightclothes, wearing a wide-brimmed hat trimmed with cherries and carrying a fur muff, did nothing to bring reality any closer.

Most of the fires were, for the moment, south of Market Street, so Nob Hill was in no immediate danger from fire. But many of the Nob Hill houses had been damaged, some more severely than others, and as he approached his own house he could see cracked walls and broken windows and, when he looked inside, the rubble of fallen ceilings, with chandeliers lying amid heaps of plaster. The front door was open, and he went inside and called Muriel's name, but there was no answer. For some reason, the house seemed to smell of decay. He climbed the stairs gingerly, afraid that his extra weight might cause the weakened beams to collapse, and when he reached Muriel's bedroom he saw that the ceiling had fallen there, too. Chunks of plaster covered her bed, which had apparently been slept in, but there was no sign of blood and no way to tell if she'd been injured. He went back to the servants' quarters, which were less heavily damaged but also empty, and after calling two or three times he concluded he was alone in the house. He was on the point of leaving when it occurred to him that it might be better to get out of his evening clothes, so he changed into street clothes, emptied the library wall safe of all its cash, and then, feeling totally at loose ends, wondered if he should pack anything to take with him. The only trouble was he didn't know where he was going; all he knew was he had to look for his wife, and he didn't have the faintest idea where to begin.

# CHAPTER 6

Henry Walden was in a deep, exhausted sleep when the wall fell on the Empire Theatre. He was aware of a thunderous crashing all around him, and of the sensation of falling, and his first thought was that it was his recurring war dream, brought on by the time at Las Guásimas when the Rough Riders walked into a trap. The shock of that engagement would probably stay with him the rest of his life: they had been marching through the jungle four abreast, exactly as though they were on parade, with no scouts and nobody covering the point or the flanks, when all of a sudden the foliage around them erupted with a blast of Mauser rifle fire. Some men were killed instantly and some were wounded; the others dove for the ground and tried to return the fire, but they were shooting blindly at an unseen enemy, and it wasn't until reinforcements came up that they were able to withdraw. A correspondent who was one of Colonel Roosevelt's devoted admirers wrote that it "was not technically an ambush, although it is true that the American troops met the Spaniards before they had expected to." To the professional soldiers it was damned well an ambush, brought on by arrant carelessness and/or stupidity.

The helpless feeling of being surrounded by an unseen enemy was at the core of Walden's nightmares, which often took the form of falling into a pit or being pinned down and unable to move, and it took him a little time to realize he wasn't dreaming. He tried to sit up, and slammed his forehead into what was apparently a beam lying across him. Something else had immobilized his legs, and although he could move his arms a little he could not get an effective grip on anything, or in any way change his position. The darkness was absolute, as was, at first, the silence; once or twice he heard a groan, and that was all. He tried shouting but received no answer, and he decided to save his breath and what little oxygen remained around him. As far as he could tell he wasn't badly hurt, and his most imminent danger was of suffocation. So he lay still and listened, and tried to think of an appropriate prayer. His church upbringing had been mandatory because his father was a vestryman, and he had long ago become cynical about the doctrine, but he felt that at the moment he needed every bit of help he could get. He prayed on the off chance that there might be something to it after all, and he ran through the Lord's Prayer with more feeling than usual, concluding: ". . . forever and ever. Amen. And, Lord, if there *is* a way out of this trap, please may it be revealed to me. Amen again." He knew better than to promise good behavior, or any such slippery currying of favor. The Lord, if He existed, was wise enough not to believe such promises, made under the duress of desperation.

After what seemed like an hour but was probably only a few minutes, he heard faint voices and the rattle and thud of debris being moved. He shouted as loudly as he could but received no reply, and he told himself he'd have to wait until they came closer before calling again. He was definitely using too much oxygen; his head ached, and the darkness was studded with twinkling blue stars, and he knew he couldn't last long if he continued at this rate. Then he lost consciousness; the blue stars faded, and everything was black. He remembered thinking of Hamlet's final line: "The rest is silence," and then he thought nothing more.

When George Bender got home, he raced into the tool shed behind the stable, picked up a shovel, then looked around for something that might serve as a crowbar. He was rummaging among the various implements and bits of hardware when Lucille came in, still in her nightclothes and looking if anything worse than before.

"Did you get it?" she asked.

"Get what?" said Bender, examining a length of lead pipe. "The elixir."

"Oh. That." He glanced around as though it might have been following him. "Yes."

"Where is it?"

"I guess it's in my jacket." He put down the pipe, and picked up a longer section. "I'll bring it later." He started out, taking the shovel and the long piece of pipe, but Lucille stopped him.

"You promised you'd bring it to me," she said.

"I *did!* It's in my jacket, over at the Empire Theatre! Now, please—I've got to get back!"

"I'll come with you."

"Not dressed like that, you won't. Put on some clothes."

"People don't care who wears what after an earthquake. For all they know, I might have just got up."

"Lucille, are you crazy? You don't move out of this house until you're dressed."

"Will you wait for me?"

"No! There's still one man buried there, and he may be dying!"

"In that case a couple of minutes won't make any difference. I'll just be a—"

"I'll see you there. But *get dressed!*" Without waiting for a reply Bender turned and ran off. Lucille watched him go, then went into the house. The brute, she thought. He has no sympathy for suffering.

When Bender got to the theater, the other men were moving rubble about in a deliberate way that suggested they weren't exactly sure what they were doing. "Have you heard him again?" Bender asked.

One of the men shook his head. "We thought we did a minute ago, but the sound always seems to come from a different place. I don't know what the hell is going on."

"I couldn't find a crowbar," Bender said. "But I thought this pipe might help, as a sort of probe. If we find where he is, we could ram it down and get some fresh air to him."

"A good idea," the other man said. "If we find where he is."

The first eight men, who had been removed earlier, had been in a section of the building where only the roof caved in, whereas Walden's room had been in a small adjunct, a sort of ell, and there not only the ceiling but also the floor had given way, making his entombment that much deeper. The only quick way to clean up the debris would have been with a Bucyrus steam shovel, such as was being used to dig the Panama Canal, but that would be counterproductive in that it would mangle any human being it touched. The only alternative, lacking any firm direction, was to move the wreckage piece by piece, and hope for the best.

"I'm going to try probing," Bender said, handing the shovel to one of the men. "It can't hurt, and who knows? If I hit him, he may yell, and then we'll know where he is."

"Make a plug for the end of the pipe you probe with," another man suggested. "That way it won't get clogged with dirt, and you can use it as an air tube if you have to."

"Good thinking," said Bender. He stuffed his handkerchief into one end of the pipe, leaving enough hanging out so he could remove it, then climbed onto the mound of debris and began to probe. He ran the pipe down as far as it would go, working it back and forth to enlarge the hole, but found nothing. He removed it, moved on a few feet, and tried again. If it weren't for the fact that a man's life hung in the balance, Bender could almost say he was enjoying himself. It was the first time since the Army that he had worked with a group of men, and he found a certain pleasure in the imagination they brought to bear on any given problem. The Army tried to tape out all the answers, and have every possible contingency covered by the book, but in actual practice it was the inventiveness of the individual that got the job done, and this inventiveness brought with it a definite satisfaction. He remembered one man, when they were in the trenches on Misery Hill overlooking Santiago, who rigged up a windmill-driven clothes washer and then, when he found there was not enough water to spare, converted it into a delousing machine by substituting currycombs for the washer paddles. It didn't work very well, but the idea was beautiful.

Bender was on his sixth probe when he saw Lucille approaching, and he was relieved to see she was fully dressed. Normally he would not have worried, but the wild look in her eye when she said she'd accompany him in her nightclothes made him wonder if perhaps she wasn't either feverish, or sick, or—he refused to let himself complete the thought. He called, "It's over there," and pointed to the fence where his jacket was hung, and saw Lucille produce a tumbler from her apron pocket as she went to retrieve the bottle of elixir. She seems all right now, he thought. But I'd better get some more elixir right away, before she finishes that bottle. He ran the probe down once more, and hit a solid beam.

When next Henry Walden regained consciousness, he was sure he was either dying or already dead. He'd heard, from men who had come close to death, that it was a sensation like rushing down a long corridor, with a slowly diminishing light at the end, and that in some cases the person felt removed from himself, looking down on the scene like a casual observer. Walden had no such feeling; he was simply surrounded by darkness, but the waning supply of oxygen gave him faint hallucinations that made him unsure of exactly what was happening. He made two or three feeble attempts to call, then gave up and resigned himself to the fact that, if he wasn't already dead, he would be very soon.

And what have I accomplished in thirty-two years? he thought. Nothing. A big, fat zero. I pissed away every chance I had to make something of myself, so sure I was a winner that I didn't even try. Well, Lord, if you're listening to me now—and I see no reason why you should be—I can tell you one thing: I would gladly be a five-dollar-a-week clerk—I would gladly dig ditches—if I were given the chance for another go-round. I don't expect to have it, but I thought you ought to know. But perhaps you'll tell *me* something: why is it that I learn these things too late? Why couldn't I have had a little common sense when it might have done some good, and not shot every opportunity almost as soon as it presented itself? And why, of all things, couldn't I have found a woman? If I'd found the right woman I might have settled down, and all these other problems would have straightened themselves out. But no; every time I got near a woman something went wrong, and so badly wrong as to make it pointless to try to see her again. There was a definite pattern there, but I'm damned if I can see the reason for it.

He remembered a time, two winters ago, when he'd met a young lady named Helen Prestwick at a dinner party. She was attractive, in a quiet sort of way, and something about her suggested there might be more beneath the surface: there were traces of humor and, every now and then, a hint of refined passion. When he'd seen her a few times and felt he knew her well enough, he asked if she would care to have dinner with him some evening.

"I'd love to," she replied. "Do you have a friend?"

"What do you mean?"

"For my sister, Grace." She indicated a tall, solemn-looking girl across the room. "Daddy insists that whenever we go out, we go together."

"Probably a good idea," Walden replied. "Yes, of course. I know a"—he thought a moment—"I have a friend who'd be happy to join us. I'll talk to him, and then we can set up a date."

He talked to his friend, whose name was Steve Gadsden, and Gadsden was dubious about the idea. He and Walden had shared a number of experiences over the years, but there was something about this one that made Gadsden tentative, and cautious.

"Actually, this Grace is not at all bad-looking," Walden told him. "I think she might be a lot of fun. And anyway, it isn't as though you were being asked to marry her. This is for one evening only, and if you don't like her you'll never have to see her again."

"Suppose you want to see more of her sister?" Gadsden replied. "From what you say, you'll need someone for Grace."

"If you don't want to, I can always get someone else. And besides, this is a sort of shot in the dark. I have a hunch about this girl, and that's all."

"All right," said Gadsden. "But if it's a washout, I'm wasting a lot of good money."

"If it's a washout I'll pay for the whole thing. You can't ask for more than that."

"I can," Gadsden replied. "But I won't."

They went to Lüchow's, and as they entered the restaurant they were greeted by the sounds of the string ensemble playing "Tales from the Vienna Woods." Grace slowed as though to stop, then continued down the long entrance hall.

"This is a German restaurant," she said.

"That's right," Gadsden replied. "The best German food in town."

"I cannot abide Germans," said Grace. "I thought this would be Chinese."

"As a matter of fact they're not Germans," Walden put in, quickly. "They're Austrians, and in some cases Swiss. And they're all naturalized American citizens. As American as corn on the cob."

"They speak German," Grace said.

"Oh, Gracie, forget it," Helen cut in. "Even if they *were* Germans, not every German is Helmut Schwanz."

"Who's Helmut Schwanz?" Gadsden asked.

"We don't speak of him," Grace replied, through clenched teeth.

"Well, now!" Walden said, brightly, when they were seated. "What would you ladies care to drink?"

Grace said, "Nothing," and Helen said, "Oh, Gracie, do have something—it'll make you feel more cheerful. Won't you join me at least in a sherry?"

"I've an idea," Walden said. "I think Steve and I will probably have champagne, so why don't you ladies join us in that? Does that appeal to you?"

"That sounds just lovely," Helen said without even looking at her sister. "We'd adore it."

"I'll go with the champagne, but I want a schnapps first," Gadsden said. "To get the ball rolling, so to speak."

"A sound thought," said Walden. "I'll join you." He turned to the waiter, who was hovering behind him. "Two schnapps right away," he said. "And then a bottle—make it a magnum—of Mumm's. Brut, if you have it."

*"Jawohl, mein Herr,"* the waiter said, and vanished.

"At least the champagne is French," Grace said, half aloud.

"Hush," said Helen. "Relax, and enjoy yourself."

It was in trying to relax that Walden and Gadsden brought about their own downfall. They had two schnapps apiece, then the better part of the magnum of champagne (Grace had one glass, and Helen two), then beer with their sauerbraten, and finally, after the flaming pancakes, they got into the brandy. Once or twice Walden had the sudden feeling that he didn't know where he was—he could have been in Vienna, or Munich, for all he knew—but then the sensation passed and he recognized Gadsden, whose eyes were becoming somewhat heavy-lidded. He wondered what Gadsden was doing at the table with him, and determined to ask later on. When coffee arrived, the ladies excused themselves to go to the powder room, and after a short silence Gadsden said, "That's probably a good idea."

"What's probably a good idea?" Walden asked.

"To go to the crapper. I'm about to burst."

"You're on. Last one there is a rotten egg."

They rose, and as they made their way down the corridor they saw that newly arrived patrons had tracked snow into the vestibule. "Hey," said Walden. "What do you know? It's snowing."

"I don't care what else is happening, I just know about my bladder," Gadsden said, and pushed open the door to the men's room. Walden followed him in.

"Remember the night we went skiing in Central Park?" Walden said, fumbling with his trouser buttons.

"Could I ever forget?" Gadsden, standing at the urinal, let his breath out in a long sigh. "Ah-h-h-h-h, that's better," he said after a few moments. "I felt as though my back teeth were floating."

"I wonder where my skis are," Walden said, moving in beside him. "That was a lot of fun, that night."

"Did you ever go skijoring?" Gadsden asked.

"What's that?"

"You let a horse pull you."

"On skis?"

"Of course on skis. What else?"

"Suppose he takes a crap."

"Just spread your skis, and straddle it."

"Where did you learn that?"

"When I was in Austria."

"Do they have horses in Austria?"

"They have horses the way other people have mice."

"Son of a gun. I always thought they just yodeled."

"Let's see if we can find your skis. Then if we can find a horse, I'll show you."

"You're on."

They left the men's room and retrieved their hats and coats, and when they reached the sidewalk it was snowing heavily. Clouds of snow whirled around the streetlamps and deadened the sounds of the traffic, and they had to walk two blocks before they could find a hansom cab. They got in, and gave the driver Walden's address, and as they sat back Gadsden said, "I'll bet one of those cabbies at the Plaza would loan us his horse."

"I don't think he'd loan it," Walden replied. "But he might rent it. People don't loan things unless there's something in it for them."

"A guy I know loaned me a goat once."

"What did you want it for?"

"Something inconsequential. I gave it back next day."

"Well, I'd loan you a horse, but I don't have one."

"Maybe this guy will loan us his. Should we ask him?"

"Let's find my skis first. After that, we'll know what we're doing."

"Where did you last see them?"

"That's the trouble. I don't remember."

"Well, not many people have skis, so it shouldn't be too hard to find them."

"I never thought of it that way. We're as good as on the slopes right now."

"I wish I hadn't had that last brandy. My vision isn't all it might be."

"What last brandy?"

"After din . . . oh, my God. Oh, my dear, sweet, ever-loving Christ."

"What's the matter?"

"The girls. We left them at the restaurant."

Walden leaped up, and rapped on the trap. "Driver!" he shouted. "Driver! Turn around!"

The trap opened, and the driver's face appeared. His hat was covered with snow. "Sir?" he said.

"Turn around!" Walden cried. "Go back to Lüchow's!"

"It's too late," Gadsden said in a hollow voice. "They'll have left by now."

A grim-faced waiter, who looked something like Bismarck, confirmed that they had indeed left, and he presented Walden with the bill.

"Did they leave any message?" Walden asked as he brought out his wallet.

"No, zir," the waiter replied. "Dey zaid dot vouldn't be necezzary."

Now, lying in the darkness, Walden felt he was close enough to death so that his whole life should be passing in front of him, as was supposed to happen in these cases. But all that came to him were bits of trivia and, try as he might, he couldn't conjure up any broad panorama, which reinforced his earlier conclusion that his life had been nothing; for all the impact he'd had, he might as well not have lived. He tried to think of what he would do if, by some miracle, he were to be saved: would he establish a scholarship for orphans, or do good works among the poor, or devote his life to medical research— how could he make his life worthwhile, when he had started out so poorly? It was idle speculation anyway, but at least it would pass the time until his final blackout.

He must have become delirious, because he had just invented the largest gold tooth in the world when he heard a scraping noise, then a rattle of falling earth, and something hard hit him on the shoulder. It pressed down, then was withdrawn, then stabbed again, and he realized that somebody, or something, must be at the other end. He gathered all his waning strength and shouted, "Hey! Cut it *out!*" There was a pause, then the thing vanished upward, and from somewhere far away he could hear voices. Dumb bastards, he thought as he closed his eyes. They could hurt a man with that sort of thing.

# CHAPTER 7

Dolly and her seven girls sat in the ruined parlor and waited—for what, they didn't know, but they instinctively clung to the shelter of the house as long as they could. The curtains, habitually kept closed, had had to be drawn apart to let in some daylight, because the gas main had ruptured and there was no illumination, and the harsh, white light of day seemed to magnify the feeling of desolation. One shaft of light was alive with motes, which hung in suspension like early morning fog, and the air was gritty and smelled of dampness, as though the falling plaster had uncovered a cesspool behind the walls.

Dolly turned to Maribelle, who was idly toying with a deck of cards. "Did your gentleman pay you before he left?" she asked.

Maribelle thought for a moment, then shook her head. "No," she said. "He was in such an all-fired hurry to get out I forgot to ask him."

"You know House Rule Number One," Dolly said. "They don't get their pants until they pay. The first thing they should do is put your *petit cadeau* on the dresser."

"I know, but last night was sort of unusual," Maribelle replied. "He had that bottle of champagne, and then he wanted to play eel, and what with one thing and another I never got around to asking him. Then this morning—" She spread her hands, and shrugged.

"Funny you should mention eels," Clarita put in. "My young man wanted to play frog. Had me jumping from one end of the bed to the other until I thought I'd scream."

Maribelle looked at Stella. "You had his friend, didn't you?" she said. "The shy one."

"Not 'arf," replied Stella.

"How was he?"

"He got over his shyness, all right. But first we had to lie on the bloody floor and laugh."

Maribelle shook her head. "It was a weird night all over," she said. "Maybe the earthquake was trying to tell us something."

"If it was, it brought its message too late," Clarita said. "I ache in every joint in my body."

"You should keep yourself in better condition," Dolly said. "Exercises every day."

"I do *those* exercises," Clarita replied. "I can pick up a single dime from the table. It's the four-footed jumping I'm not prepared for."

"A professional girl should be prepared for anything," Dolly said, with an air of finality.

"Will you do the frog act if he comes back?" Clarita asked.

"In the old days I would have," Dolly said, then changed the subject. "I wonder if there was much damage to the city."

"We'll never find out sitting here," Stella replied.

"I'll send Petunia out to see." Dolly called Petunia's name, but there was no answer, so she said, "Somebody check her room," and Lillybelle, who was nearest the door, went into the back of the house. She returned in less than a minute.

"She's not there," she said. "Her bed was slept in, but she's gone."

Dolly frowned. "That shows poor discipline," she said. "She shouldn't have left without checking with me."

"If you'll excuse me saying so, I think we all ought to leave," said Stella. "For all we know, we could be surrounded by fire this very minute."

"I haven't heard any fire engines," replied Dolly.

"That proves nothing. Maybe the fire stations all collapsed, and buried them."

"I agree with Stella," Maribelle said. "Maybe there's no city left."

"There's one thing certain," Clarita put in, "and that is we're not going to do any business today. People will have their minds on other things. I think at least we ought to see what's happening."

"All right," said Dolly reluctantly. "Perhaps you're right. But I want us all to stay together. Anyone who goes off on her own will be fined a week's take, and there will be no talking with strangers. Is that clear?"

There were murmured sounds of assent, and Dolly, clutching her ledger and her manuscript to her bosom, shepherded the girls out the door. Out of habit she tried to lock it, but the building was so badly sprung the door wouldn't even close.

It took a while for them to comprehend the scope of the disaster. O'Farrell Street was a shambles, but as yet there was no fire; debris and parts of shattered houses littered the street, and everywhere there were stunned-looking people, moving silently northward. Some carried suitcases, some had their arms full of clothes or such unlikely items as parrot cages and punch bowls, and one man had affixed roller skates to a steamer trunk, and was pushing it in the procession that moved up Taylor Street, in the general direction of Nob Hill. When Dolly and the girls looked south, across Market Street, they saw the reason for the movement: the fires that started there after the initial shock had grown and melded together, feeding on the ramshackle wooden houses and moving generally westward, fanned by the breeze that came off the Bay. Market Street, broader than most, was known as the Slot, and it looked as though everything south of it would be consumed. If the fire could be prevented from crossing the Slot, there was hope it might be partially contained; if not, the whole city might go.

Dolly and the girls stared in open-mouthed awe at the smoke that rose in towering clouds and blotted out the sun. "Jesus, Mary, and Joseph," Lillybelle whispered. "It's the destruction of Sodom as sure as Bob's your uncle. We brought it on ourselves."

"We'll have no more of that talk!" Dolly said sharply. "It's a natural disaster, and it could happen anywhere. Think of all those Italians, with Vesuvius pouring hot lava on them."

"What are we going to do?" Maribelle said. "Where should we go?"

This was a question Dolly had been trying to avoid. Looking at it realistically, it would be impossible to do any organized business in San Francisco for some time to come, so her only choice would be to relocate elsewhere. But where? Nobody knew how widespread the damage had been—whether it had flattened Oakland, and San Jose, and Santa Clara and the rest —so the only sensible thing would be to stay here, in as safe an area as possible, until the full picture could be seen.

"For the moment, I think we'll find a nice park and stay there," Dolly replied. "Then we'll see what happens after that."

"I'm going to join the Church," Lillybelle said. "You can do what you want, but I'm going to find a nun or a priest, and turn myself in."

"You'll do nothing of the sort," said Dolly. "You'll stay with the rest of us. The nuns and priests will have enough to worry about today, without adding you to their troubles."

"I'll be no trouble; I'll help them. I know when I've seen the handwriting on the wall."

"You're a silly little bitch, and you'll do what I say. What kind of church do you think would take you in?"

"Mary Magdalene had no trouble."

"And don't give me any lip about Mary Magdalene. That's sacrilegious, and you know it."

Lillybelle subsided, whimpering, and Stella said, "It's all very well to say we'll find a nice park and stay there, but what are we going to eat? And are we going to have to sleep on the bloody ground, or what?"

"How the goddam hell do I know?" Dolly shouted. "I haven't all the answers—nobody has! We'll just go with the crowd, and see what happens!"

"I think we ought to go to Oakland," Stella said.

"Maybe we will, but let's wait and see if there *is* an Oakland! Maybe Oakland is worse off than we are!"

Stella looked to the east. "I don't see any fires there."

"I'm with Dolly," Clarita said. "I think we ought to know a little more before we make any moves."

Encouraged by this support, Dolly said, "The discussion is closed. We're going to Golden Gate Park, which will be safe from the fire, and we're not going to plan one single goddam thing until we know what's going on. Now—Lillybelle, you come with me, and the rest of you follow, two by two, in line behind. There will be no talking to strangers, and no unladylike noises. Here we go—march!" An idea had been forming in her head, and as she led her column of girls into the stream of refugees Dolly began to think in terms of her book. What a sensational closing chapter, or chapters, the earthquake would make! If she could gather enough material, and make notes of everything she saw, she would have a book that would be salable on two levels, one for the prurient reader and one for the student of current events, and she might stand to make a fortune. And if she could sound penitent at the end, using Lillybelle's theory of divine retribution, she might even generate interest among the Bible-pounders. All in all it was a heady idea, and it kept her mind occupied as she and the girls made their way slowly northward.

Two blocks east of Taylor Street, Union Square had become a gathering point for the refugees from south of the Slot, but Dolly felt it was too close to the fire and would become much too crowded, so she kept on toward Nob Hill as the first stop on the way to Golden Gate Park. It wasn't the most direct way, but it was high ground, which at the moment seemed more important than anything else. They hadn't gone very far when Dolly became aware that two soldiers had spotted them, and were headed toward them with fixed bayonets. Although she didn't know it at the time, Brigadier General Frederick Funston, in command of the Presidio, had taken it upon himself to put San Francisco under military control at six-fifteen that morning, and by shortly after seven the troops had started into the city. It was some time before Mayor Eugene Schmitz found out that his city had been taken away from him, and by then it was too late to do anything about it.

The two troopers who accosted Dolly and the girls had apparently looted a saloon or liquor store, because they were glassy-eyed and truculent. One of them, a corporal, held his bayonet loosely pointed at Dolly, and said, "Where do you think you're going?"

She looked at him for an instant, sizing him up, then said, "*Pardon, m'sieu*, we wish to go to ze Golden Gate Park."

"You picked one hell of a funny way to get there. Golden Gate Park's off thataway." He flicked his bayonet to the southwest, then returned it to Dolly's midsection.

"*C'est vrai?* We are new in zees city. We work at ze French Consulate, and we—"

"Don't give me that shit. You're trying to set up an open-air cathouse, is what you're trying to do."

"*Monsieur!* I have nevaire been spoken to like zat!"

"Then it's time someone did. Frisk 'em, Charlie."

"For what?" said the other trooper, moving toward the girls.

"Concealed weapons—anything." The corporal grinned. "See what you can find." Then, to Dolly, "What are those papers you got there?"

"Zey are private—" she began as the corporal lowered his bayonet and reached for her. Quick as a cobra, Dolly lashed out; her pointed shoe whipped into the corporal's groin, and he doubled up and fell to the ground. "Don't you lay your hands on me, you son of a bitch," she said, then turned to face the other trooper, who had stopped in the middle of frisking Stella and now had his bayonet pointed toward her. "If you want the same thing, just come closer," she said.

The trooper worked the bolt on his rifle, and a round clicked into the chamber. "All right," he said. "You asked for it." He started to raise the rifle, then was aware that the mass of refugees, which had been streaming past them on both sides, had stopped, and people were crowding closer to watch. "Stand back, there!" he shouted. "Get back, or somebody's gonna get hurt!" On the ground, the corporal writhed and vomited, but the people didn't move.

"I saw what happened," someone said. "He was trying to rape her, and she kicked him in the nuts."

"Shame!" said someone else. "Don't you soldiers have anything better to do than that?"

"I said get back, all of you!" the trooper shouted, and fired once into the air. His eyes were wide with the fringe of panic, and as he worked the bolt an empty cartridge flew out and landed at Stella's feet. She picked it up, and put it in her reticule. "Back!" the trooper shouted again, but nobody appeared to have heard him.

A man, who was pushing a baby buggy full of shoes, peered down at the corporal and said, "What happened to him?"

"Tried to rape a lady," someone replied.

"Serves him right," said the man, and pushed his baby buggy back into the stream of people.

Dolly sensed that the time was right to get away. "All right, girls," she said in a commanding voice. "We're not accomplishing anything here. Let's go."

"Oh, no, you don't," said the trooper. "You're under arrest."

"For what?" said Dolly. "For fighting off a rapist?"

"For assault. Nobody was trying to rape you, and you know it."

"Who gave you authority to arrest me? Are you a policeman?"

"I can do what I goddam please. The Army is in charge here."

"Boo!" someone shouted. "Why don't you go start a war somewhere?" Others picked up the booing, and the trooper turned on them.

"I'm warning you!" he shouted. "Keep that up, and somebody's gonna get hurt!"

"You're pretty brave, aren't you?" another man said. "Put down your gun, and then let's see how brave you are!"

The corporal had managed to get to his hands and knees, but a sudden spasm of pain overcame him, and he pitched forward on his face. The trooper went to him, and at a signal from Dolly the girls broke their formation and scattered into the crowd, who laughed and applauded and closed ranks behind them, sealing them off from the troopers.

Once they were clear of the area Dolly held up her hand for the girls to gather around her, and when they were all there she said, "I think we'd better give up the idea of Golden Gate Park. It's a long way off, and those two will probably be looking for us. We'll go to Nob Hill, and see what happens after that."

"I hope we find something to eat pretty soon," Stella said. "I'm starving."

"At least you weren't playing frog all night," Clarita put in. "I can barely walk."

"The exercise'll be good for you," Dolly said. "It'll limber you up."

They heard a shot behind them, and Stella looked back. "Some poor bugger must've copped it," she said. "That trooper was bound he was going to shoot someone."

"Now you see why I don't allow enlisted men in the house," Dolly said. "No officer would've done that."

"Oh, I don't know," said Clarita. "I've known some officers who had pretty weird ideas of fun."

"Well, live and let live, I always say," Stella replied. "What's one man's meat is another man's poison."

Clarita thought for a few moments, then said, "How do you mean that?"

"Let it pass," said Stella. "I just threw it in for what it might be worth."

When they reached the top of Nob Hill, they stopped in front of the Leland Stanford mansion to rest their feet and catch their breaths. Looking back, it seemed as though the whole southern part of the city was afire: there was black smoke, white smoke, dirty gray smoke, yellow smoke, blue smoke, and red smoke, and it all blended together into a brownish mass as it rolled upward and spread out into the sky. It appeared that the fire had already crossed the Slot, which meant that the north-of-Market area was now in danger; it was a scant half mile from Market Street to Nob Hill, and with a change of wind the fire could cover that distance in short order. From Nob Hill to Telegraph Hill was another three quarters of a mile, but Telegraph Hill had the added advantage of being virtually on the waterfront, and therefore less likely to be surrounded by fire. Dolly decided to head for Telegraph Hill, and await developments there. She wanted, among other things, to start making notes; if she was going to include the fire in her book, she'd have to take down everything that had happened and everything she'd seen, or she'd forget something important when she came to write it.

The streets and lawns of Telegraph Hill were crowded with people, silently looking southward at the fire. Most of the men wore business suits and derby hats, while the women were attired as though for a shopping trip downtown; there had not been the haste to get dressed that was evident in other parts of the city, and the fire still seemed a long way away. Dolly and the girls climbed to the highest point where they could sit down, and then sank gratefully onto the grass. Clarita lay back and slowly waved her feet in the air, holding her skirt against her legs.

"Clarita!" Dolly said. "What do you think you're doing?"

"Exercising," replied Clarita. "You're always telling me I should exercise, so I am."

"Stop it this instant, and sit up like a lady."

"I thought today was a day off." Clarita lowered her legs, and came to a sitting position.

"There is no day off from acting like a lady," Dolly told her. "You never can tell who may be watching."

"Well, it may not be ladylike, but I'm going to find something to eat," Stella said. "I'm so hungry I could eat a bloody horse."

"All right," said Dolly. "But don't go far. And if you find anything, bring some back for the rest of us."

Stella drifted off, and Lillybelle looked at Dolly. "Is it all right if I just *go* to church?" she asked. "I mean, I don't think a prayer or two would hurt."

"You can pray just as well here as in church," Dolly replied. "Besides, nobody's going to be holding services today. They'll all be worried about saving the silver plate."

"I should think today of all days—" Lillybelle began, but Dolly cut her off.

"I said no, and that's final," she said. "Once you got inside a church, there'd be no telling what might happen."

Lillybelle looked glumly at the fire, which was steadily creeping closer. "We're all doomed," she said. "Doomed like the sinners we are."

"Shut up," said Dolly, opening her notebook. "I can't work with you whining in my ear."

"*Work?*" Lillybelle looked incredulous. "What kind of work can you do here?"

Dolly moistened the tip of her pencil. "I'm a writer," she replied. "Writers can work anywhere."

In the silence that followed, Clarita rolled onto her stomach and began to do push-ups. Dolores watched her for a few moments, then said, "What's that supposed to do for you?"

"Good for the arms and chest, mostly," Clarita said, beginning to turn red in the face. "It also helps the stomach muscles."

"I do sit-ups for that," Dolores said.

"Clarita, stop that!" Dolly commanded. "How many times do I have to tell you to behave like a lady?"

"Ah, *merde* on behaving like a lady," Clarita said. "How can I behave like a lady part of the time, and still be any good at my work?"

"There are plenty of ladies who are as good at that as you are," Dolly replied. "And don't you ever kid yourself."

Stella returned, holding a loaf of bread under her arm and eating a piece she'd torn off one end. "This is all I could get," she said, her mouth full. "They're setting up a soup kitchen, but so far all they have is bread and they'll only give one to a customer." She held out the loaf and Dolly took it, tore off a piece, and passed it on.

"We might as well wait till they get the soup," said Dolly. "Who's passing it out?"

"The Army, it looks like," Stella replied.

"Then the hell with it. We'll eat somewhere else."

"These blokes were all right," Stella said. "They were sober, and didn't try to get wise. They said they'd also have blankets, later on."

"I bet they will. And they'll join you on them."

Stella shrugged. "That's better than being shot for looting," she said. "I hear there's been a lot of that." She saw Dolly's notebook, and said, "What are you writing?"

"Notes for my book," Dolly replied. "The fire has given me the theme."

"What are you going to call it?"

"I haven't decided." Dolly thought a moment, then said, "What about *Out of the Frying Pan?*"

"Sounds like a flippin' cookbook. Why not *From Bed to Worse?*"

Dolly considered this. "Well, I don't have to decide now," she said. "The first thing is to get it written."

"That reminds me, I ought to write me mum. You got an extra sheet of paper?"

Dolly gave her one, and Stella looked around until she found a loose board on which she could write. She opened her reticule to get a pencil, and found the empty shell from the shot the trooper had fired. Examining it, she wondered if she should send it to her mother as a souvenir, but decided against it and dropped the shell back. Settling down with the board across her lap, she folded the paper once and began to write:

> Dearest Mum, I suppose by this time you will have heard about the terrible earthquake and fire in Frisco, which is what the Yanks call this city. Well, I'm here to tell you it is as true as I'm a foot high. The quake hit about 5 A.M. in the morning, and it was soon clear there'd be no school today. Miss LaGrange got us all up and dressed, and since the fire was

coming our way she decided we should get out, or skedaddle, as the natives put it. (Actually, I was the one who decided it, and she took my advice.) We walked for what seemed like several miles, and now we're going to spend the night on top of Telegraph Hill which has a good view of everything. They used to send messages from it, so you can see how high it must be. Some nice soldiers have offered us their blankets, so things are looking up. More tomorrow.

Later in the day a soup kitchen was set up, but the blankets never arrived, and Dolly and the girls were lucky to find an empty stable, from which the owner had taken the horse and carriage to some unknown destination. They bedded down as best they could, and watched the angry glow in the sky, and heard the far-off thumps as the soldiers began using dynamite to try to check the fire.

# CHAPTER 8

When Gresham Stoddard left his home on Nob Hill, his first thought was to go to the nearest hospital, and see if Muriel had been taken there. The fires south of the Slot did not present any immediate danger—in fact, the smoke seemed to be drifting away from the Nob Hill area rather than toward it—but all around him were signs of the staggering force of the quake. The streets, in some places, had buckled and split, leaving crevasses into which a man could very easily fall, and once or twice he saw a human hand or leg protruding from beneath a mountain of rubble. After the initial shock he found that such sights had no effect on him; his mind was stunned into accepting the catastrophe as routine, and things that would have nauseated him the day before seemed only mildly interesting. He even accepted the rats, which swarmed out of the ruptured sewers and the wreckage of Chinatown and were spreading through the city, gnawing on what carrion they could find and bringing with them the danger of bubonic plague. His mind registered this fact in a disinterested sort of way; he had his own problems, and at the moment bubonic plague was not one of them.

His thinking was somewhat beclouded by the fact he had a thudding hangover, and he wondered exactly how much he'd had to drink the night before. He dimly remembered taking a bottle of champagne upstairs with that girl who looked like Lily Langtry—what was her name? Maribelle?—but he couldn't remember if it was his second bottle or his third. Then, slowly, bits of the conversation drifted to the surface: he remembered offering to take the girl to the Yukon, or the Northwest Territory, or some such place, and her declining to accompany him outside the house. Then there was something about dreams, which led implausibly to eels, and after that he remembered very little. But he did remember the reason behind his wanting to flee to the Yukon, and even that didn't seem so terribly important in the light of later events. What did the possibility of a jail sentence matter, when the whole city was falling down around his ears? The police would have enough on their hands for the next little while, without worrying about some juggled figures at the bank. It's an ill wind that blows nobody any good, he reminded himself; this has at least bought me a little time. He knew he should be ashamed of thinking that way, but his thinking at the moment seemed beyond his control: his mind did things he never asked it to, and took off on weird and macabre tangents.

At the first hospital he came to the injured were lying in the halls, some quiet and some moaning or sobbing, and the nurses were frantically trying to give at least passing attention to each one. As one nurse hurried past him Stoddard said, "Excuse me, could you—?" but she didn't seem to hear him, and he tried another, who was bending over and sponging dirt and blood from the face of a patient who was barely conscious. "Could you tell me who's in charge here?" Stoddard asked, and the nurse glanced up at him.

"Why?" she replied.

"I want to know if a certain patient has been admitted. A Mrs. Gresh—"

"I'm sorry, we haven't had time to take names," the nurse said, and turned back to her patient. "Look around if you want to, but don't expect any names right now."

Stoddard paused, then turned and walked down the corridor, looking at the gray or bloody faces. Muriel's was not among them, which in a way was a relief, but it also meant he'd have to continue looking, with no knowledge of what he'd find in the end. He'd much rather find out for certain, one way or the other, than to have the suspense drag on. He still had the feeling that Muriel was indestructible, but he knew it was an irrational feeling, and one that was open to instant contradiction. He turned and walked back to the entrance just as a new ambulance load arrived, and he stood aside and watched the casualties being unloaded, then went out into the welcome daylight. It had been dark in the hospital, reminiscent of a Hieronymus Bosch drawing of hell, and the smell of ether and carbolic acid had almost strangled him.

When the ambulance driver came out, Stoddard stopped him and said, "Where's another hospital where someone from Nob Hill might have been taken?"

The driver looked blank, then shrugged. "You might try Letterman," he said. "Up in the Presidio. There'll be a lot get taken there."

"Thanks," said Stoddard. "I don't suppose you could give me a ride?"

"I'll take you partway. Get in."

Stoddard climbed up onto the seat, and the driver flicked the reins and they started off, bumping over the uneven streets and steering around the piles of rubble. To the south, the smoke was becoming thicker. "Do you think the fire will get up here?" Stoddard asked.

"God help us if it does," the driver replied. "Then the last resort'll be Golden Gate Park."

"Why there?"

"It's the biggest. No matter what else burns up, that'll still be safe." He thought a moment, then added, "Of course, if everyone in the city should go there, it could get a mite crowded. But then, I hear a lot are going over to Oakland."

"Is the ferry running?"

"One way only. That is, they only take passengers one way. Nobody comes from Oakland to here."

It occurred to Stoddard that Muriel might be uninjured and have already gone to Oakland, in which case the time he spent looking for her in San Francisco would be totally wasted. And the chances of his finding her, even if she had stayed in San Francisco, were about one in a thousand, given the present state of the records. He found himself thinking of the needlein-the-haystack cliché, and decided it had been the panic of the moment that had made him rush off on such a hopeless quest. If he was going to stay in San Francisco, he could put his time to better use. Just what that would be, he didn't know; his life so far had fitted him with very few side skills that could be used in an emergency.

"I been through shakes before," the driver said, to nobody in particular, "but I never seen one like this. I was here during the shake of ninety-eight, and I can just remember the shake of ninety, when I was a little shaver, but by God this one is the granddaddy of 'em all. I just never seen the likes of this one."

"Neither have I," said Stoddard, unnecessarily.

"It makes you feel small, is what it does," the driver went on. "It makes you feel like there's no point in being you, because you don't count for more'n a gnat's fart in a whirlwind. It makes you wonder why the good Lord put us here in the first place."

"It does indeed," said Stoddard.

"And all the grief it causes, and all the *work*—can you imagine the work it's going to take to rebuild this city? If I had to do it, I just wouldn't know where to start. Do I start on that block over there"—indicating a block in which only three buildings were left standing—"or do I start back there, where it's all burning? It don't make much difference, because it's all got to be done, but it's where to *start* that's got me buggered."

"Luckily, I don't have to make that decision," said Stoddard.

"Neither do I. This job here is about all I can handle. I'm supposed to have an assistant, but he got drunk last night and God only knows where he is now, so I've got to get these injured people in the wagon by myself. Usually I can get someone at the scene to help me, but a couple of times there's been nobody to help, and I'm here to tell you it's a struggle. I try to be gentle because the poor bastards have gone through enough already, but I can't always help joggling them, or dropping them, and then I feel like hell. And the ride back to the hospital is no bed of roses, either, what with the shape the streets are in, and all. It's gonna be a long day, I can tell that from here."

Stoddard made a sudden decision. "Could I help you?" he asked.

The driver looked at him. "Aren't you trying to find someone?" he replied.

"Yes, but right now I think it's hopeless. I could be of much more use if I helped you with the stretchers and—whatever."

"By God, it would be a help," the driver said. "There's no point trying to deny it."

"Then consider it done. You'll have to tell me if there's anything special I should know, because this is a little out of my line."

"Just manpower is all. That and a little finesse when the occasion requires." The driver shook the reins, and clucked at the horse. "The day is beginning to look a little brighter," he said.

Stoddard found that he took a strange delight in helping gather up the injured. He was not a morbid man, and had always flinched at the idea of suffering—possibly because he had never suffered himself, or seen anyone who was afflicted with more than a migraine headache—yet he found he was perfectly at ease with injuries the mere idea of which would have appalled him the day before. Mangled limbs, crushed pelvises, third-degree burns—he handled them all, and with a gentleness that never brought forth any outcry from the patient. He seemed to gain strength with each new incident and, having faced the fact that the job could take all day or perhaps even two, he worked without thought of a letup, carried away by the mere fact that he could be of help. Even the driver seemed to derive strength from him, and they worked together as though they had always been a team.

One call took them to a house where the front wall and most of the inside had collapsed, leaving a three-cornered shell with a mound of rubble in the center. Rescuers were swarming over the rubble, moving the larger pieces aside and burrowing down to get at the people trapped below. One victim had already been brought out, and was lying on a salvaged mattress to one side.

"How many are there?" Stoddard asked one of the rescuers.

"At least three," the man replied. "We got that one over there, and we know there are two more."

"How do you know?"

"There was one guy up on the second floor. He was trying to let himself down by knotted sheets, and these other two were coming along the street and tried to rescue him. The Goddamned fools went up what was left of the stairs, and that brought the stairs down and everything else with them. The guy on the mattress is one of the so-called rescuers."

Stoddard went over and looked at the man, and there seemed to be something familiar about him. His face was pale, and covered with dirt and plaster dust, but there was something about the shape of the nose and forehead that Stoddard thought he'd seen before. While he was trying to remember where, the man opened his eyes, and for a long minute he looked directly into Stoddard's. Finally, speaking with effort, he said, "It's lucky you got to the opera when you did, isn't it?"

"What?" said Stoddard. "What are you—? Oh." He remembered. This was the young man he'd seen last night at Dolly's, who'd been asking him about Caruso, and whom he'd also seen, briefly, in the shambles this morning. "Yes, I suppose it is," he said. "How do you feel?"

"It's hard to say. I guess I'm still numb. Have they found Art?"

"You mean your friend?" Stoddard looked back at where the men were pulling the debris apart. "No, not yet."

The ambulance driver appeared, and together they eased the young man onto a stretcher, and as they lifted him into the ambulance he said, "Let's wait until they find Art. I want to make sure he's all right."

"Well, we'll see." Stoddard went back to where the men were digging, and said, "How does it look?"

"Not good," one of them replied. "There's someone down here we're pretty sure is dead, and so far no sign of the other. It'll be a while yet."

Stoddard returned to the ambulance. "We'd better not wait

around," he said. "We'll come back after we've got you to the hospital." Then, remembering the problem when he'd been looking for Muriel, he said, "What's your name?"

"Frank Borden," the young man replied. "No relation to Lizzie."

"You'll be all right," Stoddard said as he and the driver climbed into the seat. "Anyone who can joke at a time like this can't have too much the matter with him."

The nearest hospital was St. Mary's, and when they got there they found a state of bustling confusion. The Sisters of Mercy were in charge, and Stoddard went to what appeared to be the head sister and said, "We've got a stretcher case outside. Where should we put him?"

"Oh, not another!" she cried in despair. "We're getting ready to move!"

"*Move?*" said Stoddard. "Where?"

"At the rate the fire is coming, we'll be burned to a cinder by nightfall. We're making arrangements to have our patients put on a boat."

"Do you think you could take one more? I don't think he's too badly hurt, but he needs a doctor."

"Put him in the hall here, and we'll see he's cared for. I don't suppose one more makes much difference one way or the other."

"Thank you," said Stoddard. "And, for your records, his name is Frank Borden." He almost added, "No relation to Lizzie," but checked himself in time.

"I'll try to remember," the sister said. "At this point, my records are all in my head."

Stoddard worked with the ambulance driver all that day, stopping only for a bowl of stew at one of the field kitchens. An emergency hospital was set up in Golden Gate Park, and he spent the first night there, sleeping in the back of the ambulance while the driver stretched out across the seat. Nighttime brought no real darkness with it; the glow of the fire was everywhere, and the sky burned with an angry red color. The fire was working its way north, toward Nob Hill and Telegraph Hill and the rest, and the only attempt to confine it was made along Van Ness Avenue, to the west. There the dynamite line had been set up, patrolled by troops, and there also were deployed the guns of the field artillery, to blast whatever the dynamiters missed. The theory was a sound one, to create a waste area across which the fire could not jump, but the haphazard way it was carried out often spread the fire instead of containing it. Stoddard was aware of the explosions for a while, but then exhaustion overcame him and he was aware of nothing.

Next morning, Golden Gate Park resembled a large bivouac area, or the start of the Oklahoma land rush. Several thousand people had spent the night there, along with the transportation that had brought them, and the park was jammed with people, bedding, horses, wagons, carts, broughams, luggage, household items such as bedsteads and pianos, and various cooking utensils, tools, and firearms. A few tents had been set up, but for the most part people slept either in their wagons or on the ground, the lucky ones on mattresses and the others on rolled-up coats or clothing. A miner had made a stone fireplace on which he put a huge cauldron, for maintaining a supply of hot water.

Even from a distance Stoddard could see that Nob Hill had been consumed during the night, and this led him to wonder again about Muriel. Looking around the park he realized that she might be there at this very minute, but trying to find her in the crowd would be an exercise in futility. The more he thought about it the surer he was she'd made her way to Oakland; she was probably safe and well cared for, and was wondering what in God's name had happened to *him*. The fact that he'd not come home, after promising to join her and the Neppletons for supper, gave her every reason to be furious at him, and knowing her as he did, he was reasonably certain that her fury would outweigh any concern she might have for his safety. Looking at it that way, it was probably just as well he *hadn't* found her, and the longer their meeting was postponed the more likely it would be to be civil. He found the ambulance driver, who had been off in search of a public latrine, and told him he was ready to go to work.

At the park gate they were approached by a stocky, disheveled man with a day's growth of beard, wearing a topcoat and derby hat and waving an 8 × 10 photograph. "Stop!" he cried in a rasping voice with an Italian accent. "You must take me out of here!"

"Sorry, pal," the driver said. "This is an ambulance. We don't give rides to healthy people."

"But you must! I am a friend of the President! He wants me in Washington!"

"And I'm a friend of the Queen of Sheba. Now, if you don't mind, we'd like to—"

"Look!" the man said, thrusting the picture forward. "The President signed his picture for me! I am a friend of his!"

Stoddard and the driver looked at the picture, which was of Theodore Roosevelt, and which had been autographed: "To Enrico Caruso, with best wishes." Stoddard looked again at the man and saw that he was indeed Caruso, although barely recognizable as the tenor he'd heard two nights before. His voice was hoarse with panic, and his eyes were wild and haunted.

The driver handed the picture back to him. "Sorry," he said. "If you was the President himself we might consider it, but otherwise we're not a taxi. Giddap, Mildred." He flicked the reins and the ambulance moved off, leaving Caruso staring after them.

# CHAPTER 9

When Henry Walden regained consciousness, he was dazzled by the sudden glare of daylight in his eyes. Faces were peering down at him, and hands were reaching for him, and beyond the faces was the sky, bright and clear and blue. At first he thought his hours of being buried must have been a dream, but then he focused on the rubble around him and knew they'd been real, and that he was, miraculously, alive. He felt a stab of pain in his legs when the people tried to lift him, and he said, "Take it easy. There's a beam that's got me pinned." The hands eased him back, and he heard scraping sounds as someone got to work with a shovel.

A face appeared above him, silhouetted against the sky. "How do you feel?" it asked.

"O.K., I guess," Walden replied. "My legs hurt when you tried to lift me, but that's all." He flexed his arms and hands, and found they could move freely.

Unbelievably, he heard a woman's voice above him, saying, "Would you like some elixir? It's good for pain."

He turned his head to try to see the face, but all he could see was a dark oval surrounded by soft hair. "That might be a good idea," he said, and then suddenly the face was close to him and a bottle was put in his hand. He could see the face more clearly now, and catch the faint smell of scented soap, and he thought he'd never seen anything so beautiful in his life.

"Would you like a glass?" said the woman. "I've used it, but I can rinse it—"

"That won't be necessary, thank you." Walden put the bottle to his lips and took a drink. It tasted thick and syrupy but there was also a slight sting to it, and the sensation was not unpleasant. "Thank you," he said, wiping the neck of the bottle and handing it back. "I'm much obliged."

"If you have any more pain, let me know," the woman said. "I have almost a full bottle."

"Thank you, I feel fine," Walden said, truthfully.

The men finally got the beam off his legs, and then helped him into a sitting position. "Do you think you can stand?" one of them asked.

Walden glanced around and saw the woman off to one side, watching him. "I think so," he said. "Let's see." He started to stand, but his legs buckled beneath him, and he pitched forward. The men picked him up, and he lay back and said, "My mistake. I guess I can't."

"Let's get him to the hospital," a man said. "Who's got a wagon?"

"I'll go for the ambulance, if you want," the woman volunteered. "Or we can take him to our house. Mightn't that be simpler, George?"

"He belongs in the hospital," said George, who was apparently her husband, and Walden had a small feeling of letdown. "There's nothing we can do for him the hospital can't."

"But you've got all the medicines and everything. Mightn't it be—?"

"I did have all the medicines. The shop is nothing but broken glass and crockery."

"Oh, no."

"So right now, we've got to get this guy to the hospital. I'll go hitch up the wagon."

"All right," she said. She came back to where Walden was lying, and said, "Would you like another drop of elixir?"

"No, thanks," he replied. "I feel fine. I just can't seem to stand up."

"Maybe this will help you stand. It does wonders for me."

"Well—all right." He took another swig from the bottle, and handed it back. "Thank you," he said. "It makes me *feel* as though I could stand, whether I can or not."

She looked at the other men, who were putting on their jackets and dusting themselves off. "There's no need for you to stay around," she said. "My husband and I can put him in the wagon."

"I don't mind waiting," said one of them. "I don't have the feeling I'm going to do much business today." He looked to the west, where the smoke from San Francisco spread out and covered that whole sector of the city.

Walden, who had lain back, raised himself up on his elbows. "Hey, all of you," he said. "Don't anyone go until I've said thank you. How can I say it right? How can I thank you for saving my life?"

"Forget it," said one man. "It's just lucky Harry heard you."

"Well, whichever one of you is Harry, God bless you. And that goes for the rest of you, too." He looked at the woman. "And you, too—bless you for the elixir."

"I was glad to do it," she said, looking at the ground.

"Is George a doctor?"

"No, he's a pharmacist."

"George what?"

"George Bender."

"And you're Mrs. George Bender."

She looked straight at him. "My given name is Lucille."

"Which do you prefer to be called?"

She colored slightly. "That depends."

"I see." Trying to keep his voice formal, he said, "For the record, my name is Walden. Henry G. Walden. The G stands for Godfrey. All I ask is that you don't call me Hank." As though exhausted by the speech he lay back, and looked at the sky.

"I'll remember that," said Lucille Bender.

It suddenly occurred to Walden that he was in the underwear in which he had slept, and that his clothes and all his belongings must be in the wreckage. He sat up, and looked around.

"What can I get you?" Lucille asked.

"My clothes. They must be buried here somewhere."

"They won't be much good to you now. I'm sure my husband has something that will fit you."

"But my money, and my—"

"Don't worry about that. We'll see you have what you need."

He gave her a long look. "Why?" he said. "How do you know I won't take you for all I can get, and skedaddle?"

She smiled, and said nothing, and Walden lay back and looked at the sky again.

After a while he heard the sound of an approaching wagon, and looking down the street he saw Bender driving a horse that danced and skittered like a drop of water on a hot griddle. That would be all I'd need, Walden thought: to be lying helpless in a wagon with a horse that decides to bolt. That would put a splendid climax to a day that is becoming more bizarre by the minute. The wagon came alongside and stopped, and Lucille held the horse's head and stroked its nose while Bender and the other man lifted Walden into the wagon. By now his legs were beginning to ache, and burn as though they'd been scorched, and he wondered how badly they were damaged. In his first euphoria at being disinterred he'd thought that his troubles were over, but now the possibility that he might be seriously injured—perhaps even crippled—began to occur to him. He looked around at Lucille, who was climbing onto the seat beside her husband, and said, "Do you happen to have another shot of that elixir there? I think I'm having a poor spell."

She came into the back of the wagon as Bender started the horse, and she held Walden's head while he took a swallow. "See if you can relax," she said, and he closed his eyes and moved so as to put his head in her lap. She seemed to have no objection, and they rode that way throughout the slow and bumpy drive.

When they arrived at the hospital, Bender tied the horse to a hitching rail and went inside, and Walden and Lucille stayed in the wagon. Walden was quiet, and Lucille appeared content to act as a pillow, holding his head as though that might ease his pain. After a while Bender came out, and his face was grim.

"There's no room," he said. "They've already taken some cases from Frisco, and they're shorthanded because they had to send some interns down to San Jose."

"Was that badly hit?" Lucille asked.

"No, but Agnew was. The whole damn place collapsed."

"Oh, my God. How horrible."

"What's Agnew?" Walden asked.

"The state hospital for the insane," Lucille replied.

"Those that weren't killed are running around the countryside," Bender went on. "Apparently it's a real shambles." Then he looked at Walden. "They said I should take you home, and they'd get a doctor to look at you as soon as they could. It may be a while, and in the meantime you're just to keep quiet. I'm not a doctor, but I can at least give you first aid for the time being." He untied the reins from the hitching rail, and climbed into the seat. "How do you feel?" he asked.

"All right," Walden replied. "It's just my legs that ache."

"I have a private theory about your legs," Bender said, and clucked to the horse. "Time will tell whether I'm right or wrong."

When, finally, they stopped in front of the house, Bender and Lucille managed to get Walden out of the wagon and then, with each of them supporting one of his arms on their shoulders, they half carried him into the house and put him on the sofa in the front parlor. He found that he was able, albeit painfully, to move his legs a little, but they still wouldn't support him, and when he tried to stand it felt as though they were being flayed with steel whips.

"Feel sick to your stomach?" Bender asked as Walden lay weakly back on the sofa.

"No," replied Walden. "Why?"

"That would be one sign you'd broken something. Not foolproof, but a sign."

Lucille got a blanket, and as she put it around Walden she said, "What you need more than anything is a bath. Do you think you can manage the stairs?"

"I guess I'll have to," he replied. "This is hardly the place for a sponge bath."

There was an odd note in the laugh she gave in reply, an implication of something he couldn't quite fathom, and then she was gone and in a minute he heard the water running upstairs. Bender saw the look on his face, and said, "Sometimes I think Lucille should have been a nurse."

"Oh?" said Walden. "Why?"

"She likes taking care of people."

There followed a short silence, and then Lucille appeared at the head of the stairs, looking radiant. Between them, she and Bender got Walden up the stairs, and then Bender undressed him and helped him into the bathtub. Bender examined Walden's legs, which had massive bruises across them that were already starting to discolor the surrounding flesh, and after gently touching them he said, "I don't think anything's broken. I think part of your pain is that the circulation was cut off, and it's just beginning to return."

"Whatever it is, I can tell you it's painful," Walden replied as he slid gratefully into the steaming water. "I haven't had anything hurt like this since I was in the cavalry."

"What cavalry was that?" Bender asked. It hadn't occurred to him that Walden might have been any kind of army man; he looked more like an Eastern banker, or businessman.

"The First United States Volunteer," Walden replied, his eyes closed. "Otherwise known as the Rough Riders."

"Were you with *them?*" Bender exclaimed. "Were you at Las Guásimas?"

"I was. I've never been so terrified in my life."

"I was with the Seventy-first!"

There was a slight pause, and then Walden said, "Were you the guys they sent up to help?"

"Yes! We were told we had to save you!"

After a longer pause, Walden said, "I guess you did. There was so much confusion I didn't know who was doing what."

Bender laughed. "Neither did I. I didn't even see a Spaniard until the next day, and he was a dead one."

Walden had opened his eyes, and now he closed them again. "Then I guess that makes twice you've saved me. Once at Las Guásimas, and once today."

Bender was embarrassed. "I wouldn't put it that way. The other guys heard you before I did, and I just helped. And as for Las Guásimas—" He thought for a moment, and concluded, "I don't think anyone saved anyone else. It was just a lot of people shooting at trees."

"Nevertheless, I prefer to believe you saved me, and for that I'm grateful."

Bender couldn't think of any response, so he changed the subject and said, "Is the bath hot enough? Does it help your legs any?"

"It helps everything. The only danger is I may fall asleep, and slide under the water and drown."

"I'll have Lucille—" Bender started, then stopped. "I was going to say I'll have Lucille keep an eye on you," he said, "but I guess in the circumstances that's not such a good idea."

"I'll be all right," Walden said. "I may doze a little, but I don't think I'll drown. You must have a lot of other things to do, so don't worry about me. You've done enough already."

"I ought to start cleaning up the shop," Bender said. "So I tell you what—I'll get a raincoat and throw it over the tub, and that'll keep you decent in case you want Lucille to do anything. How does that sound?"

"That sounds just fine," Walden replied. "So long as she doesn't mind if I snore."

Bender laughed. "She's used to that," he said, and went out of the room. He came back a few moments later with an oilskin slicker, which he draped across the tub in such a way as to cover Walden's midsection. It tended to sag into the water, but it made him technically decent. "There you are," Bender said, giving it a final adjustment. "If you want anything, just call, and she'll be where she can hear you."

He left, and when Walden heard the front door close he flung the slicker onto the floor, ran some more hot water into the tub, and then lay back and closed his eyes. He dozed, but in the slowly gathering dream he was once again entombed in the wreckage of the Empire Theatre, and he woke with a start. Then the drowsiness crept over him again, and the next thing he knew a voice was saying, "Is everything all right?"

He'd already said, "Fine, thank you," when he realized it was a woman's voice, and he opened his eyes and looked around to find Lucille standing in the doorway. He pulled himself upright and groped frantically for the slicker, and had just managed to get it over him when she came into the room.

"I didn't mean to frighten you," she said. "Only you were so quiet I thought you might have drowned."

"You didn't frighten me," Walden replied. "I guess I just dozed off." He looked at Lucille in embarrassment and said, "I'm afraid I'm not dressed for callers." It seemed to him he'd spent the day looking up at her, first from the hole where he'd been buried, then when he had his head in her lap, and now from a crouched-over position in the bathtub. And she looked just as beautiful this last time as she had the first.

"Don't worry about clothes," she said, as though misunderstanding his meaning. "George has plenty." She picked up his grimy underwear, and dropped it in a hamper. "I'll wash these, so you'll have a spare."

"Thank you," said Walden. "I don't mean to be so much trouble."

"If you think *this* is trouble, just think of the other people," Lucille said, looking around the bathroom as though trying to decide what to do next. Then suddenly making up her mind, she pulled a stool to the side of the tub and sat down. "Are you married?" she asked.

"Me?" said Walden. "No. Why?"

"Do you have any close friends who are?"

"Ah—yes. A few. What is this all about?"

"There are some things about marriage I'd like to know, but I can't find anyone who'll tell me. I think there must be answers, and I have the feeling that everyone but me knows what they are, and I sometimes feel like a child out alone in the woods in a rainstorm. I just don't know what to do about it."

"Can't you get George to tell you?"

"If I could I wouldn't be asking you, would I?"

"Come to think of it, I guess not."

"Although I might. There's something about you that seems sympathetic, and if only you'd been married I have the feeling you'd tell me the answers."

"Well, try me out. What are the questions?" Walden had the feeling he was losing his mind, but for some reason it was an agreeable sensation and he didn't want it to stop.

She looked at him for a moment, and her face began to redden. "No, I guess I can't," she said. "If you'd been married it would be one thing, but—" She shook her head, and clasped her hands together.

"Look, it isn't as though I'd never—uh—known any women," Walden said, at the same time thinking how often and how miserably he'd struck out. "The fundamentals are pretty much the same, no matter—"

"If you've never been married you don't know what I mean," she cut in. "We're probably not even talking about the same thing."

"I think we are. The subject doesn't have that many different aspects."

"Oh, yes it does. If you're talking about fruits you can talk about apples and oranges and limes and peaches and cumquats, but if you narrow it down and just talk about apples you can still talk of McIntoshes, Delicious, Rome—"

"Wait a minute," said Walden. "I fell off at the last turn, and you lost me."

She stopped, and her blush deepened. "I'm trying not to be specific," she said. "Because if I were, then we'd both be in trouble."

"But *how*? I don't understand!"

"That's just the tone George takes when I try to explain something to him. Don't you have any intuition?"

"Yes, but intuition isn't the same as knowledge. If you want to say something, why don't you come right out and say it?"

"Call it the laws of propriety."

"Then why'd you bring it up in the first place?"

"Because I thought you might have some understanding." She stood up. "I see I was mistaken," she said, and headed for the door.

"Wait a minute!" Walden said, turning in the tub. "Mrs. Ben—Lucille—I didn't mean it like that! Please—listen to me!"

She paused, and looked back. "Then how did you mean it?" she said. "You're the one who's been saying I should use plain English, but when you use it and I think I understand, you say you didn't mean it like that. Just what do you mean?"

"If you'll come back here, I'll explain." She came back tentatively, and did not sit down, and Walden went on, "It's just that I don't know what you're trying to say, so I can't be very helpful. I think I have intuition, but if I'm wrong, and make the wrong answer, then we'll be that much worse off than before. Can you tell me, in so many words, what it is you'd like to know?"

She moved away, and looked out the window. "I feel foolish asking this," she said. "So foolish that I can't look at you while I say it."

"All right," said Walden. "Look wherever you want."

"Well—you know what married people do."

"I've heard."

"Does that necessarily result in a baby every time?"

"Of course not."

"Why 'of course'?"

"Any number of reasons. For one thing, there are ways it can be prevented."

"There are? Are you sure?"

"Positive."

She was quiet for a moment, then said, "Thank you," and walked quickly out of the room.

Walden slid back under the water, and realized that for the first time that day he'd forgotten about his legs. Now all he felt was numb, and confused, and, for a reason he couldn't define, apprehensive. It was as though a large hole had opened up, and he was slowly sliding toward it.

# CHAPTER 10

The refugees started coming to Oakland Wednesday afternoon, first in a trickle and then in a stream that grew into a flood, until finally more than 300,000 people had crossed the Bay. Launches took some, at anywhere from fifty cents to ten dollars a head; the Southern Pacific ferry took the majority, at no charge and on a first-come-first-served basis. About half of the refugees stayed in Oakland, while the other half took the first train out they could get, regardless of where it might be going.

George Bender spent most of Wednesday afternoon cleaning up the wreckage of his shop. He filled his wagon with the debris and took it off to the city dump, then returned and with a mop and bucket set about scrubbing the floor to remove the slimy paste that covered it like a carpet. It was a long, tedious job, but he had nothing else to do, and he reasoned that it would probably be good for Lucille to occupy her mind with taking care of Henry Walden. His remark to Walden that she should have been a nurse had been truer than he'd realized; he could tell from her expression that she relished the idea of having someone to care for.

When he got home for supper that night, he saw that Walden was not on the sofa, and, looking up the stairs, he could tell there was no light in the bathroom. He went into the kitchen, where Lucille was stirring something that looked like stew, and said, "Where's Whatsisname? Walden."

"In our bed," Lucille replied, not looking up.

Bender hesitated, then said, "For the night?"

"I assume so. I figured he needed the rest."

"I'm sure he does, but—" He let the sentence trail off while he tried to think of an alternative.

"I can sleep on the sofa," Lucille went on, shaking some seasoning into the pot, "and you can sleep wherever you like."

"I see. As in, for instance, where?"

"Well, if you insist on using our bed, I suppose you could sleep with him. He's so dead to the world you could shoot a gun off in the room, and he wouldn't notice."

"You happen to know this?"

"Yes. I went in and checked from time to time."

"How did he get in our bed?"

"By himself. The bath made his legs much better."

"I see."

"If you don't want to sleep there, there's that cot up over the stable. You could bring that down, and use it."

"How long is this going to last?"

"How do I know? Until he can move around, I guess."

"He's already moving around, if he got from the tub into the bed by himself."

"Then ask him in the morning. I don't know."

"What's got into you, anyway?"

"What do you mean, what's got into me?"

"You're irritable, and—well, truculent. As though I'd done something wrong."

"How could you do anything wrong—you, of all people?"

"That's just what I mean. What are you angry at?"

She shrugged, and tasted the stew. "Life, I guess," she said.

"That makes no sense. Maybe you should take some elixir."

"I can't. Godfrey and I finished it."

"Who's Godfrey?"

"Henry Walden. His middle name is Godfrey. He'd rather be called that than Henry, because Henry leads to Hank and Hank is a name he can't stand. He had an uncle named Hank, who used to beat his horses."

"You and he must have had quite a little talk."

"It was a long afternoon. Are you going back to the shop after supper?"

"Probably. Why?"

"I could use some more elixir."

"I told you, that was the last bottle. Everything else was smashed."

She stopped, thought a moment, then said, "There's a train due in tonight from Los Angeles, with medical supplies and doctors and nurses and whatnot. Maybe they might have some."

"I doubt that elixir is included in emergency kits. You'll just have to do without until I get a new shipment." As an afterthought he added, "It might not be a bad idea if you stopped it altogether."

She looked at him, her eyes wide. "And why, pray, do you say that?"

"I think it may be addictive. I think maybe you should try something else."

"Do you have any suggestions?"

"Not at the moment. I'll see what I can find."

"I must say, I can't see the point in trying something new when I've found just what I need. I'm not a laboratory animal, you know, like some sort of rat, or guinea pig, or aardvark."

"What do you mean, aardvark? Nobody uses aardvarks in a laboratory."

"They most certainly do. I read in the paper that they're using them for tests."

"What kind of tests?"

"To see how fast they could stick out their tongues. They had an aardvark at one end of a cage and a mess of ants at the other, and then they used a stopwatch to see how fast his tongue moved. It figured out to fifty-three miles an hour."

Bender looked out the window, at the glow of the burning city across the Bay. He was quiet for a while, then said, "Where were we?"

"Where were we when?"

"Before you brought up the aardvark."

"You said you were going to get me some new kind of medicine."

"Oh, yes. Well"—he paused, and scratched a spot between his shoulder blades—"I'll see what I can do. The way things are now, though, I can't promise anything."

"You never did," said Lucille, and ladled the stew out onto two plates.

Bender had his mouth open to ask what she meant, then changed his mind and sat down at the kitchen table. Some things are better left unknown, he told himself, and began to eat his supper.

The next day, after an uncomfortable night spent on a cot in the parlor, he joined Lucille in the kitchen, where she was making breakfast. She was silent, which was not unusual, but when he started to say something she made a shushing sound and pointed to the ceiling, indicating that Walden was still asleep.

"How do you know?" Bender said in a stage whisper. "He may have got dressed and left already."

"I looked," Lucille replied, also in a whisper. "He hasn't moved."

"Maybe he's dead."

"Don't be silly."

"There's such a thing as aftershock, you know. A man can get through an accident apparently unscathed, and then—klunk —drop dead in his tracks."

"Don't say that!"

"Why not? It's true."

"Just be quiet, and eat your breakfast."

He obeyed, remarking to himself that Lucille was acting as though Walden were a visiting Balkan prince, or, on the other end of the scale, an injured kitten she'd picked up in the street. Whichever it was, it seemed clear he was the most important member of the household for the time being, so the only thing to do was accept it and carry on with other matters.

When he got outside, Bender could see that the fires were still raging uncontrolled in San Francisco, and closer at hand he could observe the effect the disaster was having on Oakland. Refugees poured off the ferries and milled about the streets; they slowly gravitated toward City Hall, where they formed a long, straggling line while they waited to register their own names and look for those of friends or relatives; and at the entrance to City Hall was a cluster of pup tents, where the militia had encamped. Word had it that the military had tried to take over, as they had in San Francisco, but Mayor Frank Mott had told them they could patrol all they wanted, but he would remain in charge of his city. All business in Oakland had been suspended on Wednesday, the day of the quake, but now everything was open again, and business was brisk.

As Bender walked toward his shop it occurred to him that, lacking any pharmaceuticals to dispense, there ought to be something else he could do to be of help. His superficial knowledge of medicine was of no use unless he had the props to go with it, so he'd probably do better in a completely different field. He swung around and headed toward City Hall, on the theory that that was the center of activity for the moment, and there he might find out what he could do. In the back of his mind, although he wouldn't admit it, he was hoping he might come up with something that would keep Lucille busy as well, and take her mind off Henry Walden.

On Telegraph Hill, across the Bay, Dolly and her girls didn't awake until the middle of the morning. Always late sleepers, they'd been so exhausted by the day before that they slept without moving, like so many gaily colored sacks of flour. Dolly was the first to waken, and it took her a moment of glancing around the stable to remember where she was. She rose stiffly, brushed the hay from her dress, went to a window, and gasped. During the night the fire had crept along the waterfront toward the foot of Telegraph Hill; it had consumed the houses on Nob Hill and half encircled the base of Russian Hill, and it was moving west in an almost straight line toward Van Ness Avenue. South of the Slot was burned out completely, and the only unburned sections she could see were west of Van Ness, and the area immediately surrounding Telegraph Hill. There seemed little doubt that those would go within the next day or so, and Dolly decided to get out while she still could. Looking down at the waterfront, she saw that East Street North as far as the Ferry Building was clear of fire, and was therefore the most logical way to go. It might take a while, because it was congested with firefighters and frantic refugees, but it was at least safe, because there was no danger of being trapped. With the Bay wharves immediately on their left, the girls could always jump into the water if the fire came too close.

"All right!" Dolly shouted, clapping her hands. "Everybody up! Rise and shine!"

She was greeted by a chorus of groans, yawns, and squeaks as the girls rolled and thrashed about and finally rose. "My God," Maribelle said, digging in one ear with her little finger, "to think—if I'd accepted that old gentleman's offer, I could've been in the Yukon by now."

"What's the Yukon got?" Stella asked, standing up and tugging her petticoat straight. "I'd sooner be in Bournemouth."

"Well, you'll both have to settle for Oakland," Dolly told them, and moved away from the window. "That is, if you're lucky."

"That's what I said yesterday," Stella replied. "What's so different about today?"

"Look out the window, and you'll see," said Dolly, and Stella obeyed.

"Crikey," she said in an awed tone. "The whole bloody town's going up, ain't it?"

"I knew it!" Lillybelle cried. "I knew it! We're all going to perish!"

"Shut up and take a piss for yourself," Dolly told her. "It'll make you feel better." Then, to the others, she said, "Let's make ourselves as neat as we can, then after that we'll have breakfast, and then start for the Ferry Building."

"I don't want any breakfast," Clarita said. "All I want is a shot of gin."

"Oh, it's going to be one of those days, is it?" Dolly said. "You'll get your gin when we get to Oakland, and not before."

"Wot's all this fancy talk about breakfast, anyway?" Stella said. "I don't see nobody offering to bring it to me in me bed."

"You'll get your breakfast at the same soup kitchen where you got your supper," Dolly told her. "Now, let's get cracking here, and save the small talk for the ferry. We've got a long day ahead of us."

"A long night I can take in me stride," Stella said, looking around. "It's these long days that are grinding me arse to a nub. All right—nobody leaves the room. Me reticule's been stolen."

"You slept on it, dimwit," Maribelle said. "Look under the hay in the corner, there."

Stella went to the dusty pile of hay where she'd been sleeping, probed around with her foot, then reached down and picked up her beaded reticule. She opened it, saw the unfinished letter to her mother, and snapped it shut. "Don't want to lose that," she said. "That's a little piece of history."

"What is?" said Dolly sharply.

"The letter I'm writing. I'm telling me mum all that's happening—could be worth a bloody fortune some day."

"Not if you write it in Cockney, it won't; nobody'll believe it. Besides, I'm writing this as part of my memoirs, so there's no point you telling the same story."

"There's as many stories as there is people, I always say. You tell yours, and I'll tell mine."

"By all means. But mine is going to be printed."

"So is the Chinatown *Gazette*. That don't make it Gospel."

Dolly smiled to imply she knew more than she was saying, and looked at the others. "All right, girls," she said. "If you're ready, we'll be going."

"What are we going to do when we get to Oakland?" Clarita asked.

"That remains to be seen," replied Dolly, picking up her papers. "The Lord has been kind to us so far; I'm sure He won't abandon us now."

"Just don't look back," said Lillybelle as they filed out of the stable. "Remember what happened to Lot's wife."

"Tommyrot," said Dolly. "A lot of idle superstition." She marched out into the daylight and the girls followed behind her, framed against the billowing smoke like seagulls in front of a storm cloud.

There was a long line at the soup kitchen, and it was an hour before they were able to file down the hill to East Street and head for the Ferry Building. Two navy fireboats had tied up at Pier 8 and their crews were running lengths of hose up to Telegraph Hill, while at various places other navy ships of the Pacific Squadron had docked, and were dispatching fire-fighting and signal crews to where they were most needed. Fleet marines patrolled the waterfront, and although at first Dolly and the girls gave them a wide berth they soon found that the marines, as opposed to the soldiers, were quiet, courteous, and well disciplined. Clarita, in fact, had to be pulled away from a particularly handsome lance corporal, with whom she'd struck up a conversation while waiting to cross the foot of Pacific Street. He was from the cruiser *Marblehead*, which by coincidence was the town in Massachusetts where Clarita's aunt lived, and she claimed this made him practically her cousin. Dolly was not impressed, and bundled Clarita off before she could find out where the *Marblehead* was berthed.

If the line at the soup kitchen had been long, it was nothing compared to the mass of people that stretched down Market Street, from Stockton to the Ferry Building, waiting to leave the city. There were people with carts piled high with bedding, people with birdcages and suitcases, people with baby buggies and steamer trunks and bicycles, people dressed as though for a ball or a funeral or the racetrack, and all of them were shuffling slowly forward, waiting their turn to board a ferry for Oakland. There were many Chinese among them—the wooden houses of Chinatown had been shattered by the initial shock, then burned to ashes in the subsequent fire—and Dolly saw four small Chinese children, each one holding the queue of the child in front of him, waiting quietly to one side, while their mother tried to balance a pile of family possessions in a wheelbarrow.

The line moved slowly, sometimes advancing no more than two or three blocks in an hour, and it was late in the afternoon before Dolly and the girls approached the gate leading to the ferries. As they were about to pass through, there came a thundering clatter down Market Street and a wagon, driven at full speed and containing three men and a driver, scattered people on both sides of its course. One of the men, who had been waving something over his head, jumped down and went to the official at the gate. He was unshaven and seedy-looking, and his eyes had the bright glint of panic.

"I am Caruso, the singer," he said, and started through.

"Sorry, Mac," the official replied, barring the way. "I don't care what you do—you gotta take your turn in line with the others."

"I am Caruso, I tell you! I am a friend of President Roosevelt—see—he gave me this!" He showed the picture and went on, "He wants to see me in Washington immediately!"

The official studied the picture, then turned and beckoned to another Southern Pacific man. "Ever hear of Caruso?" he asked.

"Sure," replied the other. He looked at the picture, then at Caruso. "If you're Caruso," he said, "let's hear you sing."

"This is preposterous! The President will—"

"Either you sing, or you go to the end of the line. Which will it be?"

Caruso glared, then took a deep breath and sang a few bars from *Carmen*. The officials glanced at each other, then the second one indicated the two men with Caruso.

"Who are these guys?" he asked. "The Nibelungen?"

"They are Antonio Scotti, a singer in my company, and Martino, my valet. They go where I go."

"All right," the official said. "Get aboard."

The three men passed through the gate, with Caruso triumphantly waving the photograph over his head, as though acknowledging applause.

"Crikey," said Stella when they had gone. "I'll have to tell me mum about that."

"Don't bother," said Dolly. "Just tell her to read my book."

Gresham Stoddard had worked with the ambulance driver all through the morning and into the afternoon, when the horse slowly came to a stop, dropped its head, and sagged in the traces, trembling on the verge of collapse. The driver got down and unhitched it, then turned back to Stoddard.

"I guess this is the end of the line," he said. "Old Mildred's likely to cash in her chips if she don't get some rest."

"Where could I find another horse?" Stoddard asked. "We can't quit now."

"I don't know about you, but I feel like old Mildred, here. If you've got the gumption to go on, more power to you, but Christ only knows where you'll find a horse. They're probably a thousand bucks a head right now."

"Still—" Stoddard looked around, as though searching for an idea. The only lucky thing, he reflected, was that they didn't have a stretcher case in the ambulance at the moment; he didn't feel that he, alone, could carry anyone five feet.

"Look at it this way," the driver went on, rubbing the horse's back with a blanket. "The Navy's got two destroyers in port, with medical teams aboard, and they and the marines have stretcher parties out in the city. I say let them take over for a while, or you and I'll become stretcher cases ourselves."

"I suppose you're right," Stoddard said. For the first time since early morning he thought of Muriel, and it seemed that she'd already become a stranger. For the past several hours he'd been living a life so different from his usual one that he might as well have been another person, and the Muriel he remembered was part of a different existence entirely. She was gone, his home was gone, and his city was rapidly going, and it was as though he'd been reborn, into a new world, with a whole new life ahead of him. He was aware that the biggest mistake of his earlier life was still shadowing him like a wolf in the woods, but with so much else going on he couldn't worry about that at the moment. It refused to go away but at the same time it hung back, as though waiting for the proper time to spring. To hell with it, Stoddard thought. I'll worry about that when the time comes.

"If I was you I'd get on over to Oakland," the driver went on. "I hear they got all sorts of facilities over there, and they're turning themselves inside out to be helpful."

"That's probably a good idea." Stoddard looked at the rolling clouds of smoke to the west, and heard the thud of dynamiting along Van Ness Avenue, and for the first time experienced a totally helpless feeling. He'd felt he was accomplishing something while the ambulance was in operation, but now, with nothing to do except stand by and watch, he was aware of the insignificance of a single person's contribution. It would be better to clear out and leave the work to the professionals, and regain his strength for whatever problems might lie in the future.

He joined the throng on Market Street and finally, as the daylight was fading, he got aboard a ferry. Nearby, the river paddle steamer *Medoc* was putting out into the Bay, and Stoddard could see her decks covered with people lying on mattresses, being tended by nurses wearing the coifs of the Sisters of Mercy. He remembered the young man they'd left at the hospital, where the sister had said they might have to transfer the patients to a ship, and he guessed that this was the ship. Then he began to worry about where he himself would spend the night, but in short order he gave that up and resigned himself to whatever might happen. This is my new life, he thought, and for the moment I have neither obligations nor responsibilities. He breathed deeply of the clean Bay air, and wondered if he would ever return to San Francisco.

# CHAPTER 11

It was Henry Walden's dream that woke him up. He dreamed he was back in Cuba, in the ambush at Las Guásimas, pinned to the ground while rifle fire and smoke spat out of the bushes and tore up the foliage around him. Then George Bender appeared, rising out of the jungle floor and coming toward him with outstretched hands, and suddenly George changed into Lucille, and she was saying something intensely provocative but Walden couldn't catch the words. He woke up in a state of high excitement that faded into disappointment and the immediate need to go to the bathroom. His legs were stiff and sore as he got out of bed, but he made it into the bathroom with no real trouble, and after a few minutes of loosening up found that he could walk with no more than moderate twinges of pain. He put some toothpaste on his finger and cleansed his mouth, washed his face and ran his wet fingers through his hair, then put on the slicker, fastened the clasps securely, and went downstairs. Lucille was in the kitchen, and her face brightened when she saw him.

"Good morning!" she said. "Did you sleep well?"

"If you want to call it sleep," he replied, feeling the stubble of his beard. "It was more like a coma. Do you think George would mind if I borrowed his razor?"

"Of course not. But don't you want some breakfast first? I can make you an omelette, or ham and—"

"Thank you, I'd rather make myself presentable first. I wouldn't want the neighbors to think you're giving breakfast to a tramp."

"Who cares what the neighbors think? It's my life."

"Then call it pride on my part. Vanity, if you will."

"The razor and mug are in the medicine cabinet, the strop is hanging on the door under his bathrobe, and I'll have to get you some of his underwear. Yours is still drying on the line."

"Thank you. I'm going to look for my clothes today, and see if I can salvage anything."

"I told you, you don't have to worry about that."

"Still, there are some personal things I'd like to find if I can."

"Of course. I'll be glad to help you."

"There's no need to bother you."

"Bother? It'll be a pleasure."

He was shaving in the bathroom, naked, when he heard her coming up the stairs. He quickly closed the bathroom door, and then listened while she puttered about the bedroom, apparently making the bed but also doing a number of other things he couldn't identify. She was humming to herself as she worked, and she took so long that he began to wonder if she'd forgotten where he was. Either that, he thought, or she has no intention of leaving, and is just killing time until I come out. He considered flinging the door open and striding out just as he was, but then reasoned it was too long a chance to be worth taking, and if it misfired it would destroy everything. And with his luck, it would be almost certain to misfire. No, he thought, no matter what she may have in mind you'd better behave like a gentleman, or you'll never be able to look in a mirror again. Bender has twice saved your life; don't repay him by knifing him in the back.

He was drying the razor when there was a tap on the door, and he jumped so that he almost cut himself. "I'll be right out," he said. "I'm just cleaning up."

"No hurry," came her voice from the other side of the door. "Everything's ready when you want to get dressed."

He heard her go downstairs, and cautiously opened the door a crack. On the bed were laid out a set of underwear, trousers, a shirt, and socks, and a pair of moccasins were on the floor. There was something on the underwear he couldn't identify, and he crossed the room and picked it up and saw that it was a blossom cut from a pear tree, which had been put dead center at the waistline, almost as though it were protruding from inside the garment. He dressed in thoughtful silence, then went to a mirror, put the pear blossom in the second buttonhole of the shirt, ran a comb through his hair, and went down to breakfast. Lucille didn't mention the blossom, and he said nothing.

Later on, while they were sorting through the wreckage of what had been Walden's rented room, he said, "I didn't know you had any pear trees on your property."

"We don't," Lucille replied, bending down and picking up a shoe. "Is this yours?"

Walden examined the shoe, which was battered and covered with dust. "It may be," he said. "But unless we find the other, it won't be much use."

"Well, let's keep looking." Lucille turned away, and poked into the rubble with a stick.

"If you don't have pear trees, where'd this come from?" Walden asked, indicating his buttonhole. Lucille looked at it as though she'd never seen it before.

"Search me," she said, then glanced where her stick had uncovered a piece of cloth. "Oh, look." She bent down, pulled the cloth, and brought a pair of trousers out from under a mound of plaster. In the back pocket was a wallet, which she opened and then held out to him. "It's yours," she said with a smile. "At least, the initials are H.G.W."

"Thank you!" Walden said, taking it from her. "I don't know what I'd do without you!" He also took the trousers, shook them out, and examined them. "Maybe they can be cleaned," he said. "At least they're not torn. Is there a good dry cleaner in the neighborhood?"

"There is, but I imagine he's too busy with other things. I'll clean them for you—they don't look too bad."

"I can't let you do *everything*," Walden protested. "I mean, you—"

"Why can't you?" She was looking directly at him as she spoke. "If I want to do things, why shouldn't I?"

He paused, returning her look, then said, "Like snipping the blossoms off pear trees?"

"Like anything I want to do. Is it against the law?"

"You sound like a suffragette."

"Do I indeed?"

"Are you?"

"I don't know what I am. I just have the feeling I've been missing something."

"Like what?"

"That's the trouble. I don't know."

Walden took a deep breath, trying to think how to phrase his next question, then stopped as he heard the rumble of an approaching wagon. He looked around and saw Bender coming toward them, and in the wagon were assorted bits of furniture such as chairs, a couple of mattresses, and an army cot. Walden waved, and when Lucille saw the wagon her face went blank.

"Doing a little looting?" Bender asked. "That's one way to get shot."

"I might ask you the same thing," Lucille replied. "We happen to be looking for Godfrey's possessions."

Bender got down from the wagon, and threw the reins over the horse's head. "I asked at City Hall what I could do to help," he said. "They said the biggest need was for housing, so I'm turning the shop into a dormitory. It occurred to me I might find some mattresses here."

"Isn't that technically looting?" Lucille asked.

"I'm making a note of every place I find something. I'll return it all when it's no longer needed." Then, to Walden, "Did you find any of your stuff?"

"Lucille found that pair of pants, and my wallet," Walden replied. "As you can see, the rest of what I'm wearing is yours."

"Except that flower in your buttonhole."

"Oh, that." Walden laughed uneasily. "I just picked that, to wear instead of a tie."

"It makes you look like a real dude." Bender glanced about,

then said, "Well, let's see what else we can find. We've still got a couple of hours' daylight left."

"Where are the refugees going?" Walden asked.

"Wherever they can. There's a camp at Adams Point, on the lake, and then there's a Chinese group at Eighth and Ninth, near the lake. The Chinese don't like to take any kind of help, but in this case they've got to. The trouble is, a camp's no good except for a couple of nights or so. What we really need is housing."

"Remember that camp at Montauk, when we came back from the war?" Walden said.

"Do I ever. That's what I mean by a camp's no good."

"I don't think civilians could ever make as much of a mess of it as that. That was worse than anything that happened during the fighting." Walden had felt a coolness creeping between Bender and himself, and he tried to break it down by reminiscing. "Remember the storm?"

"I try not to think about it," Bender replied.

"What storm was that?" Lucille asked.

"A storm hit the camp one night," Walden said. "It blew down a lot of tents and five guys drowned, mostly because the duty officer wouldn't believe there was any trouble. His hut was dry, and he didn't want to get his feet wet."

"That isn't finding us any mattresses," Bender said. "Let's all turn to here, and see what we can dredge up before it gets too dark."

Just as it had the night before, the glow from the fires in San Francisco made a rosy semi-twilight in Oakland, and they were able to work well past sunset. They found Walden's suitcase, three mattresses—one of which was covered with blood, and unusable—and four splintered chairs, which Bender kept because he thought they might somehow come in handy. He couldn't think for what, but he took the position that a chair was a chair, and in the circumstances they couldn't be too fussy.

"Don't worry about me tonight," Walden said as they were heading for the shop. "I can take care of myself."

"You'll do no such thing," Lucille replied before Bender could say anything. "You'll stay with us until you find a permanent place."

"Well—I mean—at least I won't take your bed from you. I can stay in the shop as soon as we—"

"You'll stay with us, and that's all there is to it. You can use the cot that George used last night, or you can put a mattress on the floor, but I won't hear of your wandering around alone. Who knows—your legs might suddenly give way, and you'd fall in the street and be crushed by a brewer's cart."

Walden laughed. "I don't think there'll be many brewer's carts cruising around town," he said.

"It was the heaviest thing I could think of," Lucille replied. "Anyway, you know what I mean."

Bender, who had listened quietly to the exchange, said, "The first thing to do is get the shop set up, and then I, for one, could use a smile or two."

"Good idea," said Walden. "That'll make all the decisions easier."

"What do you mean by 'smile'?" Lucille asked. "What does smiling have to do with anything?"

"A smile is a drink," said Walden.

"Oh," said Lucille. "You should have said so in the first place."

They unloaded the wagon into the shop, and did what little they could to make the place look tidy. Then they went back to the Benders' house, and while Bender stabled and fed the horse Walden and Lucille took Walden's possessions inside, and sorted through them to see which were salvageable.

"Isn't it about time for that smile?" Lucille said when the laundry and cleaning had been separated, and the rest marked for the rag bag.

"Would you like one, too?" Walden asked in mild surprise.

"I don't see why not. If I can't have my elixir, I might as well have something else. There's cooking sherry behind the bread box, brandy for the Christmas pudding above the spice chest, and whisky in the side cupboard. Take your choice."

"I think I'll go for the whisky. And you?"

She hesitated, then said, "I think perhaps a small glass of sherry. I'll get it."

They made their drinks, raised them in salute, and their eyes met briefly over the glasses. Then they each took a sip, and Lucille continued to stare at him until Walden looked away. He took another drink, a larger one, and cleared his throat.

"Who was it who said, 'Drink to me only with thine eyes'?" Lucille asked.

"I believe it was Ben Jonson," Walden replied. "Why?"

"I always thought it was a dumb remark. I didn't see how you could drink with your eyes, but maybe now I'm beginning to find out."

All right, Walden thought, if that's the way she wants to play it's O.K. with me. "Do you know what comes after that?" he said.

"What?"

"'Or leave a kiss but in the cup/ And I'll not look for wine.'"

"That's an interesting thought," she said, and moved slowly toward him.

Not right now, Walden thought, in a panic. And, of all places, not here. He took another drink, and said, "Of course, Jonson cribbed it from Philostratus."

"Did he, now? What did Philostratus say?"

"He said something to the effect of 'Drink to me with your eyes alone, and, uh, take the cup to your lips and fill it with kisses,' and so on. That was back in the third century, a long time before Jonson."

"How did you know all that?"

"Some people remember some things, other people remember others. I seem to remember poetry."

"Tell me some more."

She was now so close he could smell her scented soap, and he took a step backward just as the kitchen door opened and Bender came in. Lucille jumped as though a bolt of electricity had shot through her, and Walden turned to Bender and laughed. "I hope you don't mind that we started without you?" he said.

"Started what?" said Bender.

Walden held up his glass. "The drinks."

Bender's eyes flicked toward Lucille's glass. "What's that?" he asked.

"Just a little sherry," she replied. "It's good for the digestion."

"What would you like?" Walden asked. "I can make it for you while you wash up."

"I'll make it." Bender went to the sink and washed his hands, then poured a splash of whisky into a glass and drank half of it in one gulp.

"Hits the spot, doesn't it?" said Walden.

Without answering him, Bender turned to Lucille and said, "What's for supper?"

"I haven't even thought," she replied. "I've been busy all afternoon, and this is the first chance I've had to relax." She finished her sherry, and went to the bottle and poured another. "Sit down and take it easy, and I'll fix you something in a while."

"Is there anything I can help you with after supper?" Walden asked.

"Like what?" said Bender, still looking at Lucille.

"It doesn't matter what. I just feel I should do something to earn my keep."

"Well, we'll see." Bender drained his glass, poured a refill, then corked the sherry bottle and put it away.

"Are you telling me I can't have any more?" Lucille asked.

"Look at it any way you want. All I'm interested in is supper."

"And I said to relax. Why can't you relax?"

Bender took a deep breath, and was about to reply when there was a knock at the front door. He left the room and went to the door and opened it, and saw a stocky, middle-aged man in a bowler hat and business suit. His suit and shirt were rumpled and stained, but there was something about his face that suggested he'd be more at home in evening clothes: it was the faintly equine but jowly face one saw so often on the society page. Bender assumed he'd come with a prescription, and said, "I'm sorry, but there's nothing I can do for you. The shop was wrecked in the quake."

The man's voice was gravelly, whether from fatigue or whisky it was impossible to tell. "I don't want to buy anything," he said. "I'm looking for a place to sleep."

"Oh." Bender's mind went back to Lucille and Walden in the kitchen, and he made a sudden decision and stood back and opened the door wider. "Come in," he said. "It may be a little crowded, but we can always make room for one more."

The ferry on which Gresham Stoddard had crossed the Bay was jammed with the usual assortment of refugees, but now, after two full days of fire, a new note of hysteria had crept in: there were more and more people who were missing friends or relatives, and were frantically searching and calling as they clawed their way through the mob. One woman had a picture of a small child, which she held up and asked if anyone could recognize; a man, half crazy with grief, kept shouting, "Agnes! Agnes, for God's sake where are you?"; and a tall woman, wearing a large-brimmed hat and pince-nez glasses, sang out, "Will Evan Kilpatrick please go to the Knights of Columbus Hall in Oakland?" over and over, as she circled the ferry. Signs had been put up on the bulkheads with similar messages, and it occurred to Stoddard that, for anyone who wanted to disappear from the face of the earth, this was the perfect opportunity. Everyone was, in a sense, lost, and only those who wanted to be found need ever be heard from again. Records had been destroyed, or could be claimed to have been, and there would be a minimum of trouble establishing a new identity. He wondered what had happened to the records at his bank, and concluded it wouldn't be safe to assume that those had been destroyed, because the vaults were fireproof and probably safe from everything except a direct hit by artillery fire. Still, if he could be sure one way or the other, he would know a lot better how to proceed. The Yukon no longer seemed as attractive as it had two nights ago, but anything was more attractive than jail.

Night had fallen when he reached Oakland, and the confusion at the ferry landing was almost total. Some people shouted instructions and others shouted questions; a man with a megaphone was telling how to get to Adams Point, while another man, also with a megaphone, was giving the word about registration at City Hall; someone kept shouting, "All Chinese step this way!" and small boys darted through the crowd, passing out handbills that advertised houses for sale in the suburbs. A train was standing at the railway terminal, and several people boarded this, but Stoddard, after a moment's thought, decided not to leave until he knew a little better what was going on. He somehow felt sure that Muriel had survived, and would continue to survive without him, and the most important thing at the moment was to find out his own status in the eyes of the law.

The main stream of refugees headed toward Lake Merritt, and Stoddard had gone no more than two blocks before he decided he wasn't up to another night of sleeping in the open. His bones and muscles ached; he walked as though wearing deep-sea diver's shoes, and it seemed to him that the greatest luxury he could think of would be to find a bed—any bed, so long as it was handy to modern conveniences. He was afflicted with the problem of night rising, and his experience the previous night, in Golden Gate Park, had been an unsettling one. It turned out that several people had slept under bushes, where they were invisible to anyone standing above them, and he had been cursed in language he had thought was reserved only for the waterfront. He veered away from the refugees, and began looking for a likely house. The red glow that hung over San Francisco was reflected in the west-facing windows of Oakland houses, making it look as though they, too, were burning. Stoddard wondered briefly if he was already in hell, then decided that fatigue was beginning to make him hallucinate. He trudged on, knocking on doors where a light showed inside, and although people were sympathetic there were none who would take him in: some had already accepted as many refugees as they could handle, others were in a state of disarray brought on by the earthquake, and one householder demanded more money than Stoddard had with him at the time.

He was beginning to wonder if he might get aboard the train, if only to have a place to sleep, when he came to a house that had a stable behind it and a light on in a downstairs room. At the very worst I can sleep in the stable, he thought, and went to the front door and knocked. He heard footsteps, and the door was opened by a man of about thirty, with a thin face and a pointed nose, who apparently took him for a customer of some sort. When Stoddard explained what he wanted, the man hesitated a fraction of a second and then told him to come in. Stoddard could see a man and woman in the kitchen beyond, and wondered if they, too, were refugees.

"This is extremely kind of you," he said as he came into the house. "Having spent last night in Golden Gate Park, I'm not anxious to sleep out again."

"I don't imagine it's a great deal of fun. Come into the kitchen. Oh—I'm George Bender, and this is my wife, Lucille, and our—guest—Mr. Walden. Mr. Walden's room was wrecked in the quake."

"How do you do," Stoddard said, shaking hands with Bender and nodding to the others. "My name is—ah—Lambert. Maxwell Lambert."

"Do you come from San Francisco, Mr. Lambert?" Lucille asked.

"Alas, yes," Stoddard replied. "My house burned last night."

"Are you alone?" Lucille tried to phrase it tactfully—"I mean, do you have—?"

"My wife escaped the city earlier," Stoddard said. "And that reminds me—is there some central clearing place, where I could check on her whereabouts?"

"Try City Hall tomorrow," Bender said. "Also, people are putting up handbills with the names of those who're missing. But if I were you I'd go to City Hall first. You can register there, in case she's looking for you."

"I'll do that," said Stoddard. "But for the moment the only thing I want to do is sleep. If you would be so kind as to point me toward a bed—"

"Can't we give you some supper first? We were just about to eat."

"Well—perhaps—"

Bender glanced at Lucille, who gave him a level stare, then went to a kitchen cabinet and began to sort through the cans. Bender turned back to Stoddard. "Mr. Walden and I are having a drink," he said. "Would you join us?"

"If you don't mind my collapsing on the floor."

Bender laughed. "Don't worry about that. As I told Mr. Walden earlier, my wife really should have been a nurse, so you'll be in the best of all possible hands."

"In that case, by all means."

Bender made another drink, and as he gave it to Stoddard Lucille reached down to where he'd put the sherry, produced the bottle, and poured a glass for herself. She tapped the cork back in as though she were patting the head of a child.

"To your good health," she said to Stoddard, and drank.

"Thank you," Stoddard replied, raising his glass. "I must say, I didn't dare hope to find such a cheerful lodging as this."

"Stay around awhile," Lucille replied. "You'll find it gets positively hilarious."

# CHAPTER 12

Dolly and her girls spent their first night in Oakland at Adams Point, on Lake Merritt, and when the sun rose on Friday three of the girls were gone. Tessie and Melinda, the two silent ones who spent most of their leisure time looking at stereopticon slides, had managed, during the confusion of settling down for the night, to slip off into the crowd, where they did a brisk business in the bushes that bordered the lake. When morning came, they saw no reason to share their earnings with Dolly and struck off on their own, and it was later rumored that Tessie had married a prominent official of the Southern Pacific Railroad. Dolores, the third defector, waded into the lake to cool her feet, and became so carried away by the rustic scene that she vowed never again to return to the city. Within an hour she had hitched a ride on a farmer's wagon, and wound up in the Round Valley Indian Reservation, a hundred and sixty miles to the north.

Dolly was at first enraged when the defections were discovered, and then secretly relieved, because looking out for seven wayward girls had been a job that taxed her ingenuity as well as her patience. Now, with only four left, she had a manageable cadre with which she could survive until permanent quarters could be found. She had a feeling that her regular business might have to be suspended for a while—the matter of open-air, community living would dampen the ardor of her higher-class customers, and expose her girls only to the more feral elements of hoi polloi—but she wanted time to work on her book, and she felt that the girls could use their secondary talents in any number of ways. She decided to put Stella in nominal charge, which would free her own hands for the more important work of writing.

"Just do as I've always done," she told Stella, by way of instructions. "Make sure you don't do anything second-rate, and the world will beat a path to your door."

Stella looked doubtful. "If you say so," she said. "But do what? I'm no bloody good wif me hands."

"You used to be a hairdresser, didn't you?" Dolly replied. "At least that's what you told me."

"Oh, that." Stella made a deprecatory gesture. "That was just diddling around wif a comb."

"Well, do it again. I'm sure there are a lot of women who'll want to have their hair done."

"I'm not used to working wif women," said Stella. "I wouldn't know what to talk about."

"What do you usually talk about?"

Stella gave her a long stare. "You ought to know better than to ask a question like that."

"When I was a working girl," Dolly said, "I always had a conversational gambit ready, to put things on an intellectual plane. The war with Spain, the trial of Oscar Wilde, the relief of Ladysmith—"

"The Battle of Gettysburg," Stella put in.

"Don't be cheeky, or I'll belt you one. My point is you have to have something else to talk about, other than the business at hand. Now, when—"

"Nobody's going to be talking about anything but the quake," Stella said.

"So much the better. Let them do the talking. Let them tell you their experiences."

"All right," said Stella. "I'll give it a whirl, but I don't promise nuffink."

"And for God's sake remember your French," Dolly said. "You'll be a lot more convincing as a hairdresser if you can pretend you're French."

"Who wants to be convincing?" Stella replied. "All I want is a little rest."

"First things first," said Dolly. "Now, you keep an eye on the others, while I see if I can find us lodgings."

Stella went to where Maribelle, Clarita, and Lillybelle were standing glumly in line, waiting for a ration of an indescribable soup, ladled out by a harried militiaman. Those refugees who had brought their own provisions and alcohol stoves were cooking for themselves, but the vast majority had brought nothing, and were eating on a catch-as-catch-can basis. The scene was like that in Golden Gate Park, but without the immediacy of the approaching fire. That was a dark cloud in the west, smudging the sky and every now and then producing distant explosions, but already it represented a part of these people's pasts, and had no relation to the present or the future.

"All right, ladies," Stella said as she joined them in line. "We're all going into a new line of business."

"Like what?" said Maribelle. "Engineering?"

"Whatever we can do. The madam seems to think that I should be a hairdresser, so that's going to be my line."

"What's all this about?" Clarita asked. "Has she gone crazy?"

"No, it's just we've got no house. She's going to try to find rooms, but she'll be lucky if she gets us in the armory. You can't turn a decent trick in public, so for now we think of something else."

"It's so long since I thought of anything else that I can't think," said Maribelle. "I wish I'd said I'd go to the Yukon."

Lillybelle, who had been listening quietly, now said, "Is she serious about this?"

"Did you ever know the madam to make a joke?" Stella replied.

Lillybelle got a faraway look in her eyes, and moved out of the line. "I'll see you later," she said.

"Where are you going?" asked Stella.

"To see someone."

"About what?"

"A job."

Stella hesitated. "Well, see you come back," she said. "The madam doesn't want us scattered all over the park."

Lillybelle drifted off into the crowd without replying, and Stella watched her go. "I'd like to know what kind of job she's thinking of," she said to Clarita.

Clarita reached down the front of her dress, produced a nail file, and began to scrape at a hangnail. "With her, you never can tell," she said. "She gets some strange ideas."

Some time earlier, Lillybelle had seen one of the Sisters of Mercy moving among the people, and she now went in the direction the sister had taken. She felt that the sister's appearance had been a Sign, sent by the Lord for her to follow, and she made her way through the crowd with the calm knowledge that the Lord would guide her feet in the right direction. After about ten minutes she saw, as she had known she would, the white wings of the sister's coif, in the middle of a crowd of curious people. Lillybelle hurried to the scene, and heard the sister saying, "Will someone please get a blanket? The rest of you stand back—please—and give the lady some privacy!" She elbowed her way to the front, and saw the sister bending over a woman who was stretched out on a mattress, in labor. The woman was calm, lying still and looking at the sky, and then a contraction hit her and she closed her eyes and bit her lower lip. Lillybelle kneeled beside her, and the sister looked around in surprise.

"Are you a nurse?" she asked.

"We'll talk about that later," Lillybelle replied. "I'm here to help."

Someone produced a blanket, and the sister draped it over the woman's waist and legs, and then rolled up her sleeves, reached under the blanket, and made a manual examination. She withdrew her hands, and looked around at the spectators. "Would you all mind leaving?" she said. "If you have nothing to do here, please have the decency to go somewhere else."

Nobody moved. Lillybelle, who had taken off her jacket and rolled it up to make a pillow for the woman, turned and looked at the man nearest her. "You," she said.

"Yes?" said the man, leaning forward.

Lillybelle stood up. "You get out of here, or I'll kick your nuts up to your eyeballs, and that goes for all of you! Bugger off! This minute!" She moved toward the man, who recoiled and backed away, and the others began to disperse. Lillybelle looked at one man who hadn't moved; he was wearing sleeve garters and a derby hat, and he stood quietly by, chewing a toothpick and cracking his knuckles. "That goes for you, too," she said. "This isn't a sideshow."

"I'm her husband," he said.

"Oh," said Lillybelle. "In that case, all right."

The sister looked up at him. "Would you be so good as to get some hot water?" she said. "Or if you can't find any, then put some on to boil?"

"Sure thing," he replied, and vanished.

Lillybelle kneeled beside the woman, whose forehead was now covered with dewlike perspiration. "What's the hot water for?" she asked the sister. "You don't put the *baby* in it, do you?"

"You're not a nurse, are you?" the sister replied.

"I never said I was."

"Well, if you were, you'd know that the hot water is just to keep the husband out of the way. It gives him something to do."

"Well, well," said Lillybelle. "I guess there's tricks to every trade."

"Do you mind my asking what your trade is?" the sister said.

"Well, I'm thinking of changing it," replied Lillybelle. "I'd like to join your order."

There was a long silence, while the sister made another examination. "It requires great dedication," she said at last. "And, to begin with, true penitence."

"I'm penitent, all right," said Lillybelle. "There's no problem there."

The woman cried out as another contraction seized her, and the sister said, "See if you can find something to make pulling ropes."

"To make *what?*" said Lillybelle.

"Pulling ropes, like reins. Then we'll brace her feet, and she'll have something to pull against. It speeds the birth."

Lillybelle got up, shaking her head. "You talk about tricks of the trade," she said. "I thought I—ah, well." She looked around, then went and took down a length of clothesline someone had used to stretch a tent between two trees, and brought it back to the sister. "You mean like this?" she said.

"That's fine. Now, if you can find some place to attach it—" The woman cried again, this time a piercing shriek, and the sister reached under the blanket and said, "Never mind that now—come here!" Lillybelle joined her, and the sister said, "Put her right foot on your shoulder, and hold on—" Placing the woman's other foot on her own shoulder, the sister reached down to take the baby's head. The blanket fell away, and Lillybelle saw the wet and wrinkled figure emerge, while the sister rapidly invoked the Father and the Son and the Holy Ghost. Then the sister handed the baby to her, tied a quick knot around the cord and cut it, and said, "Wrap it in the blanket, and keep it warm," and turned her attention to the mother. "Everything's all right, dear," she said. "You have a beautiful baby boy."

Lillybelle hadn't thought of the baby in terms of gender, and as she wrapped it in the blanket she glanced down and saw that it was indeed masculine. So that's what they look like to begin with, she thought. It's a pity they can't stay that way forever. She thought of the bootees she was knitting for her sister's expected baby, and wished she'd brought them when she left the house—when? Yesterday morning? Day before yesterday? A year ago? It seemed like another lifetime.

The husband returned with a pail of steaming water, and said, "Where do you want me to put it?"

"Ask her," replied Lillybelle, indicating the sister, and as the man turned away she said, "Don't you want to see your son?" She opened the blanket slightly, and the man stopped and peered at the prunelike face and said, "I be damn. You never know, do you?" Then, to the sister, he said, "I got your water, ma'm; it's good and hot. What do you want me to do with it?"

The sister looked at the steam rising from the pail, and said, "Set it down and let it cool. You can use it to wash with later."

"If it's too hot, how come you ask me to boil it?" the man said. "If you wanted warm water, whyn't you say so?"

"There was no way of knowing how long it would take," the sister replied, standing up. Before the man could analyze her reply, she went on, "I have to go now. See that the baby stays warm, and your wife has some hot food."

"Shouldn't she see a doctor?" the man asked. "All the other—"

"Only if there's an emergency," the sister cut in. "There've been so many babies born the last couple of days there's no way to take care of them all. I'm sorry—I wish I could stay, but I can't."

She started off, and Lillybelle, who was afraid that Stella would be looking for her, said, "Sister, may I come with you?" She handed the baby to its father, and hurried to the sister's side. "I meant it when I said I wanted to join your order. I know it'll take a lot of work, but I might as well start right now. Isn't there something I can do to help?"

The sister hesitated, thinking of all the problems to be surmounted and the objections to be overcome, and she could hear the Mother Superior's voice saying, "You mean a common *tart?*" Then, in spite of herself, she smiled. "I think there is," she said. "I think there's probably a lot you can do."

When Dolly left the camp she had no precise idea where she was going, but she reasoned that the general direction of City Hall made as much sense as anything else. She had no particular desire to register, since there was nobody she could think of who might like to know her whereabouts, and the caution brought on by her trade warned her not to flaunt anything until she knew just where the authorities stood. In San Francisco she had felt secure, but for all she knew Oakland, with different officials, might have a whole new set of rules.

As she walked through the streets she saw occasional piles of rubble from fallen walls or chimneys, but compared to San

Francisco the city was virtually untouched. At one spot, on Telegraph Avenue, she was halted by militiamen, who had closed off the street while workmen with winches and cables pulled the damaged steeple off the First Baptist Church, and Dolly watched with mild interest as the steeple toppled into the street in a cascade of stone and mortar dust. She made mental notes of the scene for her book, and, not feeling she had to watch the entire demolition, took a detour around the area and continued on her way. She saw crowds of refugees gathered around schools, theaters, and public halls, and from this she inferred that the city was turning over all available space for the temporary housing of the homeless. She briefly joined the line outside the Masonic Hall, then gave up when someone near the door shouted that there was no more room. I guess it's going to depend on luck, she thought as she turned away. But then, my luck's been pretty good so far; there's no reason to think it'll desert me now. She didn't like to capitalize on other people's distress, but she couldn't help feeling that the earthquake and fire had come at the perfect time for her: they had given a point and direction to her book, which had hitherto been floundering, and had made it all but certain she would have a successful start in a new career. With her O'Farrell Street house gone, and no immediate prospect of a replacement, her old business was virtually wiped out, and this was the time to take a whole new tack. She had enough money in the bank to support herself for . . . Her plans ground to a halt as she was struck by the thought that her savings might have vanished in the fire. Frantically, she tried to think of someone she could ask—some bank official who would know what had happened to the funds. She'd heard that two tellers from the Anglo-California Bank had brought a million dollars in a wheelbarrow across the Bay by ferry to Oakland, and she hoped that someone from her bank had been as enterprising. But how to find out was something else again; in the present state of affairs it was impossible to tell how many people had survived, let alone how much money.

Sobered by the thought of having to go to work again, she

continued on toward City Hall, wondering how writers who didn't have any money made out. I guess they have to pick up something on the side, she thought; either that, or have a patron, or protector, or someone who'll foot the bills. She thought of the man who'd first suggested she write a book, and realized she should have extracted some sort of promise, or agreement, from him, which would have steered it toward publication. But now it was too late: he'd been a newspaper editor, who ran an item about the drinking habits of the wife of a local politician, and had been shot five times in the head and chest before the second edition was off the press. What she needed was a patron who knew how to keep out of trouble, but the circles in which she moved made this easier said than done.

She was walking slowly, immersed in literary thoughts, when she came to a store where two men and a woman were setting up cots and other pieces of furniture. A sign over the window read: "Geo. F. Bender Drugs & Pharmaceuticals," but there was no evidence of any drugs on the premises; the store looked more like a barracks than a pharmacy. More out of curiosity than anything else, Dolly pushed the door and went inside. A bell tinkled overhead, and the three people stopped what they were doing and looked at her.

"I'm sorry," said one of them, a man with a thin nose who looked something like a ferret, "I'm temporarily out of business. The quake—"

"I'm not looking for drugs," Dolly cut in. "I'm looking for a place to work."

There was a short silence. "What kind of work do you do?" Bender asked.

"I'm a writer. I need a place to work, and also to sleep. My—ah—home was burned in the fire."

"Well, you're welcome to sleep here," Bender said. "I don't know how mucy privacy you'll have, but in the circumstances there's not much—"

"This will be fine," said Dolly. "First-rate. How much do you charge?"

"I hadn't really got around to thinking of that. You can't very well charge people who've lost everything, can you?"

"That's up to you." Dolly looked at the woman, who was eyeing her pensively. "What are you paying?" she asked.

"I'm Mrs. Bender," Lucille replied.

"A thousand pardons," said Dolly. "My name is LaGrange—Madame Dolores LaGrange." She looked at the other man, who said, "I'm Henry Walden. How do you do."

"Enchanted, I'm sure," she replied.

"What sort of things do you write?" Lucille asked.

"At the moment, I am working on a book." Then, changing the subject, Dolly said, "How many of these beds are free? Has anyone else applied?"

"So far, you're the only one," said Bender. "Why?"

"My hairdresser needs a bed, as do two or three of her friends. We all left the city together, and spent last night out by the lake. The conditions there were deplorable."

"I can imagine," Bender replied. "Well, if they get here before anyone else applies, they're welcome. It's pretty much first come first served."

"What about Mr. Lambert?" Walden asked. "Wasn't he planning to sleep here?"

"He'll have to stay with us," said Bender. "I don't think Mrs. LaGrange would be happy sharing her quarters with an elderly gentleman."

"It makes no difference to me," said Dolly, cheerfully, "just so long as there's room for my hairdresser and her friends. I promised them I'd try to find something for us all."

"I think it would be best for all concerned if Mr. Lambert stayed with us," Bender said. "That way, there'll be no chance for embarrassment."

"Maybe he's found his wife," Lucille suggested. "Maybe we won't see him again."

"All he said was he was going to City Hall," Bender replied. "If he found his wife in that mob, it would be one shot in a million."

"I know a man who found his wife in the desert," Walden put in. "Just sort of stumbled across her."

"Was she dead?" Lucille asked.

"No, just resting. But he was surprised, because she'd told him she was going to visit her mother."

"You must know some interesting people," said Lucille. "Tell me more."

"This isn't helping Mrs. LaGrange," Bender said, and then, to Dolly, "I suggest you go find your friends—"

"My hairdresser and her friends," Dolly corrected him.

"Your hairdresser and her friends, and bring them back here as soon as you can. I'll hold the space for, say, an hour, but after that I'll have to take in anyone who asks. How many of you are there?"

"Five, counting me," said Dolly, who didn't yet know of Lillybelle's defection.

"It'll be tight, but we'll see what we can do. I suppose we can always put someone over the stable in our house."

"I could go there," said Dolly. "That would give me more privacy for my writing."

"The first thing is to get your hairdresser and the rest. We'll sort things out after that."

"Done and done," said Dolly. "I'll be back in half an hour."

She left, and the Benders and Walden went back to setting up the room. "I wonder what kind of writer she is," Lucille said, pushing a cot into one corner. "Has anyone ever heard of her?"

"I haven't," Walden replied, "but that doesn't prove anything. From her face, however, she looks as though she's lived. She might have one hell of a story to tell."

Lucille laughed. "You're an incurable romantic—or, then again, maybe you're curable. What would your guess be?"

Before Walden could think of an answer, the bell over the door tinkled, and Gresham Stoddard came in. He looked bemused, as though his mind was somewhere else.

"Ah, there, Mr. Lambert," Bender said. "Any word on your wife?"

Stoddard shook his head. "I couldn't even get near the place," he said.

"Maybe Mr. Lambert knows," Lucille said. "Have you ever heard of a Dolores LaGrange?"

Stoddard turned the name over in his mind, wondering why it sounded faintly familiar. "I don't think so," he said. "Who is she?"

"She's a writer," Lucille replied. "Or says she is. But nobody knows anything she's written."

"Unless she writes books on finance, I wouldn't have heard of her," Stoddard said. "It's a depressing thought, but there it is."

"Well, she's going to be staying here for a while, so we'll probably be able to find out," Lucille said. "She claims she's working on a book right now."

Stoddard, who had spent most of the morning trying unsuccessfully to find out what had become of his bank's records, dismissed Dolly from his mind and said, "One thing I did find out—they want volunteers to patrol the streets at night, to make sure there's no looting. I think I might give that a try."

"What's the matter with the police?" asked Bender.

"There aren't enough of them. The city's doubled in size in the last two days."

"I'll join you," said Walden. "It seems like the least I can do."

"You'll do no such thing," said Lucille. "Think of your legs."

"My legs are fine. The exercise'll do them good."

Lucille started to protest, but her husband cut her off. "He's a grown boy," he said. "They're his legs, and he can do what he wants with them."

"I'm only thinking of his own good," Lucille replied, tightly.

"When he wants you to play Florence Nightingale, I'm sure he'll ask you," Bender said, and then, to Walden, "Isn't that right, Godfrey?"

"Right as rain," said Walden. "You can bet your boots I will."

# CHAPTER 13

That was Friday, April 20, the third day of the fire. By now, the chaos in San Francisco was virtually complete: fire storms had started, forcing the would-be fire fighters to flee for their lives; refugees brought tales of rats overrunning parts of the city, and of crazed soldiers shooting or bayoneting anyone who was slow to obey orders; and volunteer vigilante groups had sprung up in a last, desperate hope of establishing order. The National Guard began looting in the remains of Chinatown, and at 5 P.M. the shelling, which had been suspended for twelve hours on the grounds that it often did more harm than good, was resumed along Van Ness Avenue. At 6 P.M. Mayor Schmitz announced that the fire was "virtually under control," a statement as wildly untrue as any that had been made in the past three days.

In Oakland, the volunteer street patrols had none of the hysteria associated with the vigilante groups, and their function was precautionary rather than corrective. When everything possible had been done to put Bender's shop in order, Henry Walden and Gresham Stoddard went to sign up for patrol duty, and received the white armbands that were their badges of office. When they'd been instructed in their sectors and their hours of duty, they decided to see if there was anyplace where they could buy food, to help restock the Benders' supply.

"It seems only fair," Walden said, "considering they're not charging us for any of this."

"I agree," said Stoddard. "And if we can't find food we

should give them money. The man's lost practically everything he owns."

"Personally, I'm not all that well heeled either," Walden replied. "I came out here to take a job, but now I don't know what I'm going to do."

"A job where?"

"With the Southern Pacific. In the main office."

"I'm sure they'll stay in business. You won't have any trouble there."

"Yes, but I'm not sure I *want* the job." He recalled his resolve, when trapped in the wreckage, to take anything that was offered him, but that now seemed less important than making sure that what he got was the best he could find. "What do you do, Mr. Lambert?" he asked.

"That's an interesting question," Stoddard replied. "Loosely speaking, I guess you could say I was in finance."

"Are you retired?"

"Very probably. It'll depend on what the fire did."

Walden considered this. "I've been in finance," he said, "but I never found it very rewarding. Of course, you'd know a lot more about that than I would."

"What sort of work have you done?" Stoddard asked.

"Oh"—Walden waved his hand back and forth—"this and that. Wall Street—mining—the war—"

"Mining where?" Thoughts of the Yukon flashed through Stoddard's mind.

"Connecticut," Walden replied. "It wasn't much. There was supposed to be a big silver lode somewhere in the area, but I saw no sign of it."

"What did you do in the war?"

"I was with Teddy Roosevelt."

"You made the charge up San Juan Hill?"

"That was a lot of fiction. We took Kettle Hill, which was off to one side, and we had the help of two Negro units doing it. San Juan was taken by two regiments from Hawkins' brigade; a Lieutenant Ord volunteered to lead the charge, and he was killed, and we got the credit. It makes me cringe every time I think of it."

"What's the difference?" Stoddard asked. "Who cares who gets the credit?"

"I do. Lieutenant Ord gets killed, and Teddy gets to be a hero. I think that stinks."

"All the papers said that—"

"I know about the papers. That Richard Harding Davis was with us, and he wrote a lot of four-ply baloney just to make Teddy look good. And Hearst—Hearst reviewed the troops before the battle, sitting on his horse as though he were some sort of general. The whole war made me wonder who's in charge of the country."

Stoddard looked sideways at him. "Did you ever think of going to the Yukon?"

"Not that I can remember. Why?"

"There's supposed to be a lot of gold there. And it's a—I guess you'd call it an untrammeled way of life. No worries."

"Except survival."

Stoddard laughed. "When you reach my age, survival isn't as important as doing what you want. Breaking out of the pattern —seeing how other people live."

"I've seen enough of that. What I'd like to do is settle down, but I want to make sure what I'm doing first."

"You're lucky to have the choice."

"I used to think so; now I'm not so sure. I used to think of myself as a Renaissance man, but I'm beginning to wonder if maybe I'm just indecisive."

They were looking, as they walked, for a place to buy provisions, but the meat markets and grocery stores had been cleaned out by people who, anticipating a shortage, had stocked up on the first day of the fire. There was no real hoarding, because most people shared what they had with others, but the fact remained that food in any large quantity was almost impossible to find. As soon as it came in it was sold, to feed the city's burgeoning population. Small, impromptu restaurants had sprung up, one of them offering "Home Made Chicken

Tamales" for ten cents, the specialty of the house being a "Large Rib Steak—25¢ with Tea, Coffee, or Milk," and for a moment Walden and Stoddard considered buying several steaks to take home, but the restaurant owner was flat in his refusal to sell more than one to a customer.

"Let's not worry about it," Stoddard said. "We'll find something we can do for them later on."

"What they need more than anything else is cots," said Walden. "At the rate people are coming in there, we'll all be sleeping on the floor pretty soon." He thought of the night he'd spent in the Benders' bed, and this led him to think of Lucille. "About that Mrs. Bender," he said. "Does she seem to you—?" He tried to think how to finish the sentence, but couldn't.

There was a pause, and then Stoddard said, "I believe I know what you mean."

"What is it? Sometimes she seems one thing, sometimes she seems another." He thought of the pear-tree blossom, and added, "I *think* I know what's on her mind, but I can't be sure."

"I'm no expert on women," Stoddard replied. "I've been married for the last thirty-seven years, and that naturally—ah—restricts one's variety of experience, but I've found that one of the hardest things to tell is just exactly what is on a woman's mind. They can say one thing and mean the opposite, and the minute you start going on that assumption they'll snap the rug from under your feet and mean precisely what they say. It's a puzzle that I daresay no man has solved to his complete satisfaction. Of course, with the coarser types—or so I'm told—there isn't this problem, but I hardly think that applies here."

"I don't know," said Walden. "I've been fooled by some of the coarser ones, too."

"I guess the only safe assumption is that nobody can be sure of anything," said Stoddard. "Always keep your guard up, and you can't be too badly hurt."

Walden remembered one night in New York, when he'd let his guard down with what had almost been disastrous consequences. He'd gone into an all-night restaurant on Fourteenth

Street for a sandwich and a beer, and taken a table next to a brightly dressed girl who was sitting alone, staring silently into an empty glass. He gave his order to the waiter, then said, "And please ask the lady if she would care to join me in a drink." The waiter relayed the message, and the girl looked at Walden and smiled.

"Thank you," she said.

"My pleasure." He cleared his throat. "Are you waiting for someone?"

"Not necessarily."

"I see. As a matter of fact, neither am I."

She smiled again, and there was a short silence while Walden went over in his mind the various possibilities that seemed to be opening up.

His pastrami sandwich and beer arrived, and then the waiter put a shot glass of rye and a glass of water on the girl's table. Walden raised his beer in salute, and the girl picked up her rye, said, "Live forever," and tossed it back. "Helps the circulation," she said, coughing slightly.

"Do you have circulatory problems?" Walden asked.

"Only every now and then. My fingers and toes get numb."

"Massage will help that."

"What kind of massage?"

"You name it."

She looked at him for a long minute, then said, "I know a number of kinds."

Walden studied his sandwich, which suddenly seemed irrelevant. He took a sip of his beer, and said, "Perhaps you'd care to show me?"

"Gladly."

He reached for his wallet, and looked around for the waiter.

"Aren't you going to finish your sandwich?" the girl asked. "It'll keep up your strength."

It occurred to Walden that this was probably a good idea, since he'd had a fair amount to drink, and a blotter of some sort was probably in order. He took the sandwich in large bites, swallowing fast, and then his throat closed and he felt he was going to strangle. With an effort he got the food down, and followed it with a gulp of beer, and when he tried to take a deep breath his chest was jolted by a hiccup. He held his breath, hiccuped again, and said, "Damn," and rose from the table.

"Are you all right?" the girl asked.

"Yes, of course. I'll be right—back." He went to the men's room, where he tried drinking water upside down, then tried holding his breath for a full minute, but the hiccups continued, and finally, in desperation, he drank glass after glass of water until his stomach was awash, and he threw up. When at last he straightened up and wiped his eyes the hiccups were gone, but it took him a while to make himself presentable. He washed his face and combed his hair, then rinsed out his mouth, gargled, shot his cuffs, and after a quick glance at himself in the mirror went back into the restaurant.

The first thing he noticed was that the girl was not at her table, but then he heard a commotion and saw other people looking at the floor, and he realized that the girl was in a rolling, gouging, biting fight with a scrawny brunette about her own age. Walden rushed over and tried to separate the two, but it was like trying to stop a dog fight. "Miss, I'm here," he said, when he thought the girl could see him. "Miss, it's me—I—I'm sorry I took so—" He saw bared fangs and fingernails and wildly flying hair, and then suddenly he was grabbed by four waiters, one of whom stabbed him in the eyes with two fingers, then the four of them lifted him over their heads like a side of beef and carried him through the door and out into the street. They dumped him in a hansom cab and one of them said, "Get him out of here," to the driver, and by the time Walden had picked himself up off the floor of the cab it was all he could do to remember his address.

Around noon the next day, feeling bruised and hung over and angry, he went back to the restaurant and accosted the manager, who was sitting behind the cash register. "I have a complaint," Walden said, "and I think it's a valid one. I've been a good customer here for—"

"I know that," the manager cut in. "I recognize you. You were going home with that dollie, weren't you?"

"As a matter of fact I was, but I don't see how that's any of your—"

"Do you know who she is?"

"Not exactly."

"She's Jack the Razor's girl. You heard of Razor Jack O'Banion?"

Walden swallowed. "Yes."

"We were doing you a favor. If he'd caught you with her, your guts would be floating out to sea by now."

"But she said she wasn't—"

"Never mind what she said. I'm telling you what could have happened."

Walden was quiet for a moment. "In that case I guess I should thank you," he said.

"I'm sorry the boys roughed you up like that. I told Luigi later he shouldn't of given you the eye-poke, but he said he figured it was the quickest way to get you out. It takes the fight out of a guy real fast."

"Yeah . . . Well, thanks again. And thank the boys—I guess."

"O.K. You want a drink?"

"I could use one, yes. Will you join me?"

The manager looked at the clock. "It's a little early, but what the hell." He motioned to Walden, who had started to reach for his wallet. "Put it away. The least I can do is give you one on the house."

Now, walking through the rubble-strewn streets with Gresham Stoddard, Walden resolved to follow Stoddard's advice: to keep his guard up, and not be lured into making any move that could lead to trouble. It seemed, on the face of it, so obvious as to be not worth mentioning, but every time he was near Lucille he could feel waves almost like electricity emanating from her, and his good intentions began to come apart at the seams. What you lack is moral fiber, he told himself.

You need to brace up, bite the bullet, and be a man. To thine own self be true, and it must follow, as the night the day, thou canst not then be false to any man. Now there, he thought, is the first time I've made use of anything I learned at Yale. Things can't help but take a turn for the better.

# CHAPTER 14

It was late afternoon when Walden and Stoddard returned to the Benders', and they could hear the distant thump of explosions across the Bay. The smoke from the fires had become diffuse; it seemed to come from the whole city rather than from separate spots, and it rose and smudged into the clouds that crept in from the west. There was a hint of rain in the air, but not enough to give any great hope. To stem the fire now, an hours-long downpour would be needed.

Walden and Stoddard, by persistent wheedling and scrounging, had managed to come up with two tins of ham, a bag of potatoes, three kippered herring, and a leg of mutton. They were sure it was not what Lucille would have ordered if she'd gone to market, but in the circumstances they felt that anything they could contribute would be a help. They went in and put their purchases on the kitchen table, then Walden called, "Hello, there! Anybody home?"

There was no answer, and Stoddard said, "They're probably back at the shop. That's going to take some looking-after, if it's full of people."

"Yes, but they still have to eat." Walden looked at the ceiling and called, "Lucille? Are you there?" In spite of himself he thought of the Benders' bed, and the pear blossom, and it was a couple of moments before he realized Stoddard was speaking.

"—at least that's what it sounds like," was all he heard.

"I'm sorry," he said. "What did you say?"

"I said it sounds as though they've put a horse up in that space over the stable. At any rate, there's something going on there."

Walden listened, and could hear a thumping, and faint voices. "You're right," he said. "Let's go look."

They went out the back door, and up the narrow stairs to the loft, and in the dim light they could see two women struggling to set up a folding cot. A chair and a packing case stood nearby, and a lighted kerosene lamp was on the floor. One of the women was Lucille, and as the two men came up the stairs she turned and beamed at them.

"Praise be!" she said. "You've come at just the right moment!"

"What's the problem?" Walden asked.

"We're trying to set up this cot for Mrs. LaGrange, and the legs won't work—I think they must be on backward."

"Let me give you a hand," said Stoddard, and as he came into the glow of the light he saw Dolly's face, and her eyes widened.

"Why, Mr. Stod—" she began, but he cut her off before she could finish the word.

"Lambert," he said. "Maxwell Lambert. Pleased to make your acquaintance."

Scarcely missing a beat, Dolly said, "How do you do, Mr. Lambert? Forgive me, but for a moment you looked like an old friend of mine."

"I'm often mistaken for other people," Stoddard replied, with an attempt at a laugh. "Now, what's the problem with this cot, here?"

"It just seems to fold wrong," Lucille said. "We're trying to set up a workroom for Mrs. LaGrange so she can have some privacy, and this is the only spare cot I could find. I think it must be left over from the war."

"Let me look at it," Walden said. "If that's the case, I should know it by heart."

He began to tug at the legs of the cot, folding them first one way and then the other, and Stoddard stepped back and glanced at Dolly.

"You say you're intending to work here?" he said.

"Yes," said Dolly, staring him straight in the eye. "I'm a writer."

"Ah, so. How clever."

"I'm writing a book."

"May I ask what about?"

"This and that."

"I'm ashamed to say I've never read any of your books," Lucille said, and then, to Stoddard, "Have you, Mr. Lambert?"

"I must confess I haven't," Stoddard replied. Turning to Dolly, he said, "But, as I said earlier, unless you've written about the world of finance it's unlikely that I would have. I'm afraid the loss is mine."

"Not necessarily," said Dolly. "I'm something of a financial buff myself. I'd like to talk with you about it some day."

"At your pleasure," said Stoddard with a slight bow.

"You know the problem with this cot?" Walden said, to nobody in particular. "It's broken."

"That's what I thought," replied Lucille. "But can it be fixed? We don't want Mrs. LaGrange to have to sleep on her desk." She indicated the packing case, on which was the folder containing Dolly's papers.

"Don't worry about me, dearie," Dolly said. "I can sleep anywhere so long as it isn't raining on me. There's a lot of people would give their eye teeth to sleep right on the floor here tonight."

"Still." Lucille turned to Walden. "Do you think you can fix it?"

"I can try," Walden replied. "Do you have any tools?"

"George keeps them in a drawer in the kitchen. What do you need?"

"A screwdriver, and probably a saw."

"Come with me, and I'll show you what we have." She went down the stairs, followed by Walden, and for a long moment Dolly and Stoddard looked at each other. Then she smiled.

"Thank you," she said.

"Thank *you*," Stoddard replied.

"What is your name these days?"

"Maxwell Lambert."

"I'll try to remember."

"About this book—is that a serious project?"

"I should hope to tell you it is. I'm starting a whole new career."

"What's it about?"

"It's the story of my life, but I think I'll begin with the earthquake and fire. I can bring in the reminiscences later."

"Using names?"

"You needn't worry. But you might help me with something."

"Anything you say."

"I don't know how I stand at the bank. I don't know if there *is* a bank. All my savings are in the Crocker, and if that's gone then I've got to go back to scratch. Do you think you could spare me a little something until the air clears?" A sudden thought struck her, and she went on, "Come to think of it, Maribelle tells me you left without paying the other morning, so this wouldn't be a loan; it would be what you might call a deposit on your account."

Stoddard cleared his throat. "To tell you the truth, I'm in somewhat the same position," he said. "I don't know how matters stand at *my* bank, and until I do there's not much—"

"But you've got credit, don't you?"

"Not under my present name."

Dolly digested this. "Oh," she said. "I see. Then—"

"But I can tell you one thing," Stoddard went on quickly. "Charlie Crocker hired a launch to take a lot of boxes and bags out into the Bay and just sit there. Nobody knows what's in them, but it sounds as though he's saved something."

"That doesn't mean my money's safe," Dolly replied. "That could be all his own loot."

"What do you need money for now, anyway? You've got housing, and there are soup kitchens, and sooner or later—"

"I need money for the long haul," Dolly said. "I need money in order to finish my book."

"Do you have a publisher? He might advance you something."

"I don't have a publisher. Clinton Wamsley was the one who told me I should write it, and you know what happened to him."

"Ah, well. In that case I don't know what to say."

Dolly picked up her folder, and riffled through the notes. "My book is going to have a very exciting opening," she said, almost as though talking to herself. "I'll start off with the night before the quake, telling who was in the house and what went on, and then go to the next morning, with everyone running around bareass trying to get out. You were a particularly funny sight, with your—"

"Maxwell Lambert was never in your establishment," Stoddard said firmly. "You know that as well as I do."

"Are you telling me that's your permanent name?"

"It may very well be."

"Then you won't mind me using your old one. Gresham Stoddard has a kind of nice sound to it."

"Now, wait a minute. I didn't say I was going to be Maxwell Lambert *forever*—it all depends on what—well, on how a certain number of things turn out. But I'm damn well not going to have you bandying my real name about, as though it were a brand of coffee. I have my rights to privacy, you know."

"When will you know how these things turn out?"

"I can't tell you. But in the Baltimore fire two years ago, they opened the safes and strongboxes before they'd had a chance to cool, and everything burned up the minute the air hit it. The same thing happened after the Chicago fire of seventy-one, so I'd like to think our people will wait awhile. It might be one week, it might be two. I simply don't know."

"I think I get the picture," said Dolly. "You're sort of in the same boat I'm in, only maybe worse."

"In a manner of speaking."

She thought for a moment. "Do you know any publishers?"

"One or two."

"Suppose you'd written a letter—before the fire—saying I

had a book you thought they'd be interested in. Do you think that might make them look at it?"

"How could I say that? I've never seen your book."

"Just say a friend of yours who should be nameless brought it to you, and you were passing it along. All I need is your name, to get me through the door. I can take care of the rest."

"But if you're opening the book with the quake, how could I have seen it before the quake happened?"

"The old opening was different. The old opening had me being raped by an Arapahoe."

"Isn't that kind of strong?"

"Well, not exactly raped. Anyway, I'm using the quake instead."

"With names?"

"That'll depend. Will you write the letter?"

Stoddard took a deep breath, and let it out slowly. "What the hell," he said. "I suppose I might as well. One little fib, more or less, isn't going to make any difference now."

"It's not a fib. A friend who shall be nameless brought it to you. Here it is." She picked up the folder from the packing case, and handed it to him. He hesitated, and she said, "And by the bye, if you think Maribelle has something worth taking to the Yukon, I'll tell you that I've forgotten more than she can ever learn. I can blow your hat off in one minute and twenty seconds, and if you think I'm kidding go get your hat and I'll show you."

"I appreciate the offer," said Stoddard, "but I'll take your word for it."

"I'm serious," Dolly said. "We writers will do anything to get our work published."

In the Benders' kitchen, Lucille saw the pile of assorted food that Walden and Stoddard had brought, and said, "What's this? Who's been here?"

"Mr. Lambert and I," Walden replied. "We thought we should contribute a little something to the larder."

"You shouldn't have!" She turned, suddenly, and kissed him

full on the mouth, clinging to him as though someone were trying to pull her away.

"It isn't much," Walden protested, with a nervous glance at the door. "I mean, it's only a few tins, and things like that. It was—" He thought he heard footsteps, and whispered, "Someone's coming!" and pulled Lucille's arms from his neck. She turned away, and in a louder voice he said, "Now let's see about those tools. Where do you keep them?"

"Over here." She pulled out a drawer containing a hammer, a screwdriver, a bag of nails, a coil of copper wire, a pair of pliers, and a folding yardstick. There were also miscellaneous items such as a clump of twine, a rusty knife blade, a scattering of assorted screws, and a drawknife handle.

Walden waited, listening, but the sound he heard was not repeated, and he bent down and poked through the drawer. "What I really need is a saw," he said. "I've got to cut a whole new leg."

"George has a saw someplace," Lucille replied, "but he never puts it in the same place twice. He leaves it wherever he's used it last."

"Where is he now?"

"At the shop. Mrs. LaGrange's hairdresser and her friends came in, and he's helping them set up. There was one less of them than expected, so they'll have plenty of room. Do you really think she's a writer?"

"Who?"

"Mrs. LaGrange. She doesn't *look* like a writer to me."

"I don't know how they look. Can you remember where George last used the saw?"

"It could have been any number of places. We'll ask him when he comes home, and meantime let's have a smile. How does that sound?"

Out of habit Walden reached for his watch fob, then remembered his watch had been lost in the wreckage. "I've got to go on patrol pretty soon," he said. "I suppose I should stay sober."

"I didn't mean get *drunk*, silly. I just meant a smile to brighten the spirit. It's been a long day."

"And it'll be a longer night. All right—just one."

Lucille went to the cupboard, where she produced a bottle of whisky and a nearly empty bottle of sherry. "My," she said, "this stuff must evaporate in the bottle. I'll have to ask George to get some more." She poured the last drops into a tumbler, then splashed whisky into a glass and said, "Water?"

"Please," said Walden, and she put in an equal amount of water.

"Here's to us," she said, handing him his glass. She took a sip, and sat at the kitchen table. "Sit down, and rest your legs. Are you sure you ought to be going on patrol?"

"It'll be good for me," Walden replied, taking a seat across the table from her. "My legs were only bruised, and this'll work the kinks out."

Lucille tasted her sherry again, and said, "Tell me some poetry."

"*Tell* you some poetry? What do you mean?"

"Recite something to me. I like it when you say poetic things."

Walden took a swallow of his drink, and said, "Like what? I can't just pick a poem out of the air."

"Pick something you think I'd like. Something romantic."

Walden thought for a moment, culling through the poems he could recite by heart, and finally settled on Shakespeare's "When in disgrace with fortune and men's eyes" sonnet. He spoke it through, and when he'd finished there were tears in her eyes.

"That's the most beautiful thing I ever heard," she said. "It's so sad in the beginning, and then all of a sudden it turns happy. Do it again."

He ran through it once more, and there was silence. He saw she'd somehow managed to empty her tumbler without his noticing, and he took a long swallow of his drink and stood up. "I've got to be going," he said.

"Don't go now." Her voice sounded almost frantic. "What time do you have to patrol?"

"Well, I'm on from eight to midnight, but I should get something to eat first, and find some heavier clothing—"

"I'll make supper for you, and get you clothes. Have another smile, but please don't leave me now."

"I don't want to drink alone, and you're out of sherry. Besides, I really—"

"I'll have a whisky with you. It's no stronger than sherry, if I put a lot of water in it. Here—give me your glass." She took his glass and her own to the sink, put whisky and water in them, and brought them back. Instead of passing his across the table, she came alongside him, and bent over to set it down. He smelled the fresh scent of her, and could feel the slight pressure of her body against his shoulder.

"Thank you," he said, taking the glass.

She didn't move. "Put your hand on my breast," she said.

"I beg your pardon?"

"I said put your hand on my breast."

Walden set down his glass, and reached up and cupped his hand against the soft bulge in her blouse. This isn't happening, he told himself. This cannot be happening to me.

"Inside," said Lucille. "I didn't say put your hand on my dress."

Crooking his arm, Walden slid his hand into her blouse, and held the warm breast with its firm nipple. He massaged the nipple with two fingers, all the while telling himself that the whole thing was impossible. Where do we go from here? he thought. To thine own self be true, indeed. What about simple practicality?

Lucille straightened up, rearranged her blouse, and returned to her seat across the table. There was silence for a few moments, and then she said, "I'm not attractive to men."

"What are you talking about?" Walden said. "Don't be absurd."

"Well, I'm not attractive to George, and I'm not attractive to you, so I'm not attractive to men."

"You *are* attractive to me! You're one of the most wildly attractive women I've ever met!"

"Then how come I had to ask you to do that? If I were attractive to you, you'd have thought of it all on your own."

"I *have* thought of it! I've thought of almost nothing but! But there's a little matter of your being married—"

"In name only," she put in.

"Nevertheless you're married, and what's more I like your husband. I owe him a great deal, and I don't think it would be fair to—to—" He tried to find the proper word.

"To what?"

"To deceive him, if you want to use the formal expression."

"You mean to take me to bed."

"Yes."

"That wouldn't deceive him, because he wouldn't know."

"That's deceiving him, if he thinks you're doing something else."

"Like what?"

"I don't care like what. It's still deceiving him."

"You see? You don't find me attractive."

"I *do*! That has nothing to do with it!"

"You just said you don't care. If you found me attractive, you'd care."

"Dear God in heaven, I've just—"

"Now you're sounding like George. He gets that same tone of voice when he's in the wrong."

"I'm *not* in the wrong! I'm—"

"You needn't shout. I'm not deaf, you know. I may not be attractive, but I'm also not deaf."

"I'm going to say this just once more. You are one of the most wildly attractive women I have ever met."

"'One of.' What about the others?"

"What others?"

"'One of' means there's more than one. Am I part of a mob, or something? That's not very flattering."

"All right. You are the single most attractive woman I have ever met."

"It took you long enough to say it."

"I mean it."

"Then prove it."

"Right here?"

"I don't care where. Make me believe it. If you were a gentleman, I wouldn't have to be pressing you like this."

"That's just the trouble—I'm trying to *be* a gentleman! I'm—"

"A real gentleman doesn't have to try. With a real gentleman it's second nature, especially where a lady is concerned."

Walden drained his drink, stood up, and went to the sink and poured another. "I hardly know how to phrase this," he said, "but just suppose, for the sake of argument, that I went along with your—uh—suggestion. What would—?"

Lucille held out her empty glass. "Does a real gentleman let a lady's glass go dry?" she said.

"Forgive me." He took the tumbler from her, made a weak drink, and handed it back. As he did, he noticed that her eyes were not quite focused on him; she seemed to be looking at something just beyond his right shoulder. "What would you think of me," he went on, "if, tomorrow morning, you woke up and realized that I had taken advantage of your should we say discontent, and had made you into what is generally considered to be a fallen woman? Would you think I was so much of a gentleman then?"

"That would depend," she replied. "But I'll never know unless I try."

Here it is, Walden thought. It is being handed to you on a silver platter, and what are you going to do about it? If you turn her down she will hate you with a deep and lasting passion, and if you go along you will be double-crossing a decent man, to say nothing of running the risk of getting shot. But if you were to do it as a favor to her, might not that be a—? His thoughts were interrupted as the front door slammed open, and Bender came in. Walden's first reaction was relief, which turned to apprehension as Bender went to Lucille, took the glass from her hand, and smelled it.

"What are you doing drinking that?" Bender asked.

In a cold, detached voice, Lucille said, "What would you suggest I do with it? Wash my hair?"

Bender set the glass down without saying anything, and looked at Walden.

"I'm sorry," Walden said. "I made it for her. There was no more sherry, and I didn't think you'd mind if I made her a weak whisky."

"I can have," said Lucille, "whatever I like. Whatever I choose, I can have." Then, looking at Walden, she added, "Or almost."

"Actually, I think the whisky is better for one than sherry," Walden said, hurrying the words to cover up her innuendo. "Sherry is rich and heavy and does terrible things to your liver, whereas whisky is more of a medicine than anything else. I remember my mother used to give me whisky when I fell through the ice or something like that in the winter. Can I make you one, George?"

"I'll get it." Bender went to the sink, held up the bottle, and looked back at Lucille. "How many have you had?" he asked.

"One," she replied. "Not counting this," lifting her glass.

"I'll get another bottle tomorrow," Walden said. "The least I can do is replace the liquor I drink."

"Some things can be replaced, others can't," Bender said, pouring the whisky. "It's fortunate that liquor is replaceable." Total silence followed this remark, and he raised his glass, said, "Here's mud in your eye—eyes," and drank.

# CHAPTER 15

That night, the glow from the fires across the Bay was not as bright as it had been the previous two nights; it was a sullen, dark red color, with every now and then an orange explosion as a building collapsed and sent a tower of sparks and flames into the air. Seen from Oakland, it was like a distant battlefield, and a low muttering came faintly across the water.

As Henry Walden patrolled the deserted back streets, armed only with a walking stick and a kerosene lantern, he wondered what he would do if he came upon a band of looters. Shout at them, probably, and hope somehow to frighten them off. Either that, or try to find a policeman, which would be like looking for a field mouse in a darkened meadow. The more he thought of it the more absurd his position became, and with that in mind he began to wonder what he was doing in Oakland anyway. If he had a brain in his head he'd leave, because he knew that sooner or later he was bound to give in to Lucille's frantic advances, and then all hell would break loose. He, whose record with women had been one mistake after another, was now having the Grand Prize almost literally thrown at his head, and all he could do was duck. There was something grossly unfair about that, he thought, but then, it was in the pattern that had been established long ago, and there was no real reason for the pattern to change. One of the few times he'd succeeded had been with a girl at whom he was angry; he'd taken her to dinner in order to tell her a few things for her own good, and had so much to drink that he blacked out, and came to in her bed, technically triumphant but totally unaware of how he'd got there. He'd always heard that such a thing was impossible, that liquor diminished performance in direct proportion to the amount consumed, but in this case the rule seemed to have worked backward, and he was left with a blank mind and a hollow victory. The girl became enamored of him, and he spent the next six weeks trying to avoid her.

Now, looking at the dying fires in San Francisco, he wondered how long it would be before life in the area resumed any faint sense of normality. It would be years before the city could be rebuilt, and in the meantime there were thousands of refugees in Oakland, camping out in whatever vacant land they could find, and it would be a long time before they could be assimilated enough so that Oakland could resume its regular pace of business. And, in the meantime, what? Would Bender's pharmacy have to suspend business while it served as a dormitory, and if so, where would the money come from to support Bender and his wife? Many people in Oakland and Berkeley owned property in San Francisco, or went to work there, and with the city virtually wiped out, what would they do for a living? Every small problem led to a larger one, and Walden was glad he wasn't the person in charge of straightening matters out. He was, for the moment, without employment, but that interested him a lot less than did the overall picture of the future. Admitting that his wisest move would be to leave, he nevertheless found himself compelled to stay, if for no other reason than to see how things would work out. Besides, if he left he'd have no place to go except back East, and that would be a defeat he was not yet prepared to admit.

He walked slowly through the streets, flashing his lantern in darkened doorways and hoping that his mere presence would discourage any potential looters. He wondered briefly about the mentality of looters, and the thin, brittle line that separates civilized men from savages, and he recalled moments during the war when that line had been shattered, and he'd seen mild-mannered youths turn into animals. It hadn't happened often, but it had been enough to show the savagery that lay beneath the surface. Come to think of it, it was something like the subterranean force that had shattered San Francisco, and he was turning this thought over in his mind when he became aware of footsteps behind him, and he turned to see a figure, also holding a lantern, approaching him. He tightened his grip on his stick and raised his lantern high, to keep the glare away from his eyes.

"Who's there?" he said, trying to sound military.

"Thieves and footpads," came Gresham Stoddard's voice. "What are you doing here?"

"Oh, it's you, Mr. Lambert. Are you through for the night?"

"No, but I think you're in my sector. Not that it makes a great deal of difference."

"To be honest with you, I don't know where I am. I've been in Oakland three days, and half that time buried in rubbish. I'm not what you'd call an expert on the city."

"Neither am I. I've just been patrolling the darkest streets, on the theory that looters wouldn't pick the bright ones."

"I was hoping I wouldn't see any looters at all."

"Same here. But since we've met up, we might as well stay together. Two'll be more effective than one."

"I think that's a splendid idea. Which way do you want to go?"

"Let's keep on down to the end of this block, and decide there. This is all a big show, anyway; I haven't heard of a single case of looting in Oakland."

"I hear they're shooting them over in Frisco. And stabbing them with bayonets."

"I wouldn't be surprised. There's nothing more dangerous than a nervous man with a gun."

Walden remembered what he'd just been thinking, and said, "Were you in the Army?"

"Lord, no. Bankers don't fight."

"I was a banker once, briefly. Come to think of it, I didn't do a great deal of fighting, either."

They walked in silence for a few moments, then Stoddard said, "Have you decided what you're going to do?"

"You mean for a job?"

"Yes."

Walden paused. "Not exactly. I'm waiting until the dust settles here."

There was another silence, and when they reached the corner Stoddard looked about, then indicated the street to the left. "Let's try this one," he said.

"How much more time do we have?" Walden asked. "I lost my watch in the quake."

Stoddard took out his watch, and held it in the light of the lantern. "Ten forty-five," he said. "We still have an hour and a quarter."

"That's not bad. We're as good as home."

Stoddard cleared his throat, started to say something, then stopped.

"I beg your pardon?" said Walden.

"Nothing. I was just thinking."

"That makes two of us."

Stoddard hesitated, then said, "Did you ever think of becoming a publisher?"

"Of what?"

"Books."

"No. Why?"

"I've just seen a manuscript—or notes for a manuscript—that might make a very successful book."

"Why not take it to a regular publisher?"

"Well . . . a number of reasons. I'd like to have some say in its final form."

"Then why don't you be the publisher?"

"Again, several reasons. It just occurred to me that you're a personable young man, you have no fixed goal at the moment, and—"

"I also have no money to speak of."

"No worry there. I can supply all of that you'd need."

"Would we do the publishing here?"

"I think not. Possibly up in Portland or Seattle—or maybe even Chicago. Our—uh—operating capital would come from Chicago." Walden looked at him with an unspoken question, and he said, "Railroad stocks. Most of my money is here, but—not knowing about the banks—" He left the sentence unfinished.

Walden thought for a few moments, then said, "This book—or this manuscript. What's it about?"

"Well, it starts with the earthquake and fire, and then it goes back and reminisces about the life of this central character, and from what I gather it's been quite a life. She was first—"

"Is this Mrs. LaGrange?"

"Yes."

"Is she really a writer?"

"Well, she's writing this."

"What else does she do?"

Pause. "She's a madam."

Walden laughed. "It ought to be quite a book."

"It isn't what you'd think. Of course, I haven't read it all, but—"

"And she hasn't written it all, either. Or has she?"

"No, no. These are just notes. But as publisher, I—we—could advance her the money to complete the book."

"And then what? Would we do others, or would this be a one-shot venture?"

"I should like to think we'd do others. I'd like to make this my—avocation, if you will—and at the same time give you something solid on which to base a career. If this book is a success, we'll have no trouble getting others."

Walden considered the idea. There was something about it that appealed to him—for one thing, its very novelty was exciting—and it would be a field where he could put his liberal arts education to its best use. His mind was exploring the various possibilities when he realized Stoddard was still talking.

"—and if Dolly's book is successful," he was saying, "then I'd like to go into something—"

"Who's Dolly?" Walden asked.

"Uh—Mrs. LaGrange. There's—"

"I take it you know her."

"In a manner of speaking. I've always felt there's a good

book to be written about the Yukon. Jack London, of course, has done one kind, but it seems to me that a more thoughtful, analytical exploration of the subject would have a wide appeal. The historical background, the geological conditions, and so on. Start with the discovery of gold—or perhaps the beginnings of gold as a precious metal—and then branch out from there. It could be the thinking man's Jack London, if you see what I mean."

"You're covering a lot of territory there," Walden observed.

"Indeed I am. But there's nothing the matter with that; it could go into several volumes if need be."

Walden thought for a while, then said, "Well, the first thing is to get this book of Dolly's written. After that, we can make other plans."

"I like your use of the word 'we,'" said Stoddard. "Does that mean what I think it does?"

"Hell, yes," said Walden. "I couldn't turn down a chance like this."

In the flickering light of their lanterns they shook hands, and Stoddard beamed. "This calls for a drink," he said. "We should celebrate our partnership."

"I don't know where we'll find one at this hour," Walden replied. "Or did you bring something with you?"

"It just so happens"—Stoddard put down his lantern, and produced a silver flask from an inside pocket—"I came prepared to ward off the cold." He unscrewed the top of the flask, and said, "Here's to the firm." He took a drink, and passed the flask to Walden.

"Here's to it." Walden drank, passed the flask back, and said, "What'll we call it? Lambert and Walden?"

"That doesn't say anything. What about Walden Press? That has a nice ring, and brings to mind Thoreau. Here's to Walden Press." Stoddard drank, and automatically held out the flask.

Walden took it, and said, "That leaves you out. What about Lambwal Books? Here's to Lambwal Books."

"Sounds like 'lamb wool.' Ah—how about Yukon Press?"

"Too remote. I know—since this whole thing was born of the fire, what would you say to Phoenix Books?"

"Books or Press? I like Phoenix Press."

"Yes, but if you say it fast it sounds like Feen Express."

"That's easy. Don't say it fast. Say Phoenix–Prress."

"Press is a sloppy word, because it doesn't mean anything. It could be a printing press, but it could also be a duck press, or a cider press, or a compress, or a press of people. 'Press not the falling man too far!' Shakespeare, *Henry VIII*. We're going to be printing books, and I think we should say so."

"Nobody said we were going to be printing ducks." Stoddard removed the flask from Walden's hand, and took a drink.

Walden was quiet while he turned the names over in his mind. "It's your money," he said at last. "I suppose we should call it whatever you want."

"Not necessarily. You're going to be the publisher. I don't mind Phoenix Books, if you think it's all that much better."

"I'm not sure it's *that* much better. I'm not going to cut my wrists if we call it Phoenix Press."

"Well, I don't mind Books. Let's call it Phoenix Books."

"All right. Let's drink to it." They drank, and Walden had to tilt his head back to get the last of the whisky. "Son of a gun," he said, wiping his mouth. "Was this thing full when we started?"

"As full as I could get it," Stoddard replied.

"It must leak. Well, thanks anyway." Walden handed the flask back, and peered down the darkened street. "What would you do if you saw a looter?"

"Tell him to stop," said Stoddard.

"How do you tell a looter from anyone else? What constitutes looting?"

"I don't know. Rummaging through houses. Carrying mattresses down the street. It all depends."

"That's a pretty thin definition. I was looking for my clothes where my room collapsed, and I could have been suspected of looting. Unless you know the person, you can't tell if he's looting or just carrying his property somewhere."

"Maybe we should do a book on looting. How to tell a looter from a law-abiding citizen—looting through the ages—famous looters of history—the theory and practice of looting—there might be a big market for it."

Walden smiled, and the light from his lantern shone up on his face, casting shadows that made him look like a Greek comedy mask. "You know something?" he said. "I think we have the beginnings of a very successful business here."

In her room above the Benders' stable, Dolly sorted through the notes and papers that Stoddard had returned to her, trying to arrange them in some sort of order. She felt it was too early to start the opening chapter about the quake and fire, and she wanted to get the rest of her reminiscences in order, so as to be able to devote all her attention to the more important parts later on. Her childhood had been a gritty one, but she saw no reason to gloss over any of the more unfortunate incidents; they might, in fact, help the reader to sympathize with her, and be rooting for her in some of the gamier sections that were to follow. She was aware that there were certain things ladies were not supposed to discuss, much less write about, but she felt that her circumstances allowed her more leeway than other female authors, and she intended to make the most of it.

She reread Chapter Two, which she had written the morning of the quake, and decided that it jumped too quickly into her encounter with Sick Wolf; she needed to start a little farther back, in her girlhood, to pave the way for what was to follow later. Taking a clean sheet of paper, she dipped her pen in the inkwell and began:

CHAPTER TWO
*I Sense a Change*
It was shortly after my eleventh birthday that I began to feel a lessening of interest in my collection of rattlesnake skins, and instead became fascinated with my brother's

She stared at the words, chewing the end of her pen, then crumpled the paper and started a new one, which read:

CHAPTER TWO
*My First Love*
After watching my father hanged by the vigilantes I felt hostile toward all men, but as I grew older I realized

No, she thought. Not far enough back. Go back to your childhood. She balled the paper in her fist, threw it on the floor, and started again:

CHAPTER TWO
*The Most Amazing Thing I Ever Saw*
I will never forget my childish astonishment the first time I saw one of

She stopped, crossed out the words, and wrote:

"Wow!" I said, as I peered into the room. "Can that be what it's all about?"

Pleased with this approach, she was about to go on when she heard voices coming from the Benders' kitchen, and although she couldn't distinguish the words she could tell there was a violent argument. It was like trying to listen to sounds under water, where the words were blurred and only the tones remained, and it was distracting enough so that she couldn't concentrate on what she was writing. I might as well hear the whole thing as a garbled part of it, she thought, and put down her pen and went quietly downstairs. Standing in the entrance to the stable she could hear more clearly, and see occasional shadows as one or the other of the Benders passed in front of the light. Dolly had a twinge of conscience at such blatant eavesdropping, then told herself it might get her good material for her book, and she listened with all the attention of a court reporter.

"What do you expect me to do?" Lucille was saying. "Do you expect me to sit home and count the bricks, while you lead the life of a man about town, giving out favors for ladies and who knows what all else?"

"What do you mean, favors for ladies?" Bender said. "What favors have I ever done for ladies?"

"You've spent your whole day setting up beds for them, for one thing. How many decent family men go around making beds for strange women?"

"Are you trying to count THAT?" Bender asked. "Are you out of your goddam MIND?"

"Don't swear at me, George Bender! You swear at me once more, and I'll—"

"Perhaps you haven't heard," Bender went on, more quietly, "but there's recently been an earthquake in San Francisco. The city has been burning for the last three days, and possibly a hundred thousand people have fled the fire and come to Oakland. It's what is called an emergency, and in an emergency people do whatever is required of them. Decent people, that is. There are some, of course, who—"

"Was that a pointed remark?" Lucille said, her voice rising. "Were you trying to imply that I am an indecent person?"

"I am trying to imply nothing, I'm simply saying that while some people are doing what they can to help the refugees, you seem to be spending your time drinking whisky with—with—"

"Go ahead, say it. With whom?"

"With a comparative stranger. You alone can judge whether you're being decent or indecent."

"Godfrey Walden is not a comparative stranger! In many ways I feel I know him better than I know you, and in many other ways I wish I knew him even better. How do you like that?"

"Well, I can't say I haven't been warned. I suppose that in itself was a decent gesture on your part."

"It wasn't intended as one."

"How was it intended?"

"It was intended to knock you off your high chair, for one thing."

"It's high horse, not high chair."

"You see? You're being condescending again!"

"I'm being nothing of the kind. I'm simply trying to point out—"

"You're trying to point out—you're trying to point out there's been an earthquake—my God, do you think I don't know there's been an earthquake? Who was it got you up that morning?"

"Oh, Jesus."

"Don't 'Oh, Jesus' me. You 'Oh, Jesus' me just once more, and you'll be 'Oh, Jesusing' to an empty room. I'm not without places to go, you know."

"For instance?"

"For instance—for instance, did you ever hear of a place called Moline?"

"Yes. What would you do there?"

"I have a cousin there. He'd be delighted to see me."

"I'll bet he would. And would he be delighted to see Godfrey, too?"

"Who said anything about Godfrey?"

"The implication was that you were going to run away with him."

"Well—" She suddenly realized that her two threats had short-circuited each other, and her only way out was to change the subject. "You deliberately misunderstood," she said. "I refuse to argue with anyone who intentionally warps my meaning."

"How did I warp your meaning?"

"By being so God-damned, all-fired holier than thou, that's how! Now, let's not hear any more about it! I'm sick and tired of talking to you!" She turned away.

He had never heard her swear like that, and he was appalled. He said, "I think your best move is to go to bed."

"I'll go when I good and damn well please. And I'll go to whichever *bed* I damn well please."

"I think your own bed would be the best. I rather doubt that Godfrey would like sleeping with a drunk."

There was silence, and Dolly, listening outside, held her breath while she waited for the reply. No words came; there was just a high-pitched shriek, followed by the crashing sounds of kitchen utensils, crockery, and glassware being hurled across the room. Quietly, Dolly went back to her makeshift desk, and resumed her writing.

# CHAPTER 16

At five o'clock the next morning the fire was checked—nearly twelve hours after Mayor Schmitz had said it was "virtually under control"—and by seven-fifteen it was officially declared out. Then, as though belatedly trying to share in the credit, rain began to fall, a fine, soaking drizzle that turned the smoke to steam and cooled the twisted girders in the wreckage. The remnants of San Francisco lay smoldering in the rain, like some giant ship that had burned and then broken up on a rocky shoreline.

In Oakland, the rain made it impossible to see across the Bay, but an unnatural quiet in the air suggested that the worst of the crisis had passed. For the past three days the distant sounds of the fire had been a background to everything else, and without them the whole atmosphere seemed to change: it was like being in a room where a fan had suddenly been turned off.

Lucille Bender came into the kitchen at seven o'clock. The backs of her eyes ached and her mouth tasted like old leather, and she found that the simple matter of walking made her heart pound and her breath come faster. She had expected to find the kitchen a shambles, but everything was in its place, and the broken crockery and glassware had been swept up and dumped into the trash bin. She assumed that George had cleaned up, and she blessed him for it; in her present condition the mere matter of bending over would have been more than she could have managed. She opened the icebox door, and the smell of food almost made her sick; lifting the lid, she saw that the ice was nearly gone, and unless it was replenished today she knew that the food would spoil. She closed the icebox door and began to make coffee, which in her condition she felt was all she would be able to handle. She hoped it would steady her nerves, because she felt as insecure as a canary in a high wind, and her stomach was trembling at the same rate as her hands. She wondered if a drink would calm her down, but the thought of whisky made her gag, and she had to go to the door for a breath of fresh air.

She was closing the door when Bender came downstairs, and he looked at her for a moment before saying, "How do you feel?"

"How do you think?" she replied, and followed him into the kitchen.

There was silence as he went to the icebox, selected a piece of sausage, and began to slice it.

"You'd better make sure that hasn't spoiled," Lucille said. "We're almost out of ice."

Bender put the sausage to his nose and sniffed it, then cut off another slice. "It seems all right," he said.

The coffee began to boil, and Lucille went to the stove and turned it off. She poured a steaming cup for herself, then without looking at Bender said, "Coffee?"

"Please."

She poured a cup for him, and when she tried to put it in front of him her hand shook so that coffee slopped out of the cup and into the saucer. "Oops," she said. "I'll get a rag."

"That's all right." Bender poured the spillage back into the cup and took an inhaling sip, drawing in more air than he did coffee. "Where are Godfrey and Mr. Lambert?" he asked. "Have they gone out already?"

Lucille looked around in surprise. "I've no idea," she said. "I thought they must be asleep."

"If they are, they're not where they usually sleep. I checked."

There was a long silence while Lucille thought about this. Then she said, "Well, I'd be the last one to know," and turned back to the sink.

Nothing more was said, while Bender ate his sausage with

bread and mustard, and finished his coffee. To hide her trembling Lucille tried to pretend she was busy at the sink, and when every now and then she sipped her coffee she used both hands to get the cup to her lips. Finally, in what she hoped sounded like her normal voice, she said, "What are you going to be doing today?"

"Well, I'm going to check the ladies and see if everything's all right there, and then I'm going to see what I can do about restocking the shop. Sooner or later, I've got to get back into business."

"You can't very well do business if the shop's full of women, can you?"

"We'll just have to see. The first thing is to order the new supplies." He held out his cup. "Do you have some more there?"

She took the cup, poured it half full so as not to spill any, and returned it to him. "Have you heard anything about the fire?" she asked.

He glanced at her strangely. "How could I? I just got up."

"I mean—I thought—it just seems to me I can't hear it any more. I wondered if it might be out."

Bender looked at the window, but could see nothing through the rain. "Can't tell from here," he said. "They ought to know at City Hall. It's got to be out pretty soon—there can't be much left to burn."

"When you think of all the people's lives it's changed . . ." Lucille let the sentence trail off.

"There's no doubt about that."

"Do you think it's changed ours?"

"How could it? The fire never got over here."

"Still . . ." There was something on her mind, but she didn't seem able to phrase it.

Bender finished his coffee, and stood up. "Well, I'm off. Expect me when you see me."

He started out, and she said, "Oh—George."

"What?" he replied, putting on his coat. She was quiet, and he said, "Did you want to say something?"

"Yes."

"What is it? I haven't got all morning."

"I just wanted to say thanks for cleaning up the kitchen."

"Think nothing of it. Any time."

"I hope there won't be another time."

"That makes two of us. But then, we can't be sure of anything, can we?"

"I don't know. Why not?"

"You went to some pains to point out that *I* can't be sure of anything—at least that's what it sounded like to me."

"Well—"

"Look—let's not open it up again, should we? You made your point, and I assume you meant it, so let's just leave it there. O.K.?"

"O.K.," she said. "If that's what you want."

"It has nothing to do with what I want. I just don't see the point in beating a dead horse."

"Thank you very much."

"I didn't mean you, I—oh, God. Here we go again. I'll see you tonight." He opened the front door, and was gone.

She stood motionless for several moments after the door had closed behind him, and then she went to the mirror in the front hall and looked at herself. Her hair, which had had a sheen to it almost like corn silk (or so she had once been told, by a sweaty youth from Tiskilwa, Ill.), was dull and matted, and there was a glaze to her light-blue eyes that suggested a fever. Her face was pale, but it was an unhealthy pallor rather than a fashionable one, and she felt she could understand why Henry Walden had resisted her advances (the memory of which, in the clammy light of a rainy day, made her squirm with embarrassment), and why her husband had treated her as offhandedly as if she'd been a hitching post. No wonder I'm not attractive to men, she thought. If I saw a man who looked like me, I'd flee into the mountains and never come out.

She was deep in these depressing thoughts when she heard the back door open, and saw Dolly come into the kitchen. "Good morning!" Lucille said, turning away from the mirror with a determinedly cheerful expression. "Did you sleep well?"

"Better'n the night before," Dolly replied, eyeing the coffee pot. "But then, nothing could've been worse than the night before, so that's not saying much. I slept—put it that way."

"Would you like some coffee? I think there's enough there, but I'm going to make another pot anyway."

"That would be fine," Dolly replied, sitting at the kitchen table. She glanced around quickly, looking for evidence of the night before, but everything seemed in order. "Where are the others?" she asked.

"My husband's gone out to check the shop, and we don't know where Mr. Lambert and Mr. Walden are. They were on patrol last night, and don't seem to have come home." She poured the last of the pot into a cup for Dolly, and set it in front of her. "How's the book going?"

"*Comme ci, comme ça*, as the French would say," Dolly replied. "There's a lot more to writing than meets the eye."

"I imagine there is." A sudden thought struck Lucille, and she said, "Your hairdresser—what's her name?"

"My—? Oh—Stella." Dolly blew on her coffee, then took a long, loud sip.

"Does she have her equipment with her?"

"What do you mean?"

"Would she be able to do my hair if I asked her to? I'd be glad to pay her."

"Dearie, I just don't know. You'd have to ask her. But if it's any fancy kind of job you're after, I suspect you'd have to bring your own tools. She didn't leave the city with much baggage."

"I have a curling iron, and a comb, and all that. I'd just like to have it done by a professional."

Dolly glanced at her hair. "I see what you mean. Well, tell Stella I told you to ask her, and see what she says. I don't know why she couldn't do it, if the mood is on her."

Lucille started another pot of coffee, and said, "Is there anything she can do about my complexion? I look as though I'd been dragged out from under a rug."

"Again, you'd have to ask her. She knows a few—ah—cosmetic tricks, and in your case I don't think she'd mind sharing them. It all depends." Dolly took another loud drag on her coffee, and said, "About Mr. Stod—whatyoumacallhim—Lambert—did he say where he was going when he went out?"

"He just said he was going on patrol. He and Mr. Walden both had an eight-to-midnight tour."

"They must've met up, if neither one is back."

"I assume so." Lucille's trembling had subsided, but it was replaced by a deep restlessness that made it hard for her to stand still. She felt she had to be doing something—anything—or she might suddenly scream. "Would you like some ham, or sausage, or kippers?" she said. "They brought a lot of stuff home with them yesterday."

"A kipper might be nice," Dolly replied. "I haven't had one of them in ages."

"A kipper it is." Lucille set about opening the tin, and Dolly decided to find out what she could about the Benders' background. Last night's fight still echoed in her ears, and she was curious to know what lay behind it. A writer, she told herself, must learn as much about people as possible, so a little snooping is all in the line of business.

"You been married long?" she asked, as Lucille struggled with the opener.

"Five years," Lucille replied. "You want it fried, or broiled?"

"Fried's fine with me. Whichever's easiest. Five years is a long time. You planning on having children?"

"Not at the moment. George feels there's too much to do at the store."

Dolly thought about this, then said, "You help him with the store, is that it?"

"No, but—it's just"—Lucille didn't feel she knew Dolly well enough to go into her various problems, and furthermore she had the suspicion that if she did, they might end up in the book—"we feel we ought to take one thing at a time, so to speak."

"He could do three things at a time, and still have children," Dolly replied. "As far as his part in it goes, he could accomplish that on the way to work. Wouldn't even have to take off his hat, if he didn't care to." As an afterthought, she added, "Lord knows, it's been done that way more than once."

Lucille could hardly believe she understood what Dolly was saying, and to change the subject she said, "What would you like with your kipper? Bread? Toast? Cheese?"

"I don't suppose you'd have an egg, would you?"

"I'm afraid not. I don't think there's an egg in the city."

"I can see why. If I was a chicken I'd hang on, too, at least until the earth quit rocking. Well, then, a piece of cheese would be fine." Lucille went to the icebox, and in an offhand way Dolly said, "Is Mr. Walden an old friend of yours?"

"Heavens, no," Lucille replied. "His rooming house collapsed in the shake, and George helped dig him out. We brought him here because he had no place else to go."

Dolly received this news in silence, and took another sip of her coffee.

"It turns out he and George were in the war together," Lucille went on, more to keep talking than for any other reason. "They didn't actually know one another, but George's company went to the rescue when Godfrey's company was caught in a trap, so they're—"

"I assume you're not talking about the Civil War," Dolly put in.

Lucille laughed. "No, the war with Spain."

"I heard something about that, but I didn't realize anyone got into trouble. I thought they all ran up a hill behind the President, and then they all came home."

"You should talk to George some time." Footsteps sounded outside, and then the front door opened and Stoddard and Walden came in. They were unshaven, and their clothes were wet and rumpled and their eyes slightly glassy, but in spite of their obviously having been drinking neither one of them could be called drunk. They were cheerful, and laughed perhaps a little too easily, but beyond that both seemed under control.

"Are we late for dinner?" Walden asked. "We got here as soon as we could."

"You're just in time," Lucille replied, relieved to see him. "I'm frying a kipper for Mrs. LaGrange—would you like something?"

"A kipper sounds fine," Walden replied, and turned to Stoddard. "What about it, Max—would you like the little lady to flip a kipper for you?"

"Anything she flips is all right with me," Stoddard replied. "Yes, please, Mrs. Bender, I would be much obliged." He dried his hands and face on a kitchen towel, then took a seat across the table from Dolly, and said, "Dolly, old girl, you now have yourself a publisher."

"You're shitting me," said Dolly. "Excuse me—who?"

"The Phoenix Press." Stoddard looked at Walden. "Or did we decide to call it Books?"

"One or the other," said Walden. "You said Books and I said Press—or maybe it was vice versa."

"I think it was Books," said Stoddard, and then, to Dolly, "We, the Phoenix Books—or Press—are going to publish your book, and possibly several others."

"Oh," said Dolly, deflated. "I thought you meant a real publisher."

"We are—or will be. We're going to incorporate, and all the rest of it."

"What do you know about publishing?"

"I have friends in the business, and I'm going to send Godfrey to learn from them. I might even hire away some of their employees. I'm going to back the company, and Godfrey is going to be the head of it."

"I thought you didn't have any money."

"My money here is—ah—in question until the banks can open. But I have funds elsewhere, and nobody need worry about one little nickel. Tell me how much you need, and it's as good as yours."

Dolly gave him a speculative look. "I'll believe that when I see the color of it," she said.

Stoddard shrugged, and said, "Very well, then, take your book elsewhere, but I don't think you're going to get anyone to print it. I—we—will guarantee to print it, which is more than you'll get from any other publisher. And we'll also advance you the money with which to finish it. You're not going to get a better offer than that."

Dolly sighed. "I suppose you're right. But will you promise to make it a pretty one, with real leather covers?"

"Real leather, no, but I can promise it'll be a handsome volume. All you have to do is put the words down."

"I was afraid of that," said Dolly. "I knew there'd be a catch somewhere."

"This was your idea, you know. Nobody is insisting you write it."

"I know." Dolly picked up a knife and fork, and began to eat the kipper that Lucille placed in front of her. "I just wish I knew a real writer," she said. "There must be lots of tricks he could tell me."

"Like what?"

"Like do you keep office hours, or do you wait for inspiration to strike. Things like that. Sometimes I can't think of a bloody thing to say."

Walden, who'd been drying himself with the towel discarded by Stoddard, said, "That's where I come in. You put down anything that comes to you, and I'll decide whether it makes sense. If not, we'll talk about it."

"Suppose I can't think of anything."

"Then just write, 'I see the cat,' fifty times, and we'll see what we can make of it."

"It seems like a kind of murky way to make a living. I like things to be more direct."

"Some things are cut and dried," Stoddard put in. "Other things have to be more flexible. Once you've tried, you'll find it's not too hard."

Dolly gave him a long look. "I don't like the expression 'cut and dried,'" she said. "It sounds like dead meat."

"Well, nobody could ever accuse you of peddling that," Stoddard replied, and Walden laughed.

"What's so bloody funny?" Dolly asked him.

"Nothing," Walden said quickly. "I just don't see you as a butcher. You have far too much class to be in trade."

Dolly considered this, and took another bite of her kipper. "You're nimble, I'll say that for you," she said at last.

"Has anyone heard about the fire?" Lucille asked from her place at the stove. "Have they managed to get it out yet?"

"They say it's out," Walden replied. "But by this time they'll say anything. We won't know until we can see."

"*I* think it's out," Lucille said. "It just kind of feels that way."

Walden glanced at her. "Are you psychic?"

"I don't know, but some days I get the feeling that I know things I don't actually see." Then, suddenly embarrassed, she turned back and took the kippers off the stove and put them on two plates. "Your breakfast, gentlemen," she said, taking the plates to the table, and then she added, "Oh, Mrs. LaGrange, I forgot your cheese."

"No matter," said Dolly. "If I eat too much I'll get bloated, and then I won't be able to write."

"You've got to keep in writing trim," Walden said, sitting down at the table. "We want to keep our writers lean and muscular."

"The muscles are no problem," Dolly replied, cheerfully. "I have muscles where most people have—oh, well, let it pass."

"Save it for the book," said Walden. "As for me, I have a feeling I may take a short nap, which makes this a midnight supper rather than breakfast." He turned to Stoddard. "In other words, Max, would you care to join me in a nightcap?"

"Why ever not?" replied Stoddard. "It should be just the thing to induce a restful snooze."

"Is there any whisky left?" Walden asked Lucille. "I promise we'll restock for you today."

"We found a place that sells it at all hours of the day and night," Stoddard said. "The man may very well be a millionaire before the week is out."

"Well, we have enough for now." Lucille produced a bottle from the cupboard, and got two glasses.

"Will you join us?" Walden asked.

"No, thank you."

"It'll clear away all those cobwebs."

"Do I look as though I need it?" Lucille had begun to tremble again.

"Everybody needs it, now and then. A little smile can brighten up your whole day."

"Well—"

"I don't mean to tempt you. I'd hate to be known as the one who led you astray."

"It isn't that. As a matter of fact, I do feel a little shaky, and perhaps just one—"

"Then what you need is a good jolt. Mrs. LaGrange, will you join us?"

"It's a little early—" Dolly began.

"You've got to drink to your publisher. Let's all have a drink to Phoenix Press—"

"Books," Stoddard put in.

"To Phoenix Books, and then we can all go our separate ways. Max and I will go to bed, Mrs. LaGrange will go to her writing, and Lucille will go to—what is it you're going to do today, Lucille?"

"I don't know for sure," Lucille replied. "There are a number of things I should be doing, but if I try to do them all I may not—" She found that her sentence was running on, with no end in sight, so she wound it up by saying, "So I guess I'll just let nature take its course."

"That seems like the most sensible idea I've heard all day," Walden said, and raised his glass. "Dangerous, perhaps, but fundamentally sensible. Here's to it."

# CHAPTER 17

With the fire finally out, the San Francisco bankers were able for the first time to look around, and try to formulate some plans for the future. Being basically conservative men most of them favored a policy of wait and see, until their vaults cooled to the point where they could be opened for inspection, but there were others who favored opening up as soon as possible, in order to take advantage of the pressing need for money. A. P. Giannini, head of the Bank of Italy, had taken all of the bank's $80,000 cash assets to his home in San Mateo, and he returned after the fire and set up in business in a new location, where he loaned money to members of the Italian community for the rebuilding of their property, and persuaded others to put their hoarded wealth in his bank as the safest place to keep it. The Anglo-California Bank had its million dollars in negotiable bonds that the two tellers had taken by wheelbarrow to Oakland; and the Hibernian Bank, only lightly damaged, had been guarded by armed employees all through the fire and was able to resume business almost at once, although it also had to serve as temporary headquarters for the Police Department, whose own building had been destroyed. The Wells Fargo Bank, on the other hand, was reduced to smoldering rubbish, and the chief cashier, one B. F. Lipman, had watched it collapse and then gone home, saying there was nothing left to do but sit and wait.

The Bank of the Pacific, of which Gresham Stoddard was a director, had suffered the same fate as the Wells Fargo. On that rainy Saturday afternoon, with wisps of steam rising from the wreckage, three of the bank's officers stood and stared in silence at the rubble-filled pit that had been the basement. They were the president, the executive vice-president, and the chairman of the board, and they had come out of some nebulous feeling of responsibility, as though attending the funeral of a colleague. Like B. F. Lipman they had nothing to do but wait, but they had an interest not only in the survival of the records, but also in what the records contained. Or at least one of them did: the executive vice-president, whose name was Slater Wallop, had not yet confided his suspicions to the other two.

"How long will it be before we can open the vault?" he said, to nobody in particular.

"I'd say two weeks," replied Norton Brundage, the president. "Sooner than that, and we're likely to lose everything."

"I'd make it three," the chairman of the board, one Lavery Whitman, said. "Don't want to take chances, you know."

"Three weeks is a long time," said Wallop. "In three weeks, almost anything could happen."

Brundage looked at him with curiosity. "Such as what?" he said. "What could happen that hasn't already happened?"

"Well—I'd just like to get at some records. I was in the middle of looking into something when the shake hit."

"Perhaps you'd better tell us," said Whitman. "What were you looking into?"

"I'd rather not say until I'm sure," Wallop replied. "I don't like to cast aspersions unless they're well founded."

"Surely you can tell us," Brundage said. "I mean, if you can't tell the president and the chairman of the board, what point is there in our being here?"

"I'd like to talk to Gresham Stoddard first," Wallop said. "There may be a very simple explanation, and I'd like to hear it from him."

"Surely you're not implying he's done anything wrong?" said Whitman in a tone of disbelief.

"I'm not implying anything," Wallop replied. "I'm simply saying I'd like to talk to Mr. Stoddard."

"If that's all you want, I'll have you over to the Club," Whitman said. "He's there most every afternoon."

"There is no more Club," Brundage reminded him. "It went the second day."

"True," said Whitman. "Damn nuisance. Well, I'll have you —someplace."

"I still want to know what this is about," Brundage said. "Why do you want to talk to Gresham Stoddard?"

Wallop drew a long breath, and let it out slowly. "Well, two weeks ago, Richardson came to me, and—"

"Who's Richardson?" Whitman asked.

"Our treasurer," Wallop replied, trying not to sound condescending. "He told me that the Auditing Committee had been puzzling over what became of some Southern Pacific bonds that Mr. Stoddard had used as collateral for a loan."

"Nothing unusual about that," Whitman said. "He's probably got them in his strongbox."

"The thing is," Wallop went on, "he's used the same bonds, over and over again, to increase the amount of the loan. He now owes the bank some four hundred and seventy-two thousand dollars, has never repaid a cent—or if he has, it's out of a new loan—and has somehow managed to make off with all the collateral. In other words, he has stuck us for close to half a million dollars."

"Good God, man, you can't be serious," Whitman said. "His father was an Argonaut."

"I didn't know *that*," said Brundage. "He's never mentioned it."

"In many ways he's a queer duck, but to embezzle money from his own bank—no. Never."

"That's why I'd like to talk to him," Wallop said. "There may be absolutely nothing wrong, but that's not the way the figures add up."

"Well, if I see him I'll tell him to call you," Whitman said. "Although if you ask me, you're barking up the wrong tree."

"Has anyone seen him?" Brundage said. "I mean, since the shake."

"Someone saw him at the opera Tuesday night," Whitman replied. "The night that wop was singing. After that, all hell broke loose." A thought struck him, and he gave a throaty chuckle. "You don't suppose the wop was the cause of it all, do you? They say his voice could shatter glass." Nobody laughed, and he cleared his throat and looked again at the wreckage.

"And all these records are now in the vault?" Brundage asked Wallop.

"That's right. I'd separated the Stoddard ones from the others—there were quite a few, as you can imagine—and put them in a folder for further study. That was Tuesday. I locked them in my own strongbox in the vault, and"—he pointed at the pit—"there they are."

"If you take my advice you'll forget about them," Whitman said. "Things are going to be hard enough for the next few months, without cluttering up the scene with a two-bit scandal."

"A half million dollars is hardly what I'd call a two-bit scandal," Brundage replied. "Furthermore, it's my—"

"Half million dollars my foot. You heard Whatsisname here—he said it's no more than four hundred thousand."

"Four hundred and seventy-two thousand," Wallop said, quietly.

"Seventy-two, sixty-four, twenty-three—who counts in nickels and dimes? The point is, you're trying to blacken a man's name without a shred of evidence."

"I'm not trying to blacken anyone," Wallop said. "I'm just trying to find out what happened to the money."

"I agree," said Brundage. "And, in the long run, it's my responsibility."

"In the long run, you'll do what the board of directors tells you," Whitman growled.

Brundage's lips turned white. "And you can have my resignation any time you want it."

Whitman turned to Wallop. "How many people know about this?" he asked.

"Well"—Wallop hesitated—"there's Richardson, and on the Auditing Committee there's Selfridge and Harkins and Knowlton and Stannard, and then there's probably the clerks, and—"

"In all, possibly a dozen?"

"Possibly. Maybe more, maybe less. After all, people have had other things on their minds these last few days, so it isn't as though they'd had time to gossip."

Whitman looked at Brundage. "Isn't there a rule that any employee of this bank who gossips is fired?"

"There is," said Brundage, "but you never can be sure—"

"If the rule is there, it's there to be obeyed. I expect you to see that it's carried out to the letter." Whitman started to walk away, then looked back and said, "And I hope you realize that rule applies to officers, too."

Brundage nodded, not trusting himself to speak. He and Wallop watched Whitman as, with his cape drawn up across his chin, he made his way through the rubble and disappeared in the misty rain, and then Brundage turned and looked at the crumbled foundations of the bank. "If this rain keeps up," he said, "it may cool things down enough so we won't have to wait too long."

# CHAPTER 18

When Stoddard and Walden had retired, and Dolly had gone back to her room over the stable, Lucille put the whisky bottle back in the cupboard, noticing that they had managed to do away with all but about four ounces. She had a thin excuse for her part in it, but she knew George would blame her without asking for an explanation, so to simplify matters she took the bottle out of the cupboard again, and poured in an equal amount of water. The drink had made her feel better in that it had reduced her trembling, and that small improvement made her feel almost euphoric. Suddenly, and for no discernible reason, the world seemed brighter, and she began to think of constructive ways to pass the time. She sang little snatches of "There'll Be a Hot Time in the Old Town Tonight" as she cleaned the kitchen and put away the dishes, and when that was done she thought of taking down the curtains and washing them. She could hear the muted snores of the two men upstairs, and decided she could probably get the curtains done before they awoke, but then, as she mounted a chair to take down the first pair, she saw a break in the clouds outside, and a small patch of blue sky above the Bay. All at once it seemed as though all her troubles were over; the fire was out and the rain had stopped, and today would be the beginning of a whole new chapter in her life. The time had come to have her hair washed and set, and have a facial massage, and prepare herself for whatever lay ahead. She got down off the chair, went upstairs and got her hairdressing equipment—comb, brush, curling iron, tortoiseshell hairpins, and hairnet—and on her way out she passed the room where the two men were sleeping. The room echoed with their snores and reeked of whisky fumes as she tiptoed in, kissed Walden once on the forehead, and then hurried out and down the stairs.

Bender didn't stay long at the pharmacy; he saw that the girls were reasonably content and had what they needed, and then he took off for the hospital, to see if he could requisition some supplies to tide him over. When he had left, Stella and Maribelle went back to the pinochle game they'd started earlier, and Clarita produced her file and began to work on her nails.

"An odd duck, that one," she said, nodding at the door through which Bender had gone. "I wonder if he'd be worth a trick or two, just for pin money."

"How yer going to turn a trick in public here?" Stella replied, sorting her cards. "It's only a bleedin' low-life'll do it in front of an audience."

"Oh, I don't know," said Maribelle, laying down a card. "I hear some of those parties up on Nob Hill get pretty randy-dandy."

"That'll be the day," Stella replied. "Besides, there is no more Nob Hill."

"That's beside the point. The longer I live the more I begin to think all men are pretty much alike."

"Well, yes. I've yet to see one with a Christmas tree where the old meat-hook should be. But it's what they do with it that's different, and there's some so shy you wonder how they know where to find it. Others, of course, are more what you might call happy-go-lucky in their approach. It all depends on their upbringing."

"You'd think that old gent I was with last Tuesday would've had a very classy upbringing," Maribelle said. "But when push came to shove, he was the one who wanted to play eel. How do you figure that one out?"

"He also wanted to go to the Yukon," Stella replied. "His upbringing must've got derailed somewhere along the line."

"I'd still like to know about this Whatsisname, Bender," Clarita said. "He fascinates me, kind of."

"What's so fascinating about him?" Maribelle played a card, then thought better of it and picked it up.

"He looks too prim to be true. I'll bet he'd be a real hot potato, if you were to get him worked up."

"What's the matter with you? Haven't you seen enough hot potatoes already?"

"Intellectual curiosity," Clarita replied, filing the nail on her forefinger. There was a silence while the other two played out their hands, and then Clarita said, "I wonder where we go from here."

"Why go anywhere?" Maribelle said. "I find this kind of restful."

"Well, we can't stay here forever. Poor old Bender's got to get back in business *some* time."

"The madam wants me to take up hairdressing," Stella said, shuffling the deck. "But I don't see there's enough money in that to keep me in the style to which I've become accustomed."

"Well, you can't keep *that* up forever, either," Clarita said. "A girl's got to have something to fall back on when the old well dries up."

"I say sufficient unto the day is the evil thereof," Stella replied. "I'll worry about that when it happens. I only wish I'd been able to get my legs around that Caruso, though; that would've been a feather in my cap, for sure. He might've even taken me home with him."

"Yeah, and he might've dropped you down that Vevusius, and burned your arse off for you."

"And he might not've, too. You heard him say he was a friend of the President—he might've taken me to the White House and then you'd've been burning *your* bloody arse with envy."

"All right, girls," Maribelle said. "Let's not spoil a restful day by getting into personalities."

"I'm not getting into personalities," Clarita said. "I just

think it's unhealthy to get ideas above your station—it makes you discontented with your lot."

"Who's discontented?" Stella replied. "A girl can dream, can't she?"

"Well, it seems to me," Clarita said, "that if ever there was a time to change professions this is it, but you don't have to get so hoity-fucking-toity you think you're going to the White House."

"I didn't say I thought I was going; I said he might have taken me. There's a difference."

"Speaking of changing professions," Maribelle said, trying to get the conversation onto safer ground, "I wonder if Lillybelle ever joined the Church."

"I wouldn't doubt it," said Stella. "She'd have done anything if she thought it'd save her soul."

"She'd probably make a good nun," Clarita said. "From what I hear she was very understanding. Sympathetic, you might say. A lot of men like that."

"What would you be if you changed professions?" Stella asked her. "What other talents do you have to offer?"

Clarita put the nail file against her front teeth, and stared out the window for a few moments. "Do you mean seriously, or do you mean if I could be anything I want?"

"Either one."

"Well, seriously, I suppose I could be a dressmaker, or something like that. If I could be anything I want, I'd like to be a general."

"A general what?"

"An army general. Wear a bright uniform with a lot of medals, ride a white horse and dash around, slashing with my sword"—she cut a broad stroke through the air with her nail file—"and have all the soldiers cheering behind me as I led them into battle." There was silence from the other two, and she went on, "I know that's crazy, but you said if I could be anything I want."

"It's crazy, all right," Maribelle said at last. "But I've got to admit, it doesn't sound bad."

"I wonder what Tessie and Melinda and Dolores are doing now," Stella said, referring to the three who had defected the first night in Oakland.

"They probably set up on their own," Maribelle said. "Tessie and Melinda don't have enough imagination to do anything else."

"What would you like to do?" Clarita asked her.

Maribelle hesitated, then said, "I'd like to raise owls. There's something very special about an owl, and besides, they eat mice. I can't stand mice."

"You'll never make a living raising owls," Stella told her. "Never in a million years."

"I didn't say I'd make a living at it; I said it's what I'd like to do. And, as you yourself just said, a girl can dream. You've got to be able to dream, or you'll get the shrieking jeebies."

Stella and Maribelle finished their pinochle game, then Stella gathered the deck together, shuffled it once, and put it aside.

"That's all for me," she said. "I haven't written me mum in three days, and it's time I got to it."

Maribelle looked at Clarita. "What do you think?" she said. "Should we hit the streets, and see if we can hustle up a buck or two?"

"I suppose we might as well," Clarita replied. "Another day of sitting around, and I'll forget how to do it."

"All I ask is don't bring them back here," Stella said, groping in her reticule for paper. "I have to be able to concentrate when I write."

"You and Dolly," Clarita said, putting away her nail file. "You'd think she was writing *Uncle Tom's Cabin*."

"Who knows?" said Stella. "Maybe she is."

"Nobody knows," Clarita replied. "But I know which way to bet."

Clarita and Maribelle tidied up their hair, straightened their dresses, and then, after checking their faces in a mirror that had been hung on the wall, they put on hats and went outside. The bell above the door jingled as they left, and Stella, glancing through the front window, noticed that the rain had stopped and the day had become perceptibly brighter. She took a sheet of paper, added it to the letter she'd started several days before, then found a pen and began to write:

> Well, here it is Saturday, and I must say I thought the week would never end. The fire has been put out, and while there isn't much left of the city it is at least better than it might have been. Miss LaGrange brought us all over to Oakland when things began to get too hot in Frisco (ha! ha!), and now we're staying in what was once a chemist's shop (they call them pharmacys over here, although I'm told the lower classes refer to them as drug stores). The owner is quite the gentleman, and has done his best to make us feel at home. Miss LaGrange has a knack for bringing out the best in men, and I must say there's been many a time

She was pondering the words, trying to decide how to finish the sentence, when she glanced out the window and saw Lucille approaching. She'd seen Lucille only once, and briefly, when they'd first arrived, and for a moment thought she might be someone looking for a place to sleep. But Lucille opened the door with such a proprietary air that Stella knew she must be the owner's wife, and then she remembered having seen her before.

"Good morning!" Stella said cheerfully. "The mister was here a while back, but then he buzzed off. I think he said to the hospital."

"He's not the one I'm after," Lucille replied, putting a drawstring bag on the nearest chair. "I'd like to talk to you."

"Wot've *I* done?" Stella said, immediately wary. She pushed the pages of her letter together, and turned them face down. "I don't know wot yer torkin' abaht." Whenever she was nervous her Cockney origin asserted itself, as though to throw up a protective screen.

"There's nothing *wrong*," Lucille said quickly. It was the first time she'd ever seen anyone afraid of her, and for some illogical reason it upset her. "I was just talking to Dolly—Mrs. LaGrange—and she said you might consider doing my hair for me. She said it would all depend on how you felt, and I said I'd be very glad to pay you, so she told me to ask you, and see what you said. Would you do it?"

"What do you mean, 'do' your hair?" Stella asked cautiously.

"Wash it and set it, and fix it so it doesn't look like an eagle's nest. And also maybe do something about my complexion, and—well, make me look a little better than I do. Do you know Charles Dana Gibson, the artist?"

"Never had the pleasure," Stella replied, casting a speculative eye on Lucille's features. She could be quite good-looking, Stella thought, but at the moment she looked frantic and blowsy, and also smelled of whisky. What she needed more than anything else was a little confidence, but that was something over which Stella had no control. Still, if she looked a little better, then maybe the rest might follow.

"I don't mean do you know him in person," Lucille said. "I don't think anyone knows him in person—I mean, obviously except his family—what I mean is, he draws pictures of beautiful women for the magazines, and I'd like to look like one of them."

"That could get expensive," Stella said. "How much were you thinking of paying?"

"What are your usual rates?"

"My usual—well, it all depends. There's lots of different jobs, and a different rate for each one. It's up to the customer. In your case"—she hesitated, wondering how high she dared go—"how would five dollars sound?"

Lucille swallowed. She had exactly five dollars with her, out of which she'd hoped to have her hair done, buy some food, and also replenish the whisky supply. "Can you guarantee it'll be a good job?" she asked.

"I'll guarantee nothing," Stella replied, "except you'll look a lot better'n you do now."

"Then let's go." Lucille removed her hat, tugged open her drawstring bag, and dumped the contents on a cot. "That's all the equipment I've got," she said. "I hope it'll do the trick." She took a chair, and sat down facing the mirror.

"If not, it won't be for lack of trying," Stella said, standing up. She looked around as though expecting something, then a smile flicked across her face. "I guess there's nobody to bring the towels here, is there?" she said.

"What do you mean?" Lucille asked, loosening her hair. "What towels?"

"Let it pass," replied Stella. "Just take off your shirtwaist, dearie, so's we don't get it all wet."

As she worked on Lucille's hair, Stella thought back on Clarita's remarks about George Bender, speculating that he might be a hot potato if aroused. Lucille certainly didn't strike her as a woman whose husband was a torrid lover, but then it was possible he was getting his action somewhere else. Somehow that didn't seem to make sense, and she wondered if Bender was simply a busy pharmacist who had no time for anything but his job. If that was so, then he was like no man she had ever come across, and must have something radically wrong with him somewhere. The whole thing intrigued her, and she decided to see what she could find out. As she was scrubbing Lucille's hair, she said, "An earthquake sure raises the old Nick with romance, don't it?"

"I wouldn't know," Lucille replied.

Oh, thought Stella. All right, then. She was quiet for a while, then said, "Have you been married long?"

"Mrs. LaGrange asked me that same question," Lucille said. "Why do people ask me that?"

"Idle curiosity, I'm sure," said Stella. "At least that's what it was on my part. No offense intended."

"I wasn't offended. I'm just curious."

"I suppose it's like talking about the weather. It just popped into my head. Take me, now, I never been married, so I guess it just occurs to me to ask about those more fortunate than I."

"Why haven't you been? I should think any number of men would like to marry you."

"Oh, they did, but I have my career to think of."

"You mean as a hairdresser?"

"In a manner of speaking. Tell me about married life—is it the bed of roses they all say it is?"

"All who say it is?"

"You know—they say a girl don't begin to live until she's been married and had children, and all the rest of it."

"Again, I wouldn't know, because my husband doesn't want to have children. Not yet, at any rate."

Stella thought for a moment, then said, "Still . . ." and let the sentence hang.

"Still nothing," said Lucille. "That's all there is to it."

Stella sensed that if she pressed any further, Lucille might get up and walk out, so she changed the subject. "Did your home take any damage?" she asked.

"No," replied Lucille. "We were lucky."

"It looks like Oakland's going to be housing most of Frisco for the next little while." Stella took a comb, and with long strokes ran it through Lucille's hair. "Everywhere you look, there's people camping out." Lucille said nothing, and Stella went on, "Do you have many staying with you?"

"Three," Lucille said. "Mrs. LaGrange, Mr. Lambert, and Mr. Walden."

"Did the gentlemen come from Frisco, too?"

"Mr. Lambert did, but Mr. Walden was right here in Oakland. His rooming house collapsed."

"He was the lucky one, wasn't he?"

"Indeed he was."

Something in the tone of Lucille's voice caught Stella's attention, and she said, "Where's he come from?"

"Back East. Originally Connecticut, and then New York." Lucille's voice was almost dulcet.

"Will he be staying with you long?"

"I really don't know. That subject has never come up."

Oh-ho, Stella thought. So here's the reason for the hairdo. I might've known it. "I guess this is no time to be making plans," she said. "We just take what the good Lord gives us, and be glad we're still alive."

"I never thought of it that way," Lucille said. "But I believe you're right."

"I mean, look at the poor blokes who've got no more choice. They say there's hundreds dead—maybe thousands—and there's lots of them as wished they'd kicked up their heels a bit before they copped it. It's here today and gone tomorrow and devil takes the hindmost, is the way I look at it, and if you can find a bit of something that makes life more pleasant, then Bob's your uncle."

"Yes, indeed," said Lucille, wondering who Bob might be.

Stella began to whistle through her teeth as she worked on Lucille's hair. "This Gibson bloke," she said after a while. "The artist. Does he live out here?"

"I don't think so," Lucille replied. "I think he lives back East."

"I don't suppose you'd have one of his pictures lying around, would you?"

"No. Why?"

"Just so's I'd have something to go by. Right now I feel like I'm working in the dark, so to speak."

"It's hard to tell you what to do. His women are beautiful, and—well, I guess *soignée* is the best word to describe them."

"You speak French?"

"Not really. Do you?"

"Put it this way: I can speak with a French accent. Dolly likes—uh—there are times when it comes in handy."

"I wish I could speak it well."

"Why? Do you know any Frenchmen?"

"No, but if I were ever to go there, I'd like to be able to speak the language."

"Do you and your husband travel a lot?"

"Heavens, no. I don't think he's been out of Oakland in five years."

Stella digested this information, then said, "To spik wees ze accent, Madame must first remembaire zere ees no 'th' sound in ze langage."

"Fine!" said Lucille, smiling. "I'll remember that."

"But if you really want to talk French, Dolly's the one you should go to. She can speak it with knobs on."

"Of course. She's French, isn't she?"

"Not exactly, but she's as good an imitation as you'll find around here."

"Well, I'll ask her. It would be fun to have a project of some sort."

"I thought you already had one."

"What do you mean?"

"Well, you're not blowing five skins just to look pretty for yourself, are you?"

Lucille found herself unable to answer, and as she searched for the right words she was aware that her face was getting hot. "Well—" she began, but Stella cut her off.

"It's none of my business," she said. "Forget I spoke."

"No, really," Lucille said, "it's just that I wanted—"

"Forget it," Stella said. "I just hope you get your money's worth, that's all."

"Well, for that matter," Lucille replied, "so do I."

Their eyes met in the mirror, and they both laughed.

# CHAPTER 19

When George Bender left his pharmacy he headed through the crowded, cluttered streets toward the hospital, hoping but not really believing that he'd get what he wanted. He was doing anything he could think of to keep his mind from coming back to Lucille, and while he knew this was probably impossible he determined to try, if for no other reason than to keep from losing his mind completely. Everything seemed to have fallen apart in the last few days, and he didn't know where to start to pick up the pieces.

That Lucille was addicted to alcohol was obvious, but beyond that what worried him most was her preoccupation with Henry Walden, and he couldn't understand her passion for a man she'd known for not quite four days. It was so meaningless, and so unlike her, that he could only assume it was the alcohol, or, worse, that she'd somehow taken leave of her senses. In either case he was at a loss as to what to do, because to him women were a breed apart, mysterious in their motivations and often irrational in their behavior, but basically decent and loyal, requiring only the steady hand of a man in times of crisis. Steady hand my foot, he thought. The minute I try to steady her she flies into a rage, and begins throwing crockery.

His theories about women were passed on from his father, who had discussed the subject with him reluctantly and only as the result of direct questioning, with little elaboration beyond the direct answers. His father, Franklin Bender, had been fifteen when Fort Sumter was bombarded, and had immediately tried to enlist in the 4th Ohio Volunteers, but the recruiting sergeant, doubting he was the sixteen he claimed to be, had demanded that he sing "The Moonlight's Fair Tonight Along the Wabash," and his voice cracked at the first high note. He was sent home to the farm, where he brooded for a year and then tried again, this time successfully. As a farm boy he was aware of the basic facts of reproduction, and from listening to his fellow volunteers he gathered there were some women who were indiscriminate in their choice of partners, but the action of the war was such that he never got to acquire any knowledge at first hand, and the whole subject remained murky in his mind. When he married, both he and his bride were nervous and apprehensive, and the result was a disaster from which it took them a long time to recover. When, finally, young George was born, it was clear he was going to be an only child.

The first time he asked his mother the "Where did I come from?" question she looked out the window, chewed on her lower lip for a few moments, then said, "Ask your father." He was eight years old at the time, and when he asked his father the reply was, "You're not old enough to know." He tried asking friends, but the answers were so diverse, and in some cases so contradictory, that he was if anything worse off than before. He concluded that the answer lay in metaphysics, combined in some arcane way with the outhouse, and was beyond his immediate comprehension. What little he could gather sounded repugnant.

At last, on the eve of his fourteenth birthday, he had picked up enough on the subject to go to his father and ask, if not for direct information, at least confirmation or denial of the various versions. His father heard him out without changing expression, then said, "I'd say you're about fifty per cent right."

"Which fifty?" George replied. "Which is right, and which is wrong?"

"You're right about the general nature of the act. You're wrong in that the baby is not born through the navel."

"Then where is it born?"

"Put it this way: Whatever goes up, must come down."

George considered this. "That sounds kind of rough on the woman."

"So they say."

"Then why do they do it?"

"They want children. Or most of them do."

"They must want them pretty bad."

"Son, I can tell you one thing—you never know what a woman wants, and what she doesn't. She can be saying one thing and meaning something completely different, and why the good Lord didn't take an extra rib from Adam to make them tell the truth, is more than I'll ever know."

"What good would having an extra rib have done?"

"It would have made them just one more step like a man."

George felt he was getting off into a morass of generalities, and said, "I've heard there are some women who do it for money. Why would that be?"

"I've told you, never ask why a woman does anything. They have their own reasons, which are kept secret from mortal men."

"But why would a woman have a baby for money? In the long run, wouldn't it cost more than she'd make?"

His father took a deep breath, and said, "There are some women who are called hookers, and they figure they can beat the odds by sheer volume. They can have only one baby at a time, but they can take in a powerful lot of money in the meantime. And if they're lucky—"

"Why do they call them hookers?"

"During the War, General Joe Hooker thought it would be better to have girls follow along with his brigade, rather than have the troops going off into the countryside and messing with the locals. So they became known as Hooker's girls, and then just plain hookers."

"Did you ever know a hooker?"

"I wasn't with his brigade."

"But did you ever—?"

"No, and that's all I'm going to tell you. You already know too much for your age."

"What does age have to do with it?"

"And if you give me any smarty talk, I'll take you out to the woodshed."

"I'm not trying to be smart, Papa. I'm just trying to learn."

"Well, there's such a thing as knowing too much. The trouble with the young today is they all want to lose their innocence. There'll be plenty of time for that later on."

"May I ask one more question?"

"What?"

"Why don't grown-ups want to talk about this? If it's something you have to be older to understand, then I should think the older people would be willing to talk about it."

"It's indecent, that's why. Now, that's the end of it."

And that was all he ever learned from his father. During his tour in the Army he learned a good deal more, although it was all second-hand and all anecdotal, and in his mind it was always a prelude to conception. Then, when he took up the study of pharmacy, he was astounded to learn that there were methods of preventing conception, but they were all either ungainly or unreliable, and strong emphasis was laid on the fact that the only 100-per-cent-effective method was continence. It gave him some restless periods, but he regarded them as tests of his willpower, which he developed to a high degree. It upset him that Lucille's willpower appeared so much weaker than his own, and he wished there were some way he could help her.

At the hospital, he found out precisely what he had feared: medical supplies were pouring in from all over the country, but they were earmarked for the disaster victims only, and individual pharmacists had no priority. President Roosevelt had put one Edward T. Devine in charge of the newly organized Red Cross, which raised $9,000,000 for general relief work; $10,000 worth of supplies were shipped up from Los Angeles; and all the relief goods and pledges were cleared through Oakland, but unless he, George Bender, was actively engaged in relief work, his only choice was to file his requisitions through the usual channels, and wait. The fact that he had refugees sleeping in his home and his store didn't set him apart from any of the other residents of Oakland; the whole city had become a refugee camp. As he walked away from the hospital, Bender reflected sourly that Roosevelt was probably going to get all the credit for the relief work, just as he had for his nonexistent charge up San Juan Hill.

He was headed for City Hall, where the line of refugees still extended halfway around the block, when he saw Gresham Stoddard coming toward him. Stoddard looked dazed, as though he had only recently awakened.

"Ah, there, Mr. Lambert!" Bender said. "Any news?"

"Of what?" Stoddard replied, looking puzzled.

"Your wife."

"Oh that. No—I—I looked for any messages, but—" He shrugged.

"I'm sure she's all right. I'll keep an eye out—what's her first name?"

"Muriel," Stoddard replied, and then, without thinking, "Muriel Stoddard."

"Would she use her maiden name?"

"Her—? Oh—yes—I mean—Muriel Stoddard Lambert."

"Well, if I see or hear anything, I'll let you know."

"That's very kind of you. Ah—how are things with the ladies?"

"If you mean at the store, they seem to be all right. I dropped in a while ago, and there were no complaints. As for the ladies at home, Mrs. LaGrange is, I assume, working on her book, and my wife—well, I honestly don't know."

"Is she all right?" Stoddard had noticed some of Lucille's eccentric behavior, but had felt it would be more tactfully ignored.

"I wish I could say. I honestly think what she needs is a project of some sort, to keep her mind occupied. She's alone a good deal of the time, and I'm afraid she gets bored."

Stoddard thought for a moment, then said, "Do you think she'd like a job? I realize some ladies feel it demeaning to work, but her duties would not be too arduous."

"What kind of job?"

"I'm setting up a small publishing firm. We're going to print Dolly's book, among others. I may have to go to Chicago shortly, and your wife's duties would be more or less to mind the store while I'm gone. She would be an executive secretary, so to speak."

"I think she'd probably love it. Have you mentioned it to her?"

"No. I—young Walden and I stayed out rather late last night, which was when we got the idea. I left him asleep, and when I got downstairs your wife had gone. I assumed she was helping you."

"No," said Bender, wondering where Lucille could be. "I haven't seen her since early this morning."

"I must say, I admire Walden's ability to sleep. When I left, he was lying as though he'd been shot."

Which is probably just as well, Bender thought. At least I won't have to worry about him and Lucille. "You said you and he got this idea," he said. "Does that mean he's going to be part of the firm?"

"He's going to be the publisher—or editor, if you will—as soon as he learns something about the work. Since I'll be supplying the money, I guess that will make me the publisher. It's all fairly loose."

"This is none of my affair, but isn't this a strange time to be starting a new business?"

"Not necessarily. A lot of businesses are going to be starting all over again, and we might as well be one of them."

"When do you plan to go to Chicago?"

"That'll depend. I may be able to do it by telegraph, and on the other hand—" He left the sentence unfinished, as he looked down the street and saw Maribelle and Clarita approaching. "Excuse me," he said. "I have a couple of things to attend to."

He hurried away, and Bender stood for a moment while he digested the information Stoddard had given him. He wished he hadn't agreed so quickly that Lucille would like the job, but at the time he hadn't known that Walden would be involved, and by now it was too late to change. Also, and unhappily, he knew that Lucille would do what she wanted whether he approved or not, so he might just as well go along with the idea and not kick up any more dust than necessary. He had always tried to be agreeable, saving his dissents for the more important things. He wondered, briefly, what would have happened if he'd taken a firmer approach a long time ago, but he realized that Lucille's style of arguing, which involved wild forays into the irrelevant, could short-circuit a firm approach in very short order. Better to be pleasant as long as possible, and hope for sanity to win out in the end. His thoughts were interrupted by a woman's voice saying, "Why, I do believe it's Mr. Bender!" and he looked around and saw Maribelle and Clarita—whom he knew by their faces, but not their names—bearing down on him.

"Good morning again, ladies," he said, tipping his hat. "What brings you into this part of town?"

"We're just taking our constitutional," Clarita replied. "A little walk for our health's sake, so to speak."

"And a good idea, too." Bender was about to move on when Maribelle spoke.

"Was that Mr. Stoddard you were just talking to?" she asked. "Mr. Gresham Stoddard?"

"No," said Bender. "His name is Maxwell Lambert. Although," he added, as a thought struck him, "his wife's maiden name was Stoddard. What an odd coincidence."

"Isn't it, though?" said Maribelle.

"I guess this is a time for coincidences," Clarita put in. "In the last few days I've seen more people I thought I knew than you can shake a stick at."

The sentence somehow reminded him of Lucille, and Bender looked at Clarita with interest. "Anyone I might know?" he said.

"Not likely," she replied. "Although I must say, you remind me of someone I knew when I was a girl—the first man I was ever in love with." She looked straight into his eyes as she said it, and he returned the stare.

"Have there been many others?" he asked.

"No," said Clarita. "He was the first and only. Until now."

"What became of him?" I can hold this stare as long as she can, Bender thought, but what in God's name is she driving at?

"Run over by a beer truck." As though explaining the accident, she added, "Drawn by eight Clydesdales."

Again that echo of Lucille, who'd been afraid Walden might be hit by a beer truck. "How very unfortunate," Bender said. Was she trying to tell him something? Was she mocking him? Just what was she doing?

"I thought I'd got over it," Clarita went on, "but now, seeing you, I guess I haven't."

"I'm sorry to bring back unpleasant memories."

"Oh, they're not all unpleasant. Only the last one. Most of them are quite beautiful."

"That's nice."

"In fact, just seeing you makes me feel like a girl all over again. I'd love to talk with you some time."

"Well—it seems to me we're talking now, aren't we?"

"Yes, but there are so many things I'd like to tell you. Some night, when you're through work, do you think we might just take a stroll?"

Oh-ho, thought Bender, at last realizing what Clarita had in mind. "I'm afraid that would be quite impossible," he said. "I'm a very busy man."

Maribelle, who had been eloquently silent, took Clarita's arm and said, "Come on, ducks, we can't keep Mr. Bender gabbing here all day. We have our constitutions to think of." She led Clarita away, and when they were beyond Bender's hearing she said, "What in the name of the gentle Jesus was all that about?"

Clarita giggled. "I was trying to get him heated up," she said.

"I know, but even he wouldn't fall for all that garbage. You were as subtle as a fire engine."

"There are times when you have to be direct. I just wanted to light a fuse, and let it smolder."

"If you ask me, you blew it out."

"We'll see. I'd be willing to bet he comes back."

"I'll take you. What do you want to bet?"

"Today's take. If he comes back, you give me what you make today; if he doesn't, I'll give you what I make."

"Let's say half the take. A girl has to eat."

"All right, half. And we'll do better if we split up than if we try for doubles."

"Right. And the day ends when—midnight?"

"Let's say sunrise tomorrow."

"Done and done."

As they parted, Clarita sighed and said, "In spite of everything, it's been a restful three days. I'm kind of sorry to see it over."

# CHAPTER 20

Bender watched the girls as they walked down the street, then he turned and slowly made his way home. His mind was a jumble of recent events—Lambert's publishing idea, Lucille's connection with it and with Walden, his worry about Lucille's health—and now, to cap it all, there was the flagrant advance that Clarita had just made at him. That had revealed her as something less than a lady, and made him wonder if Dolly and the others were all of the same general stripe. If so, then he was as good as operating a brothel, but it would be hard to prove without concrete evidence, and suspicion was not cause for turning them out. He'd simply have to keep his eyes open, and see what happened.

When he got home he found Walden puttering morosely around the kitchen, a cup of coffee in one hand and a piece of bread in the other. "I can't find the bloody peanut butter," Walden said, by way of greeting. "Do you know what happened to it?"

"It ought to be in the cupboard, there," Bender replied. "Have you any idea where Lucille is?"

"Nope," said Walden, opening the cupboard. "I haven't seen her since we went to bed."

"I beg your pardon?"

"Excuse me—since Max Lambert and I went to bed. We seem to have stayed up all night, and Lucille gave us breakfast. That's the last I remember." Walden found a knife, and began to spread peanut butter on his bread.

"I understand you two are starting a publishing house," Bender said.

Walden stopped what he was doing, and stared straight ahead. "By God, you're right," he said. "I'd forgotten all about it."

"And apparently Lucille is going to join you."

"Is she, now? Where'd you hear that?"

"I ran into Lambert, and he told me."

"Well, he knows more than I do. But then, it was his idea in the first place."

"Do you really believe Mrs. LaGrange is writing a book?"

"Well, Max thinks she is, and he's the one putting up the money."

"If you ask me, I don't think she's a writer."

"You don't have to be a writer to write a book. You just have to know how to spell. Come to think of it, not even that."

"I talked with a couple of her so-called hairdresser's friends, and if you want my opinion they're just common tarts."

Walden shrugged. "Everyone has to make a living," he said, his tongue thick with peanut butter. "As the French say, *Chacun à son goût.*"

"Yes, but I'd hate to think I was giving house room to a—"

"Wait a minute," Walden interrupted. "Let me say something."

"Go ahead." Bender wasn't sure he wanted to hear what was coming.

"You took me in, and I'm grateful. You've twice saved my life, and I'm—"

"That has nothing to do with—"

"Listen to me. You didn't ask what I did, or who I was; you helped me because I needed help. You helped Max Lambert because he needed help. Nobody knows who he is, or what he does, or anything about him except that he seems to have some money. If he doesn't have any money, no difference. You also took in these ladies—girls—whatever—and this is no time to get holier than thou just because they may be hookers. So long as they don't burn down your store, or service their customers in your front window, you have no cause to complain, because you were the one who asked them in. You're not running a girls' finishing school, and there's no reason to pretend you are. Do you understand what I'm saying?"

"You sound like Lucille."

"How do I sound like Lucille?"

"You make me out to be a pompous ass."

"Kiddo, you're the one who's doing it; I'm just reading it back to you. I don't know what's got under your skin, but you're feeling prickly about everything, and you're reacting in all the wrong places. There are some things you'd be justified in being sore about, but those aren't the things you're carping at now. You're barking up the wrong tree, and the sooner you realize it the better." Walden stopped, and looked around. "Well," he said, in a different tone. "I wonder what made me say all *that*. I must still be drunk."

"I don't think so," Bender replied. "Go on—you interest me."

"Well, I don't interest myself. I had no cause to spout off like that."

"You said there were some things I'd be justified in being sore about—can you name me one or two?"

"Not offhand, no. I just sense that you and Lucille are—well, you might say at odds."

"Has she told you anything?"

"About what?"

"What we might be at odds about."

"To the best of my knowledge she hasn't said a thing." In an attempt to keep as close to the truth as possible, Walden added, "Along those lines, that is."

"Along what lines has she talked to you?"

"Oh—general conversation. You know." Liar, Walden told himself. You'll be slapped by a bolt of lightning any minute.

"There's something wrong," Bender said, "and I'm damned if I know what it is. If she gives you any hint, I'd appreciate your letting me know."

"Uh—sure," said Walden. "Any time. But I don't really think—"

"I'm not expecting an immediate answer, mind you. But I

get the feeling she talks to you more than she does to me. That may sound strange, but it's the way I feel."

"Well, I'll certainly let you know if she tells me anything." Walden felt a sudden surge of pity, and wished there were something he could do to help. "This is none of my business," he said, "but is your—ah—romantic life—how should I say it?—complete?"

"Oh, there's none of that," Bender replied. "We don't want to have children right now."

"Yes, but—"

"Lucille understands that; there's no problem there."

"You're sure."

"Oh, yes. We've gone over it several times."

Walden shrugged, finished his peanut butter, and ran his tongue around his gums. "I'll let you know if I hear anything," he said.

The front door opened and Stoddard come in, his arms full of packages. "Ah, there, partner!" he said to Walden. "I see you're up and about."

"Just barely," Walden replied. "I see you've been shopping."

"A few provisions, to keep the home together. But I've also been making inquiries, and I think our publishing house is off to a flying start."

"In what way?"

"I've arranged for the use of a printing press, and they can put me in touch with a bindery. As soon as we get Dolly's manuscript, we can start things moving."

"What will my job be?"

"For the moment, you will be a combination editor, salesman, and general information agent. Lucille will help you arrange for the distribution of the book, and see that people know about it—that sort of thing."

"It's going to be harder until we have a book."

"We will—we will. I'm going to see the author about that right now." He put his packages on the kitchen table and hurried out the back door, and Walden saw him enter the staircase to Dolly's room.

"He's enthusiastic, I'll say that for him," Walden said, examining a package that contained five lamb chops.

"I still don't see what he wants Lucille to do," said Bender. "Just helping you is a kind of vague assignment."

"I guess that will straighten itself out with time," Walden replied. "So long as the money keeps on coming, we have nothing to worry about."

"I guess that goes for everyone."

"How are things with you?"

"Until I can replace my stock, I can't do anything. I'll just have to sit here."

"Well, if we're using your home as office space, I don't see why we shouldn't pay you. I mean, it's only fair you get something out of all this."

"We'll see." Bender seemed reluctant to commit himself, and Walden decided not to press the matter. An uneasy silence descended, and Bender began to put away Stoddard's purchases. Finally, when even the smallest noise sounded loud, Bender said, "I think Lucille's in love with you."

"Oh, pish," said Walden, feeling his throat close. "She's nothing of the kind."

"I think she is."

"There's no possible *reason* for her to be! I mean, that's the wildest thing I ever heard! Why should she be in love with me?"

"I'm not saying why, I'm just saying what I think is a fact."

"Well, I think you're wrong. In fact, I know you're wrong." Why am I saying this? Walden asked himself. The poor bastard is probably right. To Bender, he said, "It takes two to waltz, and I can promise you I've done absolutely nothing that would encourage her. Nothing. Nothing." He seized on the word "nothing" because it was the only one he was really sure of. He *had* done nothing, and he wanted to keep reminding himself. He felt as though he'd stepped into a quicksand bog, and was trying to claw his way to solid ground.

"That's as may be." Bender was putting away the last of the groceries when the front door opened, and Lucille came in. Her hair was upswept in what looked like a towering tidal wave; her cheeks were a glowing pink, and her eyebrows were darker and sharper than usual. Her upper eyelids were of a bluish tint. "Hello, honey," Bender said. "We were just talking about you, and—" He stopped as he saw the transformation that had taken place, and said, "Where in the name of God have *you* been?"

"To the hairdresser," Lucille replied, making a half pirouette. "How do you like it?"

"Like it?" said Bender. "*Like* it? I think it's the most revolting thing I've ever seen! I want you to go upstairs this minute and wash your face, and don't come back until you look like a civilized woman. Now, go!"

Lucille gasped, then turned crimson and ran upstairs, and in a moment they could hear the water running. The two men were silent for what seemed like a long while, then Walden said, "You wanted to know why you might be at odds. I think I can give you a reason."

"What?"

"Did you ever look at her side of things?"

"Do you mean why she should want to make up like a trollop?" Bender was still so angry that his eyes sparkled, and the tip of his nose was pale.

"Not exactly—well, in a sense, yes."

"There is no reason, other than that she's lost her mind."

"But why?"

"God knows. All the whisky you've fed her hasn't helped."

"*I* haven't fed it to her. All I've done—"

"Don't try to tell me that. I've seen you—I've come in here and seen—"

"All right, I've given it to her, but I never suggested it. She's always asked for it, and the reason is it's the only substitute for that elixir. It's the elixir that got her started, and if you want to know why she took *that*, I can only suggest you think back a way."

"To what?"

"Don't ask me. I don't have all the answers—my God, if I

had the answers, do you think I'd be in the position I'm in now?"

"What position is that?"

"Flopping around like a fish on a dock."

"I don't understand."

"Let it pass."

"Do you mind my saying that your omniscience gives me a royal pain in the ass?"

"I'm not omniscient—I just told you. You wanted some answers, and I was trying to find them for you."

"Well, you sounded omniscient."

"I'm sorry." There was a silence, and then Walden said, "I really am. I don't know what makes me think I can tell other people what to do."

Bender thought for a moment, then said, "Well—" and stopped. After another pause, he said, "I guess we've cleared the air, but I'm not quite sure of what."

Walden laughed. "At least that's a step in the right direction." He was about to say something more, when through the window he saw Stoddard come down from Dolly's room and hurry to the back door, carrying a piece of paper. He burst into the kitchen, waving the paper with an air of triumph.

"I have it!" he announced. "I have the first page of our book!"

"Good," said Walden. "Do you think she can keep up the pace?"

"Listen to this." Stoddard held the paper out and read: "'If I live to be a hundred and ninety, I shall never forget the morning of April eighteenth, 1906. My—'"

"That doesn't set her apart from a lot of other people," Walden observed.

"Never mind. Here's what follows: 'My first intimation that all was not well came when a prominent banker, clad only in what God gave him, came galloping out of the honeymoon suite, followed by his companion of the evening. From another room came a judge of the circuit court of appeals, banging his gavel like a man—"

"Banging his what?" said Walden.

"It says here gavel."

"What the hell had he been doing—holding court?"

"Don't ask me. 'Like a man possessed, and soon the corridor was filled with a colorful assortment of celebrities, all trying to pretend they weren't there. I often think an unclothed man is the worst liar in the world, because he is so open to correction.' "

"An interesting bit of philosophy, that," Walden said.

"Then it's true," Bender put in. "She's just a common prostitute."

"Not in the least," said Stoddard. "She is an ex-prostitute, and is in fact a very successful madam. Very high-class, as those things go."

"I gather you know her."

"In passing."

Bender glanced at Walden, and Walden smiled and said, "It's too late to do anything about it. You should have asked for their credentials before you took them in."

"Now listen to this," Stoddard said, and read: " 'They say that no man is a hero to his valet, and while this is no doubt true, one should think how much less of a hero he is to the girl he pays to indulge his passion. There are no heroes in this world; there are only heroines.' "

"She sounds like some damn feminist," Bender said. "Next thing, she'll be wanting to vote."

"Never mind," said Stoddard. "It's a refreshing point of view."

"It'll sell with the ladies," said Walden.

"I think so." Stoddard looked at the page and went on, "There are going to be a lot of things written about this earthquake, and a lot of them are going to be pretty much alike. If we can come up with something different, we may make ourselves a bundle."

"Well, keep her at it," Walden said. "Unless she goes a little faster, we'll be too old to enjoy it."

"No worry about keeping her at it. By now she considers herself a combination of Jane Austen, Emily Brontë, and Harriet Beecher Stowe."

"That's a nice combination, if she can work it. We may make more money than we think."

"Well, before we make it we've got to spend it, and my cash is running low. It's about time I got in touch with Chicago." Stoddard folded the manuscript page, put it in his pocket, and said, "I just hope I can arrange it without having to go there."

"There should be no problem with that, should there?" Walden asked.

"It may be just the slightest bit tricky. I'll start with a telegram, and see what happens."

"Are you going to do patrol tonight?"

"I'm too old to do that again. Tonight I'm going to sleep."

Walden had no particular desire to patrol, especially since it seemed like wholly wasted effort, but he didn't want to be in the house when Bender and Lucille had what was clearly shaping into a full-blown fight. His presence would only make matters worse, and he preferred to let them battle it out by themselves. "I slept late today," he said. "I think I'll sign up for an early tour, just to show them my heart's in the right place."

"I admire you," Stoddard said. "But then, that's youth. I'm going to the telegraph office, and then I'm coming back for a good long nap."

He went out, and up the stairs to Dolly's room. He took the manuscript page out of his pocket, handed it to her, and said, "This is really quite good. I have only one question."

"What's that?" Dolly asked, trying to flatten out the crease he'd made in the paper.

"I happen to know there was no judge there that morning. Is this going to be a true account, or are you writing fiction?"

"Artistic license," Dolly replied, running her thumbnail along the crease. "He's been there on other occasions, and I felt he gave a certain amount of class to this one."

"All right. That's all I wanted to know." Stoddard turned to leave.

"May I ask a favor?" Dolly said.

He stopped, and turned back. "Of course. What?"

"In the future, would you mind not folding my pages? It looks messy, and shortens the life of the paper."

"I'm sorry. I wasn't thinking."

"I can redo this page, but I'd hate to have to go over the whole thing again, just because someone had messed it up."

"Naturally. I'll tell the others."

"It's just the future I'm thinking of. The manuscript'll be worth a great deal more if it's in good shape."

"Ah, yes. Of course. I hadn't thought of it that way."

"In this business, you have to think of everything," Dolly said, and took a clean sheet of paper.

Stoddard went down and out onto the street, and headed for City Hall and the telegraph office. Going under the assumption that he would, sooner or later, become a fugitive from justice, he was trying to phrase a telegram to release his Chicago money without revealing his whereabouts, and this was virtually impossible. But until he *was* a fugitive he had no problem—except that, if he wanted it to appear that he'd died in the quake, he obviously couldn't be heard from subsequent to it. But then, nobody in Chicago would be as interested in him as they would in San Francisco, so it was possible he could— His thoughts were interrupted by someone walking beside him, and he looked around just as Maribelle said, "Well, if it isn't the old eel himself."

"Good God, where'd you come from?" he replied, trying to edge away.

"The Yukon," said Maribelle. "You want to take a little trip?"

"Thank you, no. I'm busy."

It was the first time in a long while that Maribelle had worked the streets, and she'd not made one score since she and Clarita had parted. She figured a one-time customer was her best bet, and she was reluctant to give up. "You still owe me for the other night, you know," she said. "The madam was furious I'd let you go."

"I'm sorry about that," said Stoddard. "At the time, other things seemed more important."

"If you come with me now, you'll be getting two for the price of one," Maribelle said. "Nobody can ask for a fairer deal than that."

"I said no!" said Stoddard. "Now, please! I'm busy!"

"Well, lah-di-fucking-dah," replied Maribelle, veering away. "Excuse me for drawing breath."

As he patrolled the darkened streets that night, Henry Walden thought back on his conversation with Bender, and wondered who he was to be giving other people advice. If you know so much, then why don't you do something for yourself? he thought, and this led him to wonder if it was he who was doing things wrong, or if there was a pattern to his life that led always to disaster. The fault, dear Brutus, is not in our stars, but in ourselves—but in that case, what was he to do about it? If the fault had been with his star, then the only thing would be to relax; don't kick against the pricks, and all that. But if, as he suspected, it was with himself, then what was he doing wrong? Had he set his sights too high? Was he, as he had at one time assumed, a true Renaissance man, or was he simply a dilettante with a short attention span? Until he came to some sort of conclusion there wasn't much he could do to help himself, but the answer seemed as elusive now as when he first began to wonder about it. His mind, he realized, was geared so that it always looked for an alternative: if he were in a burning building, he would be undecided as to whether to get out or to stay and fight the fire, and here was the kind of indecision that could obviously be fatal. It's a hell of a situation when you don't know when to run, he thought, but then, if everyone ran there'd be no heroes. And who wants to be a hero? Only those who are afraid of being cowards. My God, Walden, stop trying to think; it just makes matters that much worse.

The one thing he knew, without having to think about it, was that he ought to get away from Lucille. There was simply no way for that situation to end well, but how could he get away from her if they were going to be working together? Give up the whole idea; get out of town; go someplace else. Sure—and add that job to a long line of other jobs he'd tried and given up. No—he was going to see this one through as long as the money lasted, and if the firm was a bust it would at least not be from lack of his trying. Treat Lucille like any other fellow worker, and let her straighten things out between her husband and herself. That was the only sensible course, and the only one he would follow.

Refreshed at having at least made this decision, he continued his patrol until midnight, then headed back to the house. As he approached it he saw that all the windows were dark, and he was mildly irritated that nobody had thought to leave a light for him. I guess they're cutting corners in order to save, he thought as he opened the front door. He was taking off his coat when he smelled a familiar scent, and then Lucille clutched him and wrapped herself around him as though he were a tree she was trying to climb. She was wearing only a nightgown, which seemed to accentuate the contours of her body, and he barely had time to get his coat off before she wrestled him to the floor, and was all over, around, and beneath him. At first he had no time to think, and then he gave up trying.

# CHAPTER 21

On Monday, April 30, nine days after the fire had been put out, Slater Wallop and Norton Brundage drove with a crew of workmen through the ruined city to the site of the Bank of the Pacific. It was Wallop who, as executive vice-president, had first noticed the irregularities in Gresham Stoddard's records, and he and Brundage, the bank's president, were determined to open the safe as soon as they could. Nine days was perhaps crowding it a little; two weeks had been the recommended time to let the metal cool below ignition point, but they reasoned that if they could hose down Wallop's strongbox before opening it, there should be no real danger to the contents. They were shaving the margin of safety as a calculated risk, because the longer they waited the better were Stoddard's chances of getting away. And Brundage felt that Stoddard's dereliction, if proven, was a personal slap in the face, not to mention a letting down of the side. Men of his class, especially old San Franciscans, simply did not do such things.

As their wagon bumped along the rubble-filled streets, Wallop and Brundage looked in silent awe at the devastation around them. Van Ness Avenue, where they started, was a broad street lined with elaborate old homes, and while some of these had been burned or dynamited, others still stood, and stores from the ravaged sections of midtown had rented them as places of business. The White House, City of Paris, the Emporium, and other large shops had moved in their available stock, and were already carrying on almost as though nothing had happened. East of Van Ness, however, the picture changed. Here and there a house would be standing, but there were whole blocks that were nothing but mountains of smoldering debris, burned-out buildings, twisted steel beams, blackened bricks and stone, cracked and sunken streets, and twisted, leaking pipes. Then, clean as mushrooms in an unplowed field, there were small pine sheds, only a few feet square, that had been hastily put up to carry on whatever business had been destroyed behind them. Their bright boards made a cheerful contrast to their surroundings, and seemed to symbolize the rebirth of the city.

The city had set up hot meal kitchens, with long trestle tables and benches that could accommodate what looked like several hundred diners at one time, but some people preferred to do their own cooking, which by necessity had to be done outside. Some had stoves, or nickel-plated ranges, that had been carried from the ruins, while others cooked on makeshift affairs consisting of a few bricks and an oven grate, and wherever the cooking went on there were people gathered around. Everyone shared in the work and everyone shared in the food, and in many cases the normal laws of business were suspended in the interest of the common good. There were few gougers and few profiteers, because the various law-enforcers still patrolled the streets, and nobody wanted to be hauled before them. The soldiers had calmed down somewhat since the fire, but the so-called Citizens Vigilance Committee and some of the other self-appointed guardians of the law were notoriously trigger-happy. On the night of April 22 one H. C. Tilden, a prominent member of the Mayor's Relief Committee, was shot and killed by a "citizen's" guard while driving a car bedecked with a Red Cross flag. There may have been camaraderie among the refugees, but there was nothing but fear between them and the hastily deputized authorities.

When they reached the jumble of wreckage that had been the basement of their bank, Wallop and Brundage could see that the main safe was intact, although half buried in a mass of cracked marble, bricks, and mortar. They looked at it in silence for a while, then Brundage turned to the foreman of the work crew.

"What do you think?" he said. "Can you get it out of there?"

The foreman surveyed the scene, sucking on a matchstick. He wore a derby hat as his badge of office, and he tilted it over his eyes, as though looking into a sunset at sea. "It'll be a bitch of a job to get her out," he said. "I'd have to rig a block and falls, and I don't know where I'd foot the gallows. There's nothing steady down there to brace it." He rotated the matchstick to a corner of his mouth, and said, "It'd be easier just to clean all that crap away from in front, so's you could open the door and take out what you want."

"Well, do whatever you think best," Brundage said. "Just so long as you think it's cool enough."

"Can't tell that till we get down there."

"Then let's go. We're not getting anywhere standing here."

The foreman turned to one of the crew who, like all the others, wore a shapeless felt hat. "Charlie, bring along a bucket of water," he said. "The rest of you, bring the crowbars and hammers and shovels."

"Where do I find water?" Charlie asked. "There ain't a goddam faucet in miles."

"Look for a puddle. Find a leaky pipe. There's water all over —use your ingenuity. Piss in it, if you have to."

Charlie started off, dragging an empty pail by the rope on its handle. "I wish I'd joined the Army," he said. "Then I could be the one telling people what to do."

Wallop and Brundage followed the workmen across the rubble to the safe, where they all stopped and looked at it uneasily, as though it were an elephant caught in a trap. The foreman put his hand near the metal side, then drew it back. "She's still hot," he said. "Just how hot, we won't know till Charlie shows up with the water. Meantime, let's start moving some of these bigger blocks outa the way."

Using their crowbars and sledgehammers, the crew began to pound and pry at the pieces of broken brick and mortar, levering them away from the door to the safe. One man, with a shovel, cleared away the smaller bits of debris so that the crowbars could be slipped under the large blocks for better leverage. It was hard, unrewarding work, and progress was depressingly slow. It was as though they were trying to excavate a city with baseball bats, and the longer they worked the less they seemed to accomplish. The foreman stood by, offering bits of advice that were acknowledged by dead silence or by grunts, and at the same time he kept glancing up toward the street level.

"Here he comes now," he said at last, when Charlie's figure appeared lugging a pail of water. "He must've gone all the way to the Bay to get it."

Charlie made his way carefully down to where they were all standing, then set the pail on a level space, and shook his arm to restore circulation. "That sombitch gets heavy," he said.

"Where'd you go—Oakland?" the foreman asked.

"I found a cistern," Charlie replied. "It's got all the water you want."

"O.K., throw it on the door, there," the foreman said, indicating the blackened dial on the face of the safe.

"Why?" said Charlie. "One bucket of water ain't gonna cool it down."

"No, but it'll tell us how hot it is. Get with it."

Charlie sighed as though he'd just been commanded to stand on his head, picked up the pail, and threw the contents at the safe. There was a crackling hiss, and a cloud of steam.

"Christ," said the foreman. "No point trying to open *that* bugger."

"Do you think you could cool it by running water over it?" Brundage asked.

The foreman looked at Charlie. "How far away is that cistern?"

"A fair piece," Charlie replied.

"Too far to get a hose to it?"

"Depends on how long a hose you got."

The foreman closed his eyes, and appeared to be counting. "One block, two blocks—what?" he said at last.

"About a block," said Charlie. "The reason it took me so long was that was the last place I looked."

"All right," said the foreman, and turned to another workman. "Hector, you go with Charlie and see if you can scrounge up enough hose to get from there to here. If you can find a hand pump so much the better; if you can't, then rig it so's we can get a siphon going. The rest of you keep working here. It'll do no good to cool the safe if we can't get the door open."

Charlie and the workman named Hector climbed out of the rubble and started off, and the others went back to their crowbars and sledgehammers. Brundage turned to Wallop, and said, "I don't see that we're accomplishing anything here. What do you say we go for a stroll?"

"Fine," said Wallop. "Maybe we can get a snack at one of the soup kitchens—I seem to have missed breakfast this morning."

They turned away, and as they made their way back to the street Brundage said, "Trouble?"

"No trouble," Wallop replied. "I just wanted to put a notice in the paper, and since they're all printing in Oakland I had to get the copy in early."

"A bank notice?"

"No." Wallop paused, then said, "A notice asking Gresham Stoddard to contact me."

"Why'd you do that?"

"Mainly, because I wanted to see if he's alive, or still in this area. I thought that was the easiest way to find out."

Brundage was silent. "I'm not so sure that was a good idea," he said at last. "It could tip him off to what we're doing."

"Not necessarily. It would be perfectly natural for me to want to talk to him. Besides, we have no other way of finding out where he is."

Brundage thought some more. "You may be right," he said. "At any rate, there's not much we can do about it now."

"There's not much we can do about it ever, if Lavery Whitman has his way."

"That's why I didn't invite him along this morning. I want to have the cold irrefutable facts in my hand, and then go straight to the authorities. If I do that, there's nothing he can do to stop me."

"He can refuse to press a complaint, can't he?"

"Not if the facts are public. Then he'd be honor bound to press it."

Wallop considered this. "From what he said the other day, his idea of honor is to shield an old pal from harm."

"I didn't get to be president of this bank by covering up for old pals, and I'm not planning to start now. If Lavery Whitman wants to rig a deal with the police all on his own, that's his business. I'm going to do my business the way I see it, and if he doesn't like it he can get the Board of Directors to fire me."

"Are you a native San Franciscan?" Wallop asked.

"What does that have to do with it?"

"Nothing. I just wondered."

"My family came out here during the panic of fifty-seven. I was a year old at the time."

Wallop nodded, as though in sympathy. "No matter," he said. "I agree with you completely."

They returned to the work site after lunch, and found that Hector and Charlie had managed to produce enough hoses to reach from the cistern to the safe, and had bound them together in a reasonably leakproof fashion. They had also dredged up a derelict kitchen pump from somewhere, made an intake tube to drop into the cistern, and were now trying to bind the last length of hose onto the pump spout. Brundage watched them for a moment, then said, "Do you think that's going to work?"

There was a pregnant pause, and Charlie said, "If it don't, sir, then we'll just have to carry the water in our mouths."

Brundage turned away, and they made their way down to where the other workmen were still digging in front of the safe. "How're we coming?" Brundage asked the foreman.

"You can see for yourself," the foreman replied. "Once we get that big chunk outa there, there'll be room to open the door—when she's cooled off. But then I think we got another problem."

"What's that?" Brundage was impatient to get at the records, and had visualized the job as being as simple as merely opening the safe. Each new delay made him irritable to the point where he was asking stupid questions, and the knowledge that they were stupid increased his irritation. It was the first time that, as president, he'd been forced to wait for anything he wanted, and he was behaving poorly.

The foreman pointed to the safe, which was tilted down and slightly to one side. "When the foundation gave way, she settled kind of cockeyed," he said. "When you come to open the door, instead of it just swinging out it's gonna have to be lifted, 'cause its weight is holding it closed."

"Will that be so hard?"

"We'll see. That door must weigh near a ton, and it's gonna take some hefty prying to lift it."

"When do you think you can start?"

The foreman shrugged, and then, as though in answer to the question, they heard a gurgling in the hose. "Dino!" the foreman called. "Grab that hose, and point it at the safe!"

One of the workmen scrambled and picked up the hose, then said, "What part of the safe?"

"The door, you donkey! Around the edges of the door!"

The gurgling grew louder; there was a rush of air, and then water erupted from the end of the hose. It formed a limp arc that didn't quite reach the safe, and the workman took it closer until it splashed on the side of the door, sending up instant clouds of crackling steam.

"Keep it up!" the foreman commanded. "Swing it back and forth!" The workman did as he was told, and the foreman watched for a few moments and then turned to Brundage. "That's gonna take some little while," he said. "But at least this'll speed the cooling."

"Do you think you can open it today?" Brundage asked.

The foreman looked at the sky, where the sun had already sunk into an incoming fog bank. "No," he said.

"How long will it take?"

"God damn it, Mr. Brundage," the foreman said wearily, "if I was a claire voyant I could tell you what's *in* the fucking safe, and we wouldn't have to open it. I just don't know." Then, quickly, he said, "I'm sorry, sir, I didn't mean to speak that way. It's been a long day, and my piles are killing me."

"It's my fault," Brundage replied. "I didn't mean to pester you. Forgive me."

"We'll get it done just as soon as we can, and that's all I can say." Turning to two other workmen, the foreman said, "Luigi and Max, you go up and spell Charlie and Hector at the pump. We'll keep sluicing her down as long as the light lasts, and then see what she's like tomorrow morning."

"What time will you start?" Brundage asked. "I mean—I'd just like to be here when it's opened. I'm not trying to rush you."

"Well, you've got the combination, so we can't open it till you get here," the foreman replied. "We'll be here at seven-thirty."

"Fine. So will we."

Brundage slept poorly that night. He tossed and thrashed, unable to find a comfortable position, and when he drifted into sleep his dreams brought him awake again. He dreamed he was a sheriff, chasing Gresham Stoddard up into the hills and firing what turned out to be blank cartridges at him, and when finally he had Stoddard cornered Stoddard turned into Lavery Whitman, who rushed at Brundage like a mountain lion and then began to cover him with kisses. He woke up sweating from that one, and soon found himself at the bottom of a cistern in which, as the water level lowered, the drowned body of Stoddard appeared, clutching a sodden note that said, "I told you so." Finally, as the first faint light showed through the curtains, he arose and tried to dress quietly, so as not to wake his wife. A quick motion in her bed showed she was already awake.

"What's the matter with *you?*" she asked.

"Nothing," Brundage replied, stepping into his trousers. "I just couldn't sleep, that's all."

"You whimpered and whinnied and moaned like some sort of animal. You also talked."

"Impossible. I was awake practically the whole night."

"Well, somebody in your bed was talking. Did you have any visitors?"

"Don't be absurd. . . . What did I say?"

"Oh—mostly a jumble. Things like 'Catch him,' and 'Don't kiss me,' and that sort of thing. Everyday conversation."

"I think you're the one who was dreaming."

"Well, I'm not going to pry, but I think Lavery Whitman would be interested to know you dream of him."

"What do you mean by that?"

"What you said, in full, was 'Don't kiss me, Lavery.' Do you know any other people named Lavery?"

"This whole discussion is insane. Go back to sleep, and maybe you won't have such weird dreams." Brundage gathered up the rest of his clothes, and made for the bathroom. By the time he had shaved and dressed his wife was, in fact, asleep, and he was able to leave the house without any further questioning.

When he reached the bank site the crew was already there, and had a stream of water running across the door of the safe. The foreman looked up at him, and smiled.

"I think we'll be able to open her," he said. "She's still hot, but she's no longer making steam. If we're careful, we can probably swing it."

"Good," said Brundage. "Splendid. Now all we need is Mr. Wallop." It was in Wallop's strongbox that the papers were kept, so there was no point opening the safe until Wallop was there with the strongbox key. "Just keep hosing it down, and it'll be that much cooler."

Wallop appeared in five minutes, unshaven and having dressed in obvious haste. "I'm sorry to be late," he said. "I overslept—I couldn't get to sleep until about five."

"You, too?" said Brundage. "Welcome to the club." Then, to the foreman, he said, "All right. Let's give it a try."

"You better wear gloves, sir," the foreman said. "She's still a mite fiery."

Brundage took an offered pair of workman's gloves, and approached the safe. He touched the knob experimentally and felt no heat, so started to spin the dial to the combination he knew by heart. He was careful, out of habit, to stand close to the dial so as to block any bystander's view of the numbers, and he could feel the heat from the metal on his forehead. Normally, when the combination was complete, he could feel the fall of the tumblers, but with the safe at an angle the lock mechanism seemed to work differently. He tugged at the knob, but the door didn't budge. "That should be it," he said, standing back. "I don't know whether it worked or not."

"Max, try a crowbar on it," the foreman said, and the workman named Max stepped up to the door, probed the edges for a place to put a crowbar, then shrugged and gave up.

"Smooth as a baby's ass," he said.

"Maybe the heat did something to it," the foreman said. "Luigi, give it a good belt with a sledge. Not on the knob—at the edge." Luigi did as he was told, and the sledgehammer almost bounced out of his hands. "O.K., Mr. Brundage, try the combination again," the foreman said, and, when Brundage had spun the dial, "Luigi, give it one more, for good luck." Luigi did, and there was a click and the door bounced open a crack, then shut. "She's unlocked, at any rate," the foreman said. "That's at least a starter."

They managed to secure a wire to the knob and then, with two men pulling on the wire and one prying with a chisel, they got the door to come far enough ajar so that wedges and shims could be put in to keep it from closing. After that it was just a matter of brute strength, forcing it apart until it fell back against its hinges, wide open. Hot air issued from the cavernous inside, and with it the smell of blistered paint. They played the hose around the sides and the top and the bottom, and then Wallop, wearing a workman's gloves, removed the strongbox and set it on the ground. It was hosed until he could touch it with his bare hands.

"All right," he said at last, as he produced a key. "Now let's see what we've got."

The only sound was the splashing of water from the hose as Wallop inserted his key in the lock and turned it. Then slowly he lifted the lid, and the first thing he saw was brown, crumbly paper. Flinging the lid wide he reached into the box, then realized that only the paper on the top and sides had been charred by the heat; the bulk of the contents was in perfect condition. He riffled once through the papers, then closed the lid and stood up, smiling, and looked at Brundage. "Should we go?" he said.

"Yes, indeed," Brundage replied, cheerfully. As they started away, Brundage stopped, and turned to the foreman. "I want to thank you for everything," he said. "You, and"—looking at the workmen—"you have done a splendid job, and I shall recommend that you all receive bonuses. You are good fellows, every one of you." The workmen mumbled their thanks, and again Brundage and Wallop started away, but the foreman stopped them.

"Mr. Brundage," he said, "do you want to leave the safe laying open like this?"

"My God," said Brundage. "No! Close it, this instant."

"How're you going to get it open again?"

"That's no matter now. If we have to, we'll go through the whole business again. Just close the door, and spin the knob."

He and Wallop left, and the foreman shrugged and gestured the crew to comply. "That sure as hell must have been something important," he said.

Three hours later, Brundage and Wallop put the papers back in the strongbox, and put the strongbox under a pile of blankets in the cedar chest in Wallop's Menlo Park house. Wallop's wife was off doing relief work, and wasn't expected back until the end of the day. They went into the den, where Wallop poured two whiskies.

"Where do we go first?" he said. "To the police?"

"The police can be bribed," Brundage replied. "I want to go someplace where Whitman can't interfere."

"And where might that be?"

"I guess noplace, actually. But we'll stand a better chance if we go to the district attorney's office. I know Grafton Hughes there, and he'll be harder to get at than some precinct captain. All I want, really, is for it to be made public, and then Whitman won't be able to shut it up."

"If it's made public, won't that tip Stoddard off?" Wallop said. "Why don't we see if he answers my notice, and work from there?"

"All right, we'll give him a couple of days. But I want to have this evidence on file, so a warrant will be all ready if and when he shows up. I'll give it to Hughes, and tell him to hold off until we give the word."

"Fine. And if Lavery Whitman calls, we've just left town."

Brundage laughed. "You may not be so far from the truth," he said.

# CHAPTER 22

That was Tuesday, May 1. On Wednesday, Stoddard returned from a hurried trip to Chicago, having ridden on trains that were full, on the eastward run, with refugees, and, coming back, with relief workers, food and medical supplies, and journalists. San Francisco's catastrophe had made the eruption of Vesuvius seem as newsworthy as burned toast, and in the days and months and years to come some sixty-seven feature articles would be written about it, in addition to the tons of copy that were filed on the spot. Stoddard was cheered to think that his project would be the only one written from the point of view of a madam, and would therefore be unique among all the other accounts.

He went almost immediately to Dolly's room over the stable, and found her writing at her makeshift desk, a pile of manuscript pages beside her. She looked up as he came in, and without greeting or preamble said, "Did you get the money?"

"Oh, the avarice of the writer," Stoddard replied in a hollow tone. "To him, the publisher is just an endless source of money, to be scattered about like birdseed."

"I said did you get it?" Dolly demanded.

"Yes, I got it. And now, as a quid pro quo, let me see what you wrote while I was gone."

Dolly nodded at the manuscript, and as Stoddard picked it up she said, "Remember what I told you about folding. I want these pages to be preserved."

"I shall preserve them with my life, believe me."

She put down her pen, and said, "Before you go—I had an

idea you might want to use in the advertisements. See what you think."

"Isn't it a little early to think of ads?" Stoddard replied. "I mean, you've only—"

"It's never too early to think of anything. Here's the way I see it: I'll make a copy of two or three of the pages—the opening page, and a couple of others—and then we set fire to them around the edges and let them burn for just a second before we stamp the fire out. Then we take a picture of the singed pages with my handwriting on them, and use that picture as a full-size ad, giving the impression that I was writing all during the fire and barely managed to save the book. What do you think of that?"

"It's a novel approach, certainly," Stoddard said.

"Novel, hell—it'll knock them for a loop."

"Well, I'll ask young Walden, and see what he thinks. By the way, where is he—and where is everybody? There was nobody in the house when I came through."

"I don't know where they are," Dolly replied. "I'm a writer, not a nursemaid. I know that Stella is off looking for a place of her own, and—"

"Is Bender back in the pharmacy business?"

"No, but Stella wants to set up a hairdressing salon. She says she can make good money, and doesn't have to be looking at the ceiling all the time. Wants to call her place 'The Hair House,' but I tell her she's crazy. However, that's her business. She says it's something she can grow old in gracefully, and there's no denying that."

"Well, I'll look over these pages, and be back to you." Stoddard started out, but Dolly stopped him.

"I had another idea," she said. "For promoting the book. You know how at stag dinners they have a girl come out of a pie, and stuff like that?"

"I've heard," Stoddard replied.

"Well, I could go on a round of Rotary luncheons, Chamber of Commerce meetings, stag dinners, and all that, and give a little talk about how things look from my side of the fence.

Tell the kind of customers I like to have, and those I won't let in the place, and then end up by autographing the book in my own—well, however the customer wanted. That way, everyone would profit: the gentlemen would learn a thing or two for their own good, and I would sell a lot of books. How does that strike you?"

"It strikes me you've put in more time thinking about this book than you have writing it. Let's take care of one thing at a time, and not get our priorities confused."

Dolly shrugged. "I was only trying to help," she said. "It's your money." She started to go back to her writing, then saw a clipping on her desk, and picked it up. "Oh—did you see this?" she said. "Stella cut it out."

"What is it?" Stoddard asked, going back and taking the piece of paper that Dolly held out to him.

"See for yourself."

He scanned the item, which had apparently been cut from the newspaper with nail scissors, and felt the back of his scalp tingle as he read: "Will anyone knowing the whereabouts of GRESHAM STODDARD, late of Nob Hill, please ask him to communicate with Slater Wallop in regard to Bank business. Important." He crumpled the clipping, and put it in his pocket. "Thank you," he said.

"Don't thank me; thank Stella." Dolly resumed writing, and Stoddard, his mind whirling, returned to the Benders' house.

He put Dolly's manuscript on the kitchen table, and as he made a cup of coffee he noticed that his hands were trembling. Come on, he told himself. This is no time to fly apart; this is the time, of all times, you've got to be calm and careful, and not do anything without thinking it all the way through. The notice was, obviously, a lure to bring him to the surface, like a trout, and expose his whereabouts. There could be nothing Slater Wallop wanted from him other than an accounting of his legerdemain with the books, and this he was not prepared to give. It wasn't totally unexpected—in fact, he'd had it in the back of his mind all along, and had already made contingency plans—but how good were these plans? They had called, at first, for removing to Chicago, but now that he'd had to go to Chicago to cash in his railroad stocks, he'd identified himself as being alive after the fire, and could no longer pretend to have been one of the casualties. Therefore Chicago was out; he'd have to go farther East, to Boston or New York, where his face was not known and he could maintain the identity of Maxwell Lambert. But what about the book? He had no publishing connections on the Eastern Seaboard, and nobody to whom he could go for advice. It was possible that Walden might know someone, in which case everything would be easier. If not, then they'd simply have to start from scratch, but he knew that the money he now had could ease the way. All in all, it would probably be better to get out of the San Francisco area anyway, and set up in some place wholly new. He rather liked the idea of Boston, which he'd heard bore certain similarities to the Athens of the West.

He was about halfway through Dolly's pages when the front door opened, and Walden came in. Walden's face brightened, and he said, "Welcome home! How were things in the Heartland?"

"Fine," said Stoddard as they shook hands. "First-rate."

"I gather your business deal worked out."

"Oh, yes. No problem there." Stoddard was trying to think how to bring up the new problem, when Walden gave him an opening.

"Well, we've got a problem here," Walden said.

"What do you mean?"

"All the San Francisco papers are printing in Oakland, and there isn't a printing press to be had. Of course, by the time Dolly finishes her manuscript things may be different, but as of now we'd have to have the book put out by Capuchin monks."

"Hmmm," said Stoddard, trying to look concerned. "That is a poser. Well, there's more than one way to skin a cat. What would you think of printing in New York, or perhaps Boston?"

"Isn't that a long way to send the copy?"

"Not if we're there. I mean to move there, say to Boston, and set up our business on Beacon Hill. I'm told that's a fairly civilized place."

Walden was quiet while he turned the idea over in his mind. There was a good deal to be said for it, among other reasons because it would be an area that he knew, and one that was not in the throes of recovering from a major disaster. All in all, the idea made sense. "Generally speaking, I approve," he said. "But I think that, considering the kind of book we're publishing, New York would be better than Boston."

"How so?"

"Boston is very touchy on matters relating to religion or the flesh. The heavy hand of Puritanism will strangle anyone who gets out of line."

"What about New York?"

"We'd have no trouble there. In fact, I know a couple of people who might be able to help us."

"Splendid. Then that's settled. Dolly can mail us her pages as soon as we have an address."

"When do you want to go?"

"Would tomorrow be too soon?"

Walden swallowed. "I guess not," he said. "There are just—a couple of matters I have to clear up here. Can you get space on the train?"

"I think that'll be no problem."

"Great. Uh—have you seen Lucille?"

"No. I've seen only you and Dolly."

"Well, if you see her would you tell her I'd like a word with her?"

"I imagine she'd probably like a word with you."

Walden tried to think of an answer, but could find none. He had, for the last ten days, done his best to avoid being alone with Lucille, simply because every movement of her face and every posture of her body was directed at him. Now and then he would look up from something he was doing, and see her staring at him across the room, her mouth partly open and her eyes showing a strange smoky quality, and he'd have to look away for fear she might start toward him. They'd been lucky that Saturday night in that everyone else had remained asleep, but that was not the kind of luck one could count on, and he had a feeling that one more encounter might make him never want to stop.

He ran into her about an hour later, on her way back from the shop. She had clearly been to see Stella, but just as clearly had told Stella to go lightly on the cosmetics. She looked radiant, and when he told her he wanted to talk to her she was at first delighted and then, when she saw his face, wide-eyed and apprehensive.

"It looks as though we're going to be leaving," he said as they took a street leading to the Bay.

"Who's 'we'?" she asked.

"Max and I."

"Why?"

"We can't get printing facilities here."

"Where are you going?"

"New York."

"You mean the firm is going to New York?"

"If you want to call us a firm."

"Well, I'm part of the firm. Can't I come, too?"

"I don't see how. We're going to stay there, and your home is here."

"If you ask me to, I'll come."

"How can I ask you to? That would be sheer insanity."

"I know, but I'd still come."

"I can't ask you. It's impossible."

"Don't you want me?"

"Of course I—I'd love to have you, but—no. This is where you belong."

"Will you ever come back?"

"I have no way of knowing. I'd like to think so."

They walked in silence for a while, and she reached out and held his hand. "When are you leaving?" she asked.

"Tomorrow."

"Oh."

"If Max can get space on the train, that is."

"I can always hope it'll be wrecked before it gets here."
"What good would that do?"
"Just give a little more time."
"It isn't as though we'd been doing anything the last ten days, you know."
"You don't have to tell me that. You've been avoiding me."
"No, I haven't. I've just—"
"Yes, you have, and you know it."
"I was just afraid to see you alone, for fear . . ."
"For fear what?"
"For fear I might lose control."
"Would there be anything so bad about that?"
"There are certain times and certain places where certain things are simply out of the question. I shouldn't have to tell you that."
"I know. But to every rule there's the exception that proves it."
"Well, I'm sorry."
"Now you're angry at me."
"I am not."
"You certainly sound it."
"I'm sorry if I sound it. I'm not. I just don't see there's anything else I can do."
"I suppose not." She was quiet for a long time, still holding his hand as they walked, and finally she said, "You know, I have a theory. It just came to me."
"What is it?"
"I have a theory that a girl has just one real love in her life, and that's all. It may be the man she marries and it may not, but there's room in her life for just one love, and in my case it happens to be you."
"You don't know me well enough for that."
"I know you better than you think."
"Are you trying to tell me you don't love George? Because he's—"
"Of course I love George, but not the way I love you. And you don't have to tell me what George is, because I know."

"But still—"

"Don't hem and haw about it. You said you don't want me to come to New York with you, and I accept that—"

"I didn't say I didn't *want* you to come; I said it would be impossible."

"It comes to the same thing. If you'd really wanted me, then nothing would have been impossible. I've said I accept that, and you're probably right."

"I'm glad you agree."

"What I'm saying is I can live more easily with George, now that I've got something better to remember. Any time I think I'm going crazy I can remember Saturday, and I'll know it's possible for everything to be glorious. You don't know what you did for me that night."

"It wasn't all one-sided, you know. What I did was not exactly an act of philanthropy."

"I'm happy to hear it."

They were at the water's edge, and Walden looked across the Bay at the ruins in the distance. "Well—it's an ill wind—" he said. Then he turned, and formally put Lucille's arm in his. "We've got to get back, or people may be thinking scandalous thoughts about us."

Lucille giggled. "Let them. I have better memories than they can even dream."

The train left Oakland, and headed northeast toward Sacramento and the Donner Pass into Nevada. George and Lucille Bender, who had watched its trail of smoke as it dwindled into the distance, started slowly home, each one immersed in private thoughts.

"He said an interesting thing the other day," Bender said.

"Who did?" Lucille was only half listening.

"Godfrey."

"Oh?" Now she was all attention. "What did he say?"

"He said I should try to put myself in your place. Do you know what he meant?"

"I have no idea." Her mind was racing, trying to find a clue.

"We'll, I've been trying, and all it's done is make me think the better of him. Doesn't that seem odd?"
"Not necessarily."
"I see."
"Possibly, but don't worry about it."
"You're sure?"
"I'm positive."

Ahead of them, a newsboy was calling out a new edition, hot off the press, and as they passed him Bender saw a picture on the front page, and said, "Hey—look at that!"

"Look at what?" Lucille had gone back into her own thoughts.

"Max Lambert!" Bender gave the newsboy a coin, and took the paper and opened it. There was a two-column headline that read: "MISSING BANKER SOUGHT BY POLICE," and then a cut of Gresham Stoddard, and a story that began:

> Gresham Stoddard, well-known financier and member of the Board of Directors of the Bank of the Pacific, is being sought by police for questioning in connection with a shortage of funds from that bank amounting to some half million dollars. Mr. Stoddard and his wife, Muriel, a prominent patron of the San Francisco Opera and other artistic and charitable institutions, have been missing since the earthquake and fire, when their Nob Hill mansion was destroyed, and while there is no evidence of their having died in their house, neither is there any evidence that they survived. Bulletins requesting information as to their whereabouts have been unproductive, and police theorize that

"Well, what do you know about that?" Bender said, folding the newspaper and putting it under his arm. "I would have sworn that was a picture of Max Lambert."

"It was," said Lucille. "I thought you knew."

On the train, Walden and Stoddard looked out the windows at the vineyards and citrus groves on either side of the tracks that rose slowly toward the foothills of the Sierras. Neither one spoke for the better part of an hour, and then Stoddard said, "I feel as though I'd been over this route just a couple of days ago. Pretty soon I'll know every tree by heart."

"Maybe this'll be the last time," Walden replied. "Maybe you won't have to come back."

Stoddard knocked on the wooden chair arm. "With any luck," he said.

"Just be glad you're not the conductor. Think how many times he has to do it."

Stoddard started to say something, stopped, then took a deep breath and started again. "There's something I suppose you ought to know," he said.

"I guess there's a lot I ought to know," Walden replied. "What, specifically, are you thinking of?"

"If we're going to be partners, I suppose you should know that I'm wanted by the police. Or if I'm not, I very shortly will be."

Walden digested this, then said, "I wondered about that. I thought our exit was a little hurried." He looked out the window, and said nothing more.

"Don't you want to know why?" Stoddard asked.

"Does it have anything to do with the publishing house?"

"No."

"Then I don't care. That's my job, and that's all that interests me."

"Oh, my," said Stoddard. "With an attitude like that, I don't see how we can fail."

# CHAPTER 23

The town of Tijuana consisted of one dusty street, with a sprinkling of adobe huts on either side. Chickens and goats made up the bulk of the traffic, with an occasional burro standing in what shade it could find, and the only sign of human habitation came when an irate mother, in the dark interior of one of the huts, berated a child in a shrill cackling of Mexican Spanish. The town seemed to be waiting for something to happen, and hoping it wouldn't.

Five miles to the west, the Pacific surf washed at the beach with a stately, monotonous rhythm, ending the journey for waves that had traveled the six thousand miles of open water from Japan, and dispersing them in a sudden rush and rattling of pebbles. Fishermen's boats bobbed on the swells offshore, and on the beach, up beyond the surf line, were shacks where the fishermen mended their nets and, in some cases, lived. Here and there were more substantial dwellings, leftovers from a time when someone had thought of establishing a seaside colony. The idea had not caught on, and the cottages had either been left vacant or rented to mad *norteamericanos*, who didn't care what they did with their money.

On the patio of one of these, Leffert Neppleton sat with his back against the wall and his feet on the rail, moodily drinking a bottle of *pulque*, which was beer made from cactus juice. It was still midmorning, too early to start on the tequila, but the servant he'd sent to market had not yet returned, and all that was left was the *pulque*, which had been a last resort even when he'd bought it. Some of the Mexican beer was splendid, but the *pulque* left a great deal to be desired; it tasted like old laundry water that had turned sour. The servant, a failed bandit named Jesús Gómez, had more or less come with the cottage, and Neppleton had arranged with the border authorities that he be allowed transit back and forth to San Diego to buy those necessities of life not available in Tijuana. Since American money was used in the transaction there was never any argument, and although Neppleton was sure that Gómez was taking a big cut for himself, he never gave him enough to tempt him to run away. He would mentally calculate what the purchases would cost, add five dollars coming and going as a tip to the border guards, 15 per cent for Gómez to steal, and be grateful for whatever change was returned. Once or twice Gómez had hinted that Neppleton should perhaps give him a little more, *"para emergencia,"* but Neppleton simply smiled and waved him away, and Gómez also smiled, and shrugged.

From behind the house Neppleton heard the soft sounds of a burro approaching, and he swung his feet off the rail and stood up. Emptying the last of the *pulque* onto the sand he went around to the rear, where Gómez was unloading the baskets that were slung on either side of the burro's haunches. "Well, now!" Neppleton exclaimed jovially. "*Como usted* make out?"

"*Muy bien, señor,*" Gómez replied, unloading six bottles of real beer and one of tequila.

Neppleton eyed the groceries, which had undoubtedly been bought in Tijuana, and for which he would be charged San Diego prices. "You had enough *dinero*, I assume," he said.

"*Sí, señor,*" said Gómez. "*Escasamente.*" He reached in his drawstring purse, fished out two nickels and a dime, and handed them to Neppleton. "*Su periódico, señor,*" he added, producing a folded newspaper from the basket, and presenting it with a flourish.

"Thank you very much," Neppleton said, putting it under his arm. "*Muy gracias*. The *señora* will appreciate that." Knowing that the newly arrived beer would be hot and foamy, he decided to make himself a long tequila drink while he read the paper, and he accordingly went into the kitchen, put tequila and lime juice into a glass, and poured in a splash of bottled water. He then returned to the patio, put his feet on the rail, and, after taking a sip of his drink, opened the paper. There, staring at him, was a picture of Gresham Stoddard, accompanying a story that had been taken from the San Francisco paper. His feet came down from the rail with a crash, and he leaped from his chair and ran into the cottage, shouting, "Muriel! Muriel! Guess what!" He flung open the bedroom door, and in the cool darkness of the room saw Muriel Stoddard pulling herself into a sitting position.

"What is it?" she asked. "What happened?"

"Look at this!" He tossed the newspaper at her, then opened the shutters to let in the daylight. The bedroom, which had seemed as cozy as a womb, now looked garish and untidy.

Blearily, Muriel stared at the newspaper story in silence, and then said, "Well, I will be everlastingly. He must have been keeping a woman."

"You don't suppose he ran away with Phyllis, do you?"

"Not likely. That would be too much of a coincidence. But I wonder where he did go."

"It's possible he didn't survive."

Muriel shook her head. "Not him. He's the kind who always survives."

"But now we don't have to be so careful. Nobody wants *us* for anything. We can get out of this dump, and go where we want."

"What about Phyllis?"

"She's told me several times, she has so much money she doesn't give a damn what I do. I intend to take her up on that, and make her stick to her word."

Muriel laughed, and held out her arms. "My God, you're wonderful," she said. "If Gresham had had your kind of spirit, my life would have been a breeze."